CW01509097

DUKE WITH A DEBT

WICKED DUKES SOCIETY
BOOK TWO

SCARLETT SCOTT

Happily Ever After Books

Duke with a Debt

Wicked Dukes Society Book 2

All rights reserved.

Copyright © 2025 by Scarlett Scott™

Published by Happily Ever After Books, LLC

Edited by Grace Bradley and Lisa Hollett, Silently Correcting Your Grammar

Cover Design by Wicked Smart Designs

This book or any portion thereof may not be reproduced or used in any manner whatsoever without the express written permission of the publisher except for the use of brief quotations in a book review.

The unauthorized reproduction or distribution of this copyrighted work is illegal. No part of this book may be scanned, uploaded, or distributed via the Internet or any other means, electronic or print, without the publisher's permission. Criminal copyright infringement, including infringement without monetary gain, is punishable by law.

This book is a work of fiction and any resemblance to persons, living or dead, or places, events, or locales, is purely coincidental. The characters are productions of the author's imagination and used fictitiously.

Scarlett Scott™ is a registered trademark of Happily Ever After Books LLC.

For more information, contact author Scarlett Scott™.

https://scarlettscottauthor.com/

For all the historical romance readers out there.
Long live carriage bangs, icy dukes and smoldering gaming hell
owners, crowded ballrooms and alcove kisses, marriages of
convenience, fiery governesses and wicked rakes, daring gowns and
loosened cravats, and all the things that make us swoon and sigh as
we turn the pages.
I'll keep writing as long as you keep reading.

🤍

CHAPTER 1

*T*he African grey parrot balanced calmly on its perch was glaring at him.

"Gormless shite," the bird pronounced, flapping its wings as if to punctuate the words.

Stuart Gilden, Duke of Camden, glared back at the feathered creature who had just paid him insult, walking slowly toward it, hands clasped behind his back. He stopped before the parrot, cocking his head and holding its unique silvery stare.

"Do you know," he said pleasantly, "I could wring your neck with one hand?"

"Landlubber," the parrot squawked. "Pistols at dawn."

His eyes narrowed. "Did you just challenge me to a duel?"

Incredulousness rose within him. This was indeed the strangest bird he had ever met. Intelligent, complex, and just a touch mad. Rather like its owner, whose presence he was awaiting.

"Megs want a biscuit," the parrot told him.

"I haven't a biscuit," he said. "And to be perfectly candid, if

I had one, I'm not sure I'd share it with you. You've been rather rude thus far, haven't you?"

"Gormless shite," the parrot said, extending its wings again.

"Megs, my love, I've told you about your language."

The familiar, feminine voice had Stuart turning away from the feathered menace to find Miss Rosamund Payne gliding toward him. It had been some time since their paths had crossed, for their circles had only overlapped thanks to his brother Wesley. But little had changed since he had seen her last.

Her hair was the same, indistinct shade of neither gold nor red, but an odd color all its own. Her eyes were sharp and dark in her pale face. Her chin was stubborn, her forehead high. She still had the mouth of a courtesan, the only overtly sensual feature she possessed and quite incongruous with her unassuming spinsterish air. Her figure was trim yet curvaceous as he preferred, her breasts high swells hidden in her modest silk bodice, her height slightly taller than most ladies' and yet still no match for his. No one could ever call Miss Rosamund Payne a great beauty.

Still, there was something compelling about her. He had always found her presence magnetic in a painfully unwanted way. She had been meant to be his sister, and it hadn't been his place to notice her. Yet, notice her, he had.

But she scarcely seemed to take note of Stuart now as she hastened past him to her infernal parrot.

"Do be a good parrot, and I'll give you a pistachio," she purred in a tone that would have been better suited to a lover than a feathered beast.

"Megs want pistache," the African grey declared.

Stuart stepped to the side, granting Rosamund and her bustle more room, trying not to take note of her perfume, which also had not changed—a decadent blend of rose, violet, bergamot, and ambergris that was rich and alluring.

"Will Megs behave?" she asked the parrot, holding up a small pouch.

"Megs behave," the bird chirped, then whistled.

Rosamund carefully removed one small oval nut and offered it to the parrot, who gleefully took the object in its beak. Stuart was distinctly aware that he was being ignored, and the novel sensation wasn't a pleasant one.

Rosamund trailed an elegant finger over the bird's head. "What a good bird, Megs."

And then, at last, ever so slowly, she turned the full force of her attention upon him, her dark stare burning into his. "Good afternoon, Camden. I cannot think of a single reason you would have for paying a call upon me."

No curtsy. Nary a smile. Not a *Your Grace*, and most definitely not a hint of welcome. Stuart wasn't certain what he had expected.

"Rosamund," he greeted in turn, offering a slight bow. "It is good to see you."

She arched a brow. "Is it?"

Heat crept up his throat.

"Of course," he fibbed.

She pursed her lips. "I suppose we should sit. Comfort is important when one is being lied to, I find."

Her observation was more piercing than any blade.

But he was at her mercy, and far more than she yet realized.

He inclined his head. "As you wish, madam."

"I've called for a tray of tea as well," she said coolly before swishing past him.

She moved to the seating area across the room and gingerly settled on a settee, smoothing her seafoam-green skirts. He followed, folding his taller frame into a narrow chair nearby, sparing her his proximity on her seat even as part of him was tempted to do otherwise. Belatedly, it occurred to him that her navy bodice bore the outline of gold scales as if she were a mermaid, the entire affair accented with seafoam ribbon on the sleeves and decolletage.

The fanciful dress, so incongruous with what he knew of her, took him by surprise.

"I must thank you for accepting my call," he forced himself to say, though they were both more than aware that she had kept him waiting, in the presence of the insult-wielding parrot, for half an hour.

"It was unexpected." She watched him, unsmiling, so very poised. "And not entirely pleasant, if I am honest."

Her forthright nature was something he recalled well. But what disturbed him now was that he also remembered her tears, the accusation in her eyes. He remembered how shattered she had looked, like a hand mirror that had been dropped upon a stone hearth.

Stuart brushed aside the memory as he winced. "I'll admit that I had harbored some hope that the intervening years might have rendered you more amenable to a tête-à-tête with me."

She laughed then, the sound throaty and pleasant and full, before her levity faded, and she continued regarding him with her unnerving gaze. "I regret to report that they have not."

God. She would not make this easy on him, then. Why had he supposed she would?

He gripped the arms of his chair. "I am sorry for that, Rosamund."

"As am I," she said, unsmiling. "Actually, I'm sorry for a great many things."

"A great many things," the parrot chimed in, apparently having finished with its pistachio.

Rosamund's searing stare made his neckcloth feel more like a noose. He turned his attention to the African grey for a moment to find the bird was watching him as closely as its mistress was.

"Gormless shite," the bird repeated, before issuing another whistle.

He clenched his jaw and snapped his attention back to Rosamund. "It would seem the bird has made his opinion of me quite clear."

"*Her* opinion," Rosamund corrected. "Megs is a female parrot. She was also quite bonded to her former master, who was a sea captain, hence some of her more...*colorful* vocabulary."

Stuart was suddenly dying to know how an heiress dressed as a mermaid had acquired a sea captain's foul-mouthed parrot, but the question would have to wait. He had far more pressing matters to attend to at the moment, none of which were pleasant.

"I beg your pardon. I assumed the creature was male."

"Naturally." She gave him a pained smile that was more of a taunt than aught else, those full lips that would have been better served on a courtesan distracting him.

Her one-word response felt like an insult, and Stuart knew he ought to let the matter go, but he was as obstinate as she, and he couldn't.

"Why do you say that?" he asked.

"Because it is very much like a man to assume that every creature in his path must also be male, in his mold," she said.

"Your opinion of my sex is clearly poor."

Again, her brow arched upward. "Can I be blamed?"

The past lay unspoken, a heavy burden. They stared at each other, two unsmiling enemies—Rosamund with her shrewd gaze and the airs of a queen and Stuart with his swallowed pride and a disgust for his scoundrel of a brother that surely rivaled hers.

"Of course not," he relented. "What my brother did to you was unconscionable."

Her smile was serene. "What he did made me stronger and wiser."

She was utterly unflappable, and this was new. He did not remember such self-possession in her, the ability to flay a man with nothing more than her eyes and tongue. The line of buttons bisecting her bodice drew his attention as she inhaled, the urge to undo them, to muss her irritating perfection perversely rising from nowhere.

"I am relieved to hear it," he forced out.

A tap at the door heralded the arrival of the tea tray. They were silent as a servant bustled in, laying the tray on the table separating them before excusing herself with a curtsy. The dishes of tea that had been laid out looked as if they were antiques, fashioned of fine porcelain lined with gold and decorated with enamel Libra scales on the cup and a water carrier on the saucer. He watched as she prepared his tea precisely as he had always liked it: a splash of milk first, followed by tea and two lumps of sugar.

She had remembered.

Her attention to detail felt somehow strangely intimate, particularly when their fingers brushed as she handed him his tea. The sweet bergamot of Earl Grey rose from the steaming cup.

"Thank you," he said, deciding the fine porcelain he held was likely Meissen.

He wondered if Rosamund had purchased the cups and saucers herself or if they had belonged to her father, whose eccentricities and affinity for collections had been rather notorious.

She finished preparing her own tea. "You are most welcome. To the tea, if not at my home."

The reminder that they were bitterest enemies was pointed. She would serve him tea and recall precisely how he liked it made, but she drew the line at false pleasantries.

"Megs want tea cake," the parrot called from across the room, reminding him of her presence.

Well, at least she hadn't called him a gormless shite again.

Progress.

"You shall have some in a few minutes, darling," Rosamund returned, her voice gentling as she responded to the bird.

And Stuart was suddenly, irritatingly envious of the feathered menace still glaring at him from her perch.

"Now then," Rosamund said suddenly, returning the full, disconcerting force of her attention upon him. "I don't imagine you came here for idle conversation or tea. What is it that brought you to me, Camden?"

His heart thumped hard. Here was his opportunity. And yet, the words felt thick and heavy and improperly formed. His tongue was stuck, his mouth dry. He, who had faced death and destruction and the hells of war, was terrified of four little words that, taken separately, were all rather inconsequential, save one.

He could do this.

He *had* to do this.

The contents of the latest letter he had received yesterday were still burned upon his soul.

Stuart took a deep, steadying breath, holding Rosamund's dark stare. "Will you marry me?"

∾

INTO THE SHOCKED silence that had descended following the Duke of Camden's improbable proposal, Megs interjected, "Gormless shite! Megs want pistache."

The diversion was comedic for its timing. It was also just what Rosamund needed.

"You'll not be having any pistachios if you insist upon paying our guest insult," she chided her beloved parrot, her mind whirling.

He was jesting.

Surely.

Playing a terrible joke upon her.

The Duke of Camden was a devoted sybarite, as cold and jaded and arrogant as they came. He didn't want to marry anyone, least of all a plain spinster whose foolish heart had been shattered by his cruel scoundrel of a younger brother.

"Megs sorry," the African grey said, her apology accompanied by a cheerful whistle that suggested her contrition was based solely upon her desire for another nut.

Rosamund rose from her seat as if it suddenly had been set alight and moved across the room to Megs, intent upon giving her reward, only to realize that she had left the pouch of pistachios on the table by the tea set.

With an irritated sigh, she turned back to the abandoned nuts, only to find the Duke of Camden standing as well, his pale-blue eyes upon her, so different from his brother's, which were hazel, ringed with gray. In her stupid love for Lord Wesley, she had once written a sonnet devoted to the mercurial nature of his eyes. Pity she hadn't realized his eyes were a metaphor for his honor.

"What is it?" she demanded, flustered.

"It is rude to sit in the presence of a lady." He extended his arm, her pouch dangling from his long fingers. "Also, I do believe the pistachios you seek are to be found within."

He had noticed where she kept them. And that she had

forgotten them in her haste to flee him and his ridiculous proposal. But then, he had always been far too observant.

She snatched the pouch from his grasp. "Thank you."

Whirling about, she returned to Megs, extracting a pistachio that she offered up. The parrot took it in her beak, nibbling.

"Does she never move from her perch?" Camden asked, his voice far too near.

He had followed her, rather in the vein of a tiger stalking its prey. A big, powerful beast, sleek and magnificent and yet capable of so much strength and ruthlessness. She didn't even need to look to know what she would see. The Duke of Camden was tall, broad-shouldered, lean-hipped, and powerfully built. Unlike his younger brother, his was not a classical masculine beauty.

Camden was all hard angles and merciless planes: a firm, square jaw, an unforgiving blade of a nose, high, sharp cheekbones, and an incongruously sinful mouth that looked as if it might leave a bruise. His hair was a dark, rich mahogany with a slight wave, so unlike Wesley's long, blond locks, which had been a source of colossal vanity. And the duke was taller and stronger, an immense monolith of a man.

She turned back to him, the familiar sound of the parrot enjoying her treat of little comfort, and realized that in her discomfiture she had quite forgotten what Camden had asked of her.

"I beg your pardon?" she queried.

"The bird," he offered, nodding toward Megs. "She has been on her perch for nearly an hour. I merely thought it unusual that she hasn't chosen to flit about or wander."

He was not wrong in his assessment. And the reminder of the lack of care Megs had endured still left her heart hurting. She and the parrot had found each other when they had needed companionship and understanding the most.

9

"Before the sea captain took her in, she was kept too long in her cage by her previous owner," she explained. "Continually being confined weakened her ability to fly."

"A shame," he said softly.

She wondered if he meant it or if he was simply mouthing words like so many other people. No one else seemed to appreciate her bond with Megs the way she did. It was difficult, if not impossible, to explain. It simply was.

"Yes, it is," she agreed, gesturing toward the abandoned tray. "Shall we continue our tea?"

"I was hoping we might further our conversation instead," Camden said, his voice, like his expression, hardened and severe. "Specifically, I was keenly waiting for your answer."

Dear God.

She hadn't misheard him, then.

Nor did he appear to be jesting. If anything, the Duke of Camden was joyless, utterly unsmiling. So serious that his countenance might crack.

"I don't understand."

She skirted him, suddenly needing air. Distance. His size and his presence were duly overwhelming. Not that she feared him but that he was so very…masculine. So different from Wesley, who had been teasing and charming, filled with irreverent quips and longing glances that had lit her from within.

All a guise, as she had later learned. Everything about Lord Wesley Gilden had been contrived for the purpose of securing England's wealthiest heiress as his wife. And he had nearly accomplished the feat.

"Rosamund, don't run from me."

Camden was following her, his voice near, and her awareness of him made her heart stutter into a faster pace and a languorous bud of heat unfurl deep within her at the same time. The duke had always been dangerous to her. When she had been engaged to his brother, she had noticed him. He had taken all the air from every room he inhabited, intrigued her in a way that had been most improper. She had forgotten those restless feelings he'd inspired, dismissed them along with her betrothal.

But whatever she was, Rosamund Payne was no coward. She had faced almost every shame imaginable and held her head high. So she stopped and spun back to face Camden, and with so much haste that they collided, her bouncing off his granite wall of a chest.

"Oh," she said, the startled exclamation fleeing her.

She should remove her hands from his coat. Cease touching him. Step away. But he was hotter than the most comforting winter's fire in the grate. And he smelled delightfully manly, like shaving soap with a tinge of sandalwood and musk.

"I can explain," he said, a muscle in his wide jaw tightening.

She forced a laugh she didn't feel, intent upon showing him nothing but sangfroid. No emotion. Not a hint of anything other than what she wanted him to see.

"I do not see how you possibly can," she said honestly.

For there was not a world that existed in which the arrogant Duke of Camden wanted to marry his younger brother's plain, spinster castoff. No matter how much money she promised to bring to their union. Unless...

She searched his gaze, looking for affirmation. Finding it.

"You need funds," she guessed, almost breathless at the thought.

"I do." His hands had clamped on her waist to steady her, but that was where they remained, holding her to him.

Not tightly. She could escape. And yet, she made no move to do so. There was a shocking intimacy to the way he held her, wrapped in an arrogant assumption.

11

Part of Rosamund wanted to push away from him; his grasp was gentle enough, and she could extricate herself with ease. But part of her wanted to linger. To keep her hands on his chest, where his heart was thumping every bit as hastily as hers. He was not as unaffected as he pretended either.

That didn't change her inevitable answer. "I'm afraid that marriage no longer holds the allure it once possessed for me. And as for the notion that I must be wanted for my fortune alone, well, as you can imagine, Your Grace, that has grown particularly hateful. I am no longer willing to give a man my fortune in exchange for his name. It is a terrible business decision."

And she *did* have a flair for business. That was one realization she could thank Lord Wesley Gilden for, even if she would sooner blacken his eye than admit it aloud.

The duke's pale eyes burned into hers. "Never imagine I come to you without something to offer in return."

"I have no interest in being a duchess. I am perfectly content to be Miss Payne until the day I die. Titles mean less than nothing to me, particularly when the title in question belongs to a member of the Gilden family. Plainly, you and your offer of marriage and title and scoundrel brother can all go rot."

"Go rot," Megs chimed in from her perch. "Gormless shite. Megs want tea cake."

Rosamund chose to ignore her beloved parrot for the moment, knowing that Megs was nettled because she was.

Camden's lip curled, and he released her, taking a step back. "I do not fault you for that opinion."

"I wouldn't care if you did."

"Brava." A small smile played with the corners of his lips. "The tigress has emerged at last."

"Tigress?"

"You were always so quiet and placid, allowing Wesley to

12

trod all over you and doing so with a smile. But I saw beyond your polite façade. I very much doubt he ever did. If you had married, he would have destroyed you. You would have been miserable as his wife."

The tea was cooling. And in truth, it was a source of comfort for her—the preparation of a cup, the slow and careful movements, the joy of drinking it. She had grown accustomed to hiding herself behind the trappings of civility. Most people never looked beyond them.

The Duke of Camden, however, was not most people.

Her chin went up. "How fortunate, then, that his mistress sent me a letter before I was foolish enough to marry him."

Although the missive had long since been tossed angrily into the flames, she knew every word of it by heart. *He loves me, though he will wed you to provide for our little family.*

Our little family.

Three words that had broken her heart open like a ripened peach dropped from lofty heights. How she had loved Lord Wesley Gilden. He'd been out of her reach, charming and handsome, and his attention had gone straight to her head, rendering her quite witless for a woman who prided herself on her intelligence. That fact still grated raw upon her nerves now—that she had known better, had been wiser, and yet still he had outmaneuvered her with such devastating ease. Oh, how she loathed her own stupidity—to this day, a perennial thorn in her side.

Camden's smile faded, his unusual eyes still holding her in their piercing thrall. "You are right to be angry with him. My brother is a bastard."

"Right bastard," Megs said, whistling. "Megs want pistache."

"Language, Megs," she chided before she surrendered to the African grey's demand.

Breaking the hold Camden's stare had on her, Rosamund

moved past him to where Megs watched them from her perch, her head cocked, her silvery gaze somehow both curious and knowing.

"Megs want pistache," the bird repeated, apparently having changed her mind about the earlier request for tea cake.

"And you shall have it, but you must behave," she crooned, stroking Megs's silken head with a crooked finger.

She picked up the pouch from the table where she had left it and extracted one nut, offering it to the parrot, who eagerly took it in her beak. As she stood with her back to him, Rosamund could feel Camden's stare on her as if it were a touch. Swallowing down a rush of unwanted emotion, she spun about to face him again, pinning a polite smile to her lips.

"Oh my, look at the time. Regretfully, I have other engagements awaiting me today, Your Grace."

His expression was unreadable, his harsh face drawn, and she could not deny the compelling figure he made, standing in her drawing room as if he belonged there, tall and elegant and haughty. He was more handsome than she had recalled, and it disturbed her to make that acknowledgment. To recognize that she was aware of him as a man.

That perhaps she always had been, even when she'd believed herself in love with his brother.

"I'll take my leave, but I would remind you before I go that if you marry me, you'll have the one thing you have been coveting these last three years."

She laughed bitterly. "If you think it was the illustrious Gilden family name I was after, you are wrong, Your Grace."

"Not my name." He smiled again, but it didn't reach his eyes. "Revenge."

CHAPTER 2

"*F*or you, Your Grace."

Stuart accepted the correspondence from his butler, Fleetwood, his gut tightening at the familiar scrawl on the missive atop the proffered silver salver.

Another one.

He was careful to keep even a hint of his concern from showing on his face. "Thank you, Fleetwood. Has Lord Wesley come home yet this afternoon?"

"His Lordship has not," his butler said, confirming Stuart's suspicions.

Curse him. It would seem Stuart had no means of keeping his brother from ruining him, save locking the bastard in a room, and he had already made unsuccessful use of that tactic. Wesley had climbed out the bloody window.

He forced a polite smile for Fleetwood's benefit, but he knew damned well he wasn't fooling the shrewd old retainer. "I trust you will notify me if he does?"

The butler sketched a bow. "Of course, Your Grace."

He nodded. "Thank you. That will be all."

As Fleetwood disappeared with a discreet snick of the

door closing once more, Stuart ground his molars and hissed out a frustrated breath from between clamped teeth.

"Fucking damn it," he muttered, then raked his fingers through his hair, no doubt leaving it unkempt.

But there was no one to impress in the hollow, painfully bare confines of the study that had once been his father's, and, before that, his grandfather's, now his. The dark squares and rectangles on the ancient damask wall coverings mocked him. These were spaces where priceless paintings had hung, long since removed and sold off in an attempt to ameliorate his father's mounting debts.

Wishing for a whisky—or better yet, one of his old chum King's infamous concoctions designed to numb the mind— he forced himself to read the latest letter. All the spirits were gone anyhow.

To His Grace, the Duke of Camden,
Five thousand pounds shall be delivered to Messrs.
Dolan and Rowe by the end of the month or a
letter concerning all pertinent information will be
delivered to The Times.

An icy tendril of dread licked down his spine at the threat. The bastard was growing bolder.

The end of the month.

He had mere weeks to gather up a small fortune and deliver it, just as he had for the past few months. The initial letter had spelled out, in intricate detail, what the sender knew and what he was willing to do unless his demands for payment were met. Stuart's initial shock had given way to rage and a determination to do something, anything, to keep this unknown monster from revealing the truth. Only to realize that his hands were tied. He had no recourse. He couldn't go to Scotland Yard or anyone else with the threats because that would reveal the reason for the blackmail, and while Stuart could weather any scandal, Mother could not.

And so, he answered every letter with the required payment, draining his already scanty funds as surely as Wesley did and their father before him.

Stuart didn't have five thousand pounds, of course. He'd scarcely summoned the three thousand pounds for the last request. Damn Wesley for putting them in this tenuous circumstance.

And curse Miss Rosamund Payne for refusing his proposal. It had, perhaps, not been one of Stuart's finer ideas. But when one needed enough funds to rival Croesus himself, one had few options. Rosamund's wealth was tremendous. It would have been the solution to his problems, a means of relieving himself from the burden of debts, mortal and otherwise, that Wesley and their father had amassed.

Oh, there was another solution, to be sure. But Stuart hadn't the stomach for murder. There was also a problem with such a tactic. He didn't know who was behind the blackmailing.

But he hadn't the time to agonize over the letter or the threats at the moment. He had a ball to attend. Because that was how utterly ridiculous his life had become. Fending off creditors and blackmailers in the morning and afternoon, then feigning a smile and waltzing by the evening.

Gritting another foul curse, Stuart rose from his desk, crumpling the letter in his fist as he did so. No need to preserve the words; they were tattooed upon his very brain. Grimly, he stalked across the room to the low fire burning in the grate and pitched the balled missive within. Flames took a moment to lick at the paper before engulfing it, the entire thing diminishing to ash in seconds.

If only he could apply the same hasty banishment to his unknown foe.

Until that day came, he had no recourse, save trying to persuade Miss Rosamund Payne to change her mind.

Stuart passed the next two hours in the prodigiously painful preparations. His valet, Sharpe, fretted over his evening finery with the fastidious devotion of a true dandy. In the end, it was formal blacks with a white necktie, but the first waistcoat he'd donned had been dismissed by Sharpe.

"Too garish, Your Grace, if you will forgive me for saying so."

Stuart had glanced bemusedly down at himself, thinking the waistcoat perfectly suitable.

"And a wrinkle," Sharpe worried. "It must be pressed anew, I fear."

He would have argued that no one would spy the wrinkle as it would be hidden well beneath his coat, but Stuart held his tongue. He knew there was no winning a battle with his determined valet.

"So much lint," Sharpe had proclaimed at the replacement, his worries no more assuaged as he shook his head and all but wrung his hands in despair. "I fail to see where it all has come from. No, no, no. This one shan't do, Your Grace."

A third had finally passed muster, and now, Stuart prowled the absolute crush of Brandon's ball, overheated, annoyed, and desperately in need of a drink. Anything to bring him oblivion. Only, he couldn't imbibe. Not now, not yet. He had a plan of battle to attend.

And fortunately, his quarry stood just on the periphery of the dance floor, conferring with the widowed Countess of Grenfell, whose fiery tresses made her stand out in any crowd. How fortunate.

The air was scented with a cloying blend of sweat, hair grease, champagne, and perfume, the gas lamps blazing hot as Hades overhead. But as he drew nearer to Miss Payne, those unfortunate details concerned him significantly less. She was smiling at something Lady Grenfell had said, and it was genuine rather than feigned, unguarded and guileless. It was decidedly not how she had looked at him during their meeting.

There had been pistols at dawn in her eyes. Her smiles had been small, tight, and forced. Her posture had been that of a soldier about to march into battle, tense and poised, ready for action. She saw him as her enemy, and he couldn't blame her for that.

In a way, he was. What he wanted from her was what most men wanted from her, what Wesley had wanted from her—her fortune. She hadn't minced words. And, as always, he'd been impressed by her. Miss Rosamund Payne was stronger and far more confident than she'd been three years ago. She was harder too. Where once she'd worn her softness with naïve unawareness, now she had donned her armor. He hated how poorly Wesley had treated her during their doomed betrothal, but he was also glad that she'd taken up the cudgels for herself.

By the time he reached Rosamund, Lady Grenfell had conveniently ventured elsewhere, leaving Rosamund alone. Her dark eyes widened at his approach, and he forced a smile of his own, bowing.

"Miss Payne."

She offered him a punctuated curtsy in return. "Duke."

A painfully polite silence descended. His fault. All the practiced flattery in his head had vanished the second he was in proximity. Thank Christ she didn't have the parrot with her. He had half expected to find the rude little creature perched on her shoulder, glaring at him with smug, silvery eyes as it called him a gormless shite.

A small victory.

The orchestra struck up a cotillion, prodding him into action.

"Would you do me the honor of dancing with me?" he asked, feeling like a nervous suitor courting his first debutante. This sort of nonsense wasn't his preference at all.

"I don't dance."

He knew that for a lie. He'd seen her dance with Wesley on numerous occasions, and she'd been elegantly graceful.

Stuart raised a brow. "Then why attend a ball?"

She pursed her lips, thinking for a moment before responding. "Boredom, I suppose. And the opportunity to wear a new gown."

Those notions didn't persuade him any more than her assertion she didn't dance had.

Stuart shook his head, absurdly amused. "Those reasons seem painfully vacuous for a woman of your intelligence, Miss Payne."

And Rosamund Payne was nothing if not a clever woman. One conversation with her, and it was clear. How she had fallen prey to Wesley remained a mystery he wasn't certain he would ever solve. But she wasn't alone in her plight.

Her eyes narrowed. "Must I have a reason to attend a ball, Your Grace?"

There was her fighting spirit, in full renaissance. He couldn't deny it; there was something undeniably alluring about her when she was determined, her jaw clenched, her shoulders drawn back in a pugnacious stance. She was a woman who had learned how to defend herself, to fight her own battles.

Stuart tilted his head in acknowledgment. "One must always have a reason for everything one undertakes in life. Even if it's not a good one."

Her chin went up. "Oh? And what is yours, then, for approaching me this evening?"

She had him there, but he wasn't ready to admit defeat.

He summoned the charm that he had once possessed and smiled as if he hadn't a care. "To dance with you, of course."

She laughed at him. The utter daring, to laugh at him, the Duke of Camden, in the midst of a crowded ballroom.

"If you expect me to believe that rot, then you must think me every bit as foolish as I was three years ago," she said, her tone rather biting.

He clenched his jaw. "Brandon is my friend, of course. I would attend regardless of your presence here, but I'm being honest when I tell you that there is not another soul in this ballroom I would dance with other than yourself."

Her lips parted, and for a moment, she stared at him, her gaze searching, and it was in that same breath that he noticed she had depths of honeyed amber in her dark-brown eyes. But then she clamped her lips into a tight line, and she stiffened her spine.

"You want to dance with me because you need my fortune," she countered, her voice hushed. "Do not pretend to court me like a lovestruck swain. It only makes me long to punch you in the nose."

He had no doubt that she would do it too.

Stuart was bemused by this new Rosamund. He hated that his brother's betrayal was the cause of it. But he also heartily approved of her unfailing confidence, which had been previously lacking. Even if she'd been forced to acquire it through her own heartbreak. Stuart was quite familiar with that sort of pain, which was why his own heart was cold and dead. Lady Flora Seaton had seen to that.

"I would prefer not to go about the ball with a bloodied nose, if you don't mind," he told Rosamund, keeping his tone mild. "But perhaps we might take a walk in the gardens and talk privately, without fear of our conversation being overheard."

He knew the confines of Brandon's town house—inside and out—quite well. They'd been chums since their Eton days. But more than that, they were also clandestine business partners, along with four other friends. He had no doubt that the others—the Dukes of Kingham, Whitby, Riverdale, and Richford, in no particular order—were mingling somewhere in the throng as well.

Her eyebrows rose at his suggestion—a bold one, he knew. "Have we not said everything there is to say?"

She would give him no quarter. Of course not.

"Must I prostrate myself before you to persuade you to lend me a few more moments of your time?" he asked.

Between the letters, the threats, Wesley's profligate gambling, and his ever-growing mountain of debt, Stuart had no remaining pride. He would likely kiss Miss Rosamund Payne's hems if she demanded it of him, with the entire ballroom as witness too.

The burden of duty was oft a suffocating, humiliating one.

She hesitated in her response, and he seized his opportunity.

"Oh, look," he said lightly, looking over her shoulder as if he spied someone approaching. "Here comes the Marchioness of Seabury headed in this direction. The august lady looks as if she is in desperate need of a tender listening ear. I trust you can provide her with one."

Rosamund's brows crashed inward in a sudden frown. "Not Lady Seabury. The last time she cornered me at a ball, I couldn't rid myself of her for a full hour."

He remembered, because it had happened when he had hosted the ball in honor of Rosamund and Wesley's betrothal. He felt slightly guilty at using Lady Seabury in his effort to further his campaign, for she had recently met an untimely end. But Rosamund didn't appear to know that salient fact, and he was shamelessly using it to his advantage.

"Fine," she growled. "Take me outside if you must. Anything to listening to her opine on the finest feathers for adorning a hat. I have no wish to make a row with her today."

Among her faults, Lady Seabury had been dreadfully loquacious, with a tendency to force anyone she could to listen to her sermons on fashion.

He offered Rosamund his arm. "Allow me to save you, dear lady."

She hesitated, eyeing him sternly for a heartbeat, her hand outstretched, before she settled it in the crook of his elbow. "Do kick your noble steed into a gallop, sir. I have no wish to spend the rest of my evening trying not to take note when Lady Seabury breaks wind."

Her declaration startled a laugh from him. "I knew she was notorious for her lengthy discussions, but I hadn't quite heard *that* before."

A becoming flush tinged Rosamund's cheeks. "I suppose that was badly done of me."

Not as badly done as him lying about a dead woman approaching them just so he could get Rosamund alone.

Stuart gave the hand resting on his arm a serene pat. "Never mind that, my dear. I'm happy to be of service."

Hellfire. He was no better than his scoundrel brother.

THE NIGHT AIR was cool as it kissed Rosamund's cheeks, which was just as well because the combination of the ball's crush, the blazing chandeliers, and the Duke of Camden's sudden appearance at her side had rendered her thoroughly overheated. Likely, venturing outside with him had been a mistake. But it was one she couldn't rectify, now that she walked with him on the gravel path beneath the silvery glow of a watchful moon.

A heavy silence had descended between them as Camden had expertly weaved them through the throng of fellow revelers and out the door into the gardens, punctuated by the gurgling of a small fountain. He brought them to a pause before it, the Roman goddess of the hunt presiding over them, reaching for her quiver.

"Ah, Diana," Camden drawled. "Goddess of wild beasts. Rather an appropriate place for our discussion, I think."

"Which one of us is the wild beast, Your Grace?" she couldn't help asking.

"There is one within us all, at least to a certain extent. Would you not agree?"

His voice was low, and although he hadn't said a suggestive word, something within her quickened. The Duke of Camden possessed a pleasant, deep voice that slid over her senses like a silken caress.

"Perhaps," she allowed, mindful that every minute she spent alone in his presence in the moonlight was fraught with danger. "But I do think it would be prudent to save such debates and to talk about what you wished to discuss with me instead. Our time here in the gardens must be limited."

"Good of you to remind me." His tone was wry as he turned to face her instead of the fountain, forcing her hand from its resting place on his arm. "As you might have guessed, I wished to speak with you about my offer."

His proposal of marriage, he meant. And she couldn't deny it—she remained cautiously intrigued by the prospect, for two very private, wholly different reasons. The old dream she'd once had of a family, children of her own, had reemerged like a perennial bursting through the crust of winter's soil to sprout anew. At thirty, she had quite surrendered that dream and her shattered heart. But now, the lure was there, the opportunity to seize what had been denied her.

And then there was the other potent temptation, not nearly as noble—gaining her revenge upon the man who had once brought her to her knees. But as much as she loathed Lord Wesley Gilden for his lies and betrayal, she could not, even in her weakest moments when the need for vengeance burned hottest, reconcile sacrificing the rest of her life to obtain it. Nor was she certain that she would wish to have children with the Duke of Camden, of all men. It was foolishness to hope, and she recognized that weakness in herself that made such a union seem possible.

There was only one sound response to give him.

"I'm afraid my answer must remain the same, regardless of whatever you would impart," she told him quietly.

"A chance," he said. "A few moments of your time to explain myself. That is all I ask of you now."

When he phrased it thus, she felt a curmudgeon for denying him. The yearning within her roared back into a flame from a tiny ember.

Rosamund inclined her head. "If you must, but I can assure you, there's nothing you can say that will alter my mind."

He caught her hand in his suddenly, his grasp gentle and yet shocking, the urgency and intimacy sending a dark thrill through her when she least wanted it.

"Please, Rosamund."

He was being far too familiar with her. She shouldn't like it, and yet some perverse part of her did. She would be lying if she said she had never taken note of her former betrothed's handsome older brother. But she had been in love with Wesley, loyal to him, and her admiration had never gone further than a frank intellectual acknowledgment that the Duke of Camden was a handsome man.

She forced out a sigh, vexed as much with herself as with him. "If you insist."

"I do." He gave her fingers a tender squeeze. "Thank you. I understand your feelings where Wesley is concerned. My brother is in the mold of my father. A wastrel, who was a wastrel before him."

His candor took her by surprise.

"That is unkind of you to say," she observed nonetheless, although without bite.

Behind them, the din of the ball was faded and yet an omnipresent reminder that they weren't far from a room filled with lords and ladies. The Duke of Camden was still holding her hand in his, and she was oddly reluctant to sever the connection. Perhaps she had consumed too much champagne.

"The truth is not often kind," Camden said, his voice stern, with a harsh edge that she knew wasn't reserved for her. "He's also a liar, a reprobate, and a terrible gambler as well, but I was aiming to be politic."

"If so, I do believe you fell short of the mark." She raised a brow at him, even if he couldn't see her in the moon's pale illumination. "Not that I mind, of course. My own opinion of your brother is anything but polite, as you no doubt are already aware."

"And you have every reason to feel so. What he did to you was unconscionable."

Something occurred to her then, which had not in the gloomy days of despair when she had first learned of Wesley's perfidy. "You knew what he was doing, didn't you? You knew he had no desire to marry me at all, that he only wanted my fortune and he was willing to lie to me and use any means possible to persuade me to wed him."

"Any means?" A muscle ticked in his jaw. "Surely he did not coerce you into anything...untoward?"

"If you are wondering whether your brother forced me, the answer is no. He did not." She summoned a smile that she knew was bitter, filled with fury for Lord Wesley's careless manipulations and how effortlessly she had been his dupe. "He wouldn't have done, or so he told me in his own words. He isn't partial to plain, big-nosed spinsters."

The duke muttered an oath. "Your nose isn't overly large."

Camden's firm pronouncement took her off guard, as did the anger lacing his voice. It was almost as if he were furious on her behalf. But that made no sense. He was Lord Wesley's brother. Surely his loyalty lay firmly with his own family.

She tamped down any feelings of gratitude toward the duke for coming to her defense. After all, telling her that her nose wasn't large was hardly a compliment.

"Thank you, Your Grace. I am unbearably flattered."

"Christ. That's not how I meant it."

She wouldn't take pity on him; she couldn't. His rogue of a brother had left her with none.

"Oh?" she asked lightly. "It sounded rather how you meant it to me. But you needn't feel as if you must pay me false compliments or issue untruthful odes to my beauty. Your brother did all that well enough, and I'm quite inured to it now, I assure you."

"What I meant," he said emphatically, giving her fingers another urgent but gentle squeeze, "is that the insults he paid you were untrue. You are a lovely woman in your own right."

She wasn't lovely, and Rosamund knew it. Some women were. Her friend Lottie, the Countess of Grenfell, for instance, was beautiful. Rosamund was more than aware of her own appearance, in sharp contrast. Her hair was neither golden nor red but some shade vaguely in between, and it held no natural curl. Her eyes were dark and common as mud, her face unique rather than pretty. That, she blamed on her Payne blood. Her father's family all possessed sharp, angular features. High foreheads, stern brows, long noses, and rigid jaws.

She had inherited many of their characteristics. She wasn't a particularly soft and demure woman. She was opinionated, intelligent, and independent. Business thrilled her, not balls. One of her most beloved companions was a parrot with a shockingly vulgar vocabulary. She was only palatable to polite society because of her few, treasured polite society friendships and the fact that she had first possessed a massive dowry and later inherited the remainder of a vast fortune from her father upon his death.

Her allure, in short, was not her looks. It was her funds. Her endless funds. Once, she had been naïve enough to believe otherwise, persuaded by a handsome man who danced attendance and kisses on her.

Never again.

"Pray don't insult me with lies, Your Grace. It is beneath the both of us," she told Camden cooly.

"Paying you insult was not my intent, and let me assure you that I'm not lying."

She didn't believe him, of course. But she was growing weary of this game they played, and the longer they lingered in the darkened garden, the greater their chances of being caught became.

Rosamund shook her head. "Regardless, you must understand my hesitancy to remain here with you, when all you have to offer me is false flattery and the concession that your brother is a scoundrel."

"But I have more to offer you, if you will but listen," he insisted. "All our lives, my brother has wanted everything that is mine. It started with a set of wooden toy soldiers our father bought me on a whim, and it went on to include the title I was set to inherit and, later, the woman I loved. He has done everything in his power to ruin me."

The raw bitterness in the duke's voice was undeniable. Here, in the silvery moonlight, it was as if he had finally taken down the arrogant mask he wore.

"The woman you loved?" she pressed, morbidly curious.

"My brother seduced her and then refused to marry her, all to spite me. He took great enjoyment from my pain."

The revelation should not shock her; she knew Wesley was capable of anything. And yet, it somehow did.

"Was this before or after our betrothal?" Rosamund asked, wanting to know and yet hating herself for it.

The answer had no bearing upon her. It changed nothing. "Before."

She swallowed against an unwanted rush of feeling, hating that after three years, Wesley's betrayal still affected her. "Still, I fail to see what this has to do with your proposal."

"Everything. Do you not see? If you marry me, he will covet you. And yet, he will never have you, because you are too wise for his tricks. Seeing you as my duchess will be a constant reminder to him of what he lost through his own ruthless manipulations. It would be the greatest form of revenge he can be dealt."

For the first time, she understood what the duke offered her, completely and without question. And she couldn't deny it—there was a certain forbidden allure to the notion.

But Rosamund remained unconvinced that consigning herself to a loveless marriage for the rest of her life all to enact vengeance on Lord Wesley Gilden would be a worthy trade. Even if it would give her the chance for the family she had always longed for.

"Although revenge is tempting," she said, "I remain a businesswoman, Your Grace. One who cannot see the value of her fortune and freedom equaling mere retribution. You require my fortune. I, however, do not require anything."

Except children of my own, she thought, but she wisely kept that to herself.

"Do you deny that the thought of holding the purse strings where my brother is concerned is not appealing?" he asked.

"Yes, but I am not the one who would be holding them, would I? If I married you, then you would be in possession of not just my funds, but my independence as well. And I can assure you that my autonomy is worth far more than any amount of gold or petty reprisal."

"A marriage contract would assuage all your concerns."

Rosamund was about to answer when the cacophony of the ballroom suddenly became louder, punctuated by the tinkling laugh of a woman on the veranda beyond the fountain. Another couple had come into the gardens, presumably for privacy. Perhaps for a tryst. One simply never knew what manner of mischief was afoot at a ball, particularly one hosted by the notorious Duke of Brandon. A masculine voice could be heard, followed by the crunch of gravel on soles.

She inhaled sharply, fear that they would be caught freezing her in place.

But Camden took her hand in his, lacing their fingers together, and tugged her deeper into the shadows. She couldn't deny the sudden spark of awareness that lit within her at their entwined hands, even as he pulled her rudely down the path. The giggling lady grew louder.

"Who's there?" asked a male voice.

Panic assailed her. They were about to be caught! She had no wish to be forced into marriage with the Duke of Camden. She would sooner spend the rest of her life in ignominy and disgrace.

Camden startled her by whirling her around and pinning her neatly to the solid stone statue at her back.

"Hush," he whispered, his head bent toward hers as if he

meant to kiss her, his hot breath coasting over her lips in the prelude to something she was sure she should not want.

And yet her pulse leapt. Her nipples went embarrassingly hard beneath the rigid boning of her corset. Deep in her belly, heat blossomed. Everything within her felt as if it were tightened, like the string on an instrument pulled excruciatingly taut. Was it anticipation, fear, or shock that made her feel thus? Or was it the Duke of Camden's lean, muscled strength crowding her into the marble base of the statue, a wall of cool stone at her back in stark contrast to the warmth blazing from him? His scent curled around her, mingling with the damp night air and the light perfume of blossoming roses—sandalwood and musk.

She inhaled, painfully aware that his mouth was near enough that she could rise on her toes and press her lips there, on that stern line that was so oft unsmiling. Such a strange intimacy, kissing. The sharing of breaths and lips and tongues. Would he kiss her?

Did she want him to?

Yes, answered the whisper of some insidious longing inside her. She did want him to. Very much. She scarcely heard the approaching couple over the relentless pounding of her heart.

"Apologies, old chap," came the same masculine voice from somewhere in the darkness beyond the wall of Camden's chest.

He was blocking her from view, she realized.

Protecting her.

The discovery was as shocking as her desire for him was.

Another feminine giggle broke the silence, and then the crunching of gravel signaled that the couple was headed in a different direction, no doubt in search of their own privacy. Camden didn't immediately move. Instead, he remained as he was, his big body pinning hers to the statue, his hands on the marble at either side of her, keeping her there.

The air between them turned heavy. A frisson of yearning she had no right to feel swept over her. Would he kiss her now?

He lingered, his eyes glittering in the pale light, burning into her, his lips so close. And then, as if a spell had suddenly been broken, he raised his head and stepped away from her, leaving her bereft, the statue keeping her from falling unceremoniously to her rump.

"Consider what I've told you before you make your final decision," he said coolly, as if what had just happened between them had been one-sided. "We should return to the ball now before someone else happens upon us. We were fortunate enough with this interruption."

He offered his arm to her.

Rosamund shook herself from the grips of whatever delirium had possessed her. "We should go back in alone."

Camden gestured for her to proceed. "You first, and then I'll follow you in a few moments."

She swallowed hard against another rush of unwanted longing. "Good evening, Your Grace."

As she gathered what remained of her tattered pride and swept past him, she heard him call her name.

"Rosamund."

She turned back to find him watching her, the moonlight lovingly silhouetting his tall figure.

"You still owe me a dance."

She didn't bother to argue, and neither did she answer him. But when Rosamund returned to the ball, she found her mother, who was in her cups and tittering with a pair of dowagers who had similarly enjoyed more than their fair share of champagne.

"I'm calling for the carriage," she announced.

"Must we go already?" her mother asked, sounding dismayed.

Since Father's death, Mother relied upon societal diversions to keep her from melancholy.

Rosamund thought of her strange interlude with the Duke of Camden and his determination to dance with her. She didn't think she could risk being held in his arms. Her ability to remain impervious was in severe jeopardy, as was her rational thinking. Too much champagne and bracing air outdoors. The moonlight had made her maudlin.

"Yes," she said firmly. "I'm afraid that we must."

She needed to escape before she did something more foolish than agreeing to wed Lord Wesley Gilden— promising to marry his forbidding older brother.

CHAPTER 3

*H*e had almost kissed Rosamund.

What the devil had he been thinking?

Stuart was still chastising himself for his own stupidity the day after Brandon's ball as he stalked toward his sleeping brother, pitcher of water firmly in hand. Wesley was sprawled on one of the few remaining pieces of furniture in his barren library, booted feet crossed at the ankles, wearing clothing that was at least three days old, snoring loudly enough to wake the dead. The whole bloody room smelled of sour spirits, sweat, and dirty boots.

He *hadn't* been thinking, and that was a problem. He needed to remain calculated and collected if he was to persuade Rosamund to marry him. She was balking at the notion—and far too much for his peace of mind. He couldn't go about kissing her in gardens or performing any of the other acts that might have accompanied those kisses and about which he would absolutely *not* think just now on account of the snoring, drunken wastrel he was about to wake.

Stuart stopped before his brother, watching him for a

moment. When Wesley slept, it was the only time he wasn't reaping more debts he couldn't pay or getting himself thoroughly soused or causing some other manner of mayhem. There was a dark bruise beneath his brother's left eye and a split above his upper lip.

A drunken fight of some sort, no doubt.

Or perhaps Wesley had bedded another man's wife, and the fellow hadn't been impressed. Whatever had happened to him, his brother wasn't dead, which was what Stuart often feared when Wesley disappeared for days at a time. He was alive and breathing and snoring on Stuart's Grecian couch instead of lying in a ditch somewhere, a bullet or a blade in his back. But whilst the initial relief had been strong at being informed that Wesley had returned relatively unscathed and was *presently inhabiting the library*, as Fleetwood had so politely phrased the situation, all such comfort had gone. Fury was its omnipresent replacement.

Stuart lifted the pitcher over his brother's head and tipped it. Liquid poured from the spout, sluicing over Wesley's greasy blond hair. His brother came to life with a snort and a howl, spluttering on water.

"What the bloody hell, Stuart?" he demanded furiously, shaking like a soaked dog emerging from an unwanted bath.

Droplets sprayed all over the threadbare Axminster.

"Wake up," he said without sympathy.

"Fuck you," Wesley growled. "I *am* awake. And thoroughly goddamned sopping."

"At least you're alive," he said, unmoved by his brother's ire. "Where have you been these last few days?"

He could imagine, of course, but usually, reality was so much worse, and Stuart preferred to know what he was dealing with when it came to Wesley.

"I was having a run of good fortune, if you must know,"

Wesley said, dashing more water from his eyes. "I won a thousand pounds."

Whenever Wesley won, he neglected to take into consideration the many thousands of pounds he'd lost over the years in the name of securing that futile victory. It was the disease of the gambler, to forever be chasing that ever-elusive luck, the one hand of cards or roll of dice that would make his every sacrifice worthwhile.

Only, too often, that halcyon moment never arrived.

"You haven't the funds to gamble," he reminded his brother grimly.

And meanwhile, Stuart had depleted his coffers of what he had gleaned from the Wicked Dukes Society. Not that it signified. Nothing stopped Wesley from doing whatever the hell he wanted, regardless of how damaging it was to those around him.

"I've funds aplenty," Wesley countered. "How do you think I won the thousand quid?"

"One of the few acquaintances you have remaining whom you haven't yet beggared?" he guessed unkindly. "Or perhaps you're selling yourself as a stud to unsuspecting widows."

Wesley's eyes narrowed, and he shot to his feet, a bit unsteady. "I'm not a whore, you pompous prick."

Stuart shrugged. "You've already sold your soul. I was merely thinking of what could be left of value that you might pawn."

Wesley's lip curled as he swayed drunkenly to his right. "You haven't an inkling of what it's like, standing there, the Duke of Camden, so damned smug. Three years' difference, and I would be in your shoes. An accident of birth has kept me from all that should be rightfully mine."

Stuart couldn't help but to think of another for whom three years had made a great difference. Rosamund could assume the role of an icy queen all she liked, but he had seen hints of vulnerability hiding just beneath her emotionless façade. She had been suffering in the wake of Wesley's betrayal. It had left her reeling.

But that was often the way of the world. The victim was left to pay the price for the crime visited upon them, whilst the criminal could blithely carry on with life.

He held his brother's bloodshot gaze. "I do know what it's like to be the elder brother, forced to shoulder your debts and pay for your exploits and to soothe Mother's fears whilst you're gallivanting about London, whoring and gambling and Christ knows what else."

"Ah, yes, our sainted mater." Wesley stumbled to the sideboard, presumably searching for spirits when more was the last thing he needed. "How is the old bird today, hmm? Still hiding in her chamber like a frightened mouse?"

Their mother was not well, and she hadn't been for years. His brother's casual insults stung on her behalf. Stuart longed to stalk across the library to grasp Wesley by the back of his rumpled coat and shake the devil out of him before tossing him into the street.

Instead, he remained where he stood, flexing his fingers at his sides, forcing himself to maintain the pretense of a calm he was incapable of feeling. "Mother is as well as can be expected. She worries over you and wishes you would pay her a call."

Wesley laughed bitterly. "She's never given a damn about the spare. She only ever loved the heir."

That wasn't true. Their mother loved Wesley, and with a dedicated determination and unwillingness to see any of the villainy within him that sometimes made unwelcome surges of jealousy eat Stuart up inside.

"She loves you," he continued, balling his hands into impotent fists. "It would do her spirits some good to see you."

"It would do her spirits some good to get out of that

fucking room," Wesley returned snidely, swiping his arm through empty crystal glasses and sending them crashing to the floor. "Where the hell is the brandy?"

"Gone," he said, pleased with himself for finally deciding to remove all sources of temptation from the town house. "You drank the last of it, and we haven't money for more."

"Then I reckon my thousand pounds will have to fetch me some. I'm ill. I need my medicine."

Brandy was no panacea for Wesley. He'd been getting deeper into his cups every night. His dissipation was beginning to show on his face and around his middle.

"You drank too much," he said curtly. "Again."

"On the contrary. I didn't drink *enough*, and that is why I feel like donkey shite." His brother waved an arm in the air and stumbled into the half-empty bookshelves.

"You look worse than it," he couldn't help pointing out. "You need breakfast, some sleep, and a bath, Wesley."

"Oh, do I? Thank you, wise brother duke, for telling me." He leaned against the shelves, presumably to keep from toppling to his arse. "I'll come to you for counsel on my life when you seek me out for advice on how to keep the woman you love from sucking your brother's cock."

The dull anger that had been growing within Stuart raged into a roaring blaze. It took every modicum of restraint he had to keep from leaping across the room like a wounded animal and throttling his brother.

"Do not speak of it," he warned.

"Or what?" Wesley grinned. "You'll stop paying my debts? You'll toss me into the street? We both know you won't." He pushed away from the shelves, his face turning white as he did so. "Fucking hell, I think I'm going to retch."

It would serve him right, but Stuart's domestics were spread painfully thin. The maid would already have to clean up the broken glasses. He had no wish to ask her to clean up his brother's vomit as well.

He closed the distance between himself and Wesley in a few hasty strides, thrusting the empty pitcher forward. "Use this. We can't afford to replace the carpets."

"How kind of you, brother," Wesley said and then promptly held the pitcher to his face and emptied the contents of his stomach into it.

Feeling ill himself and anything but kind, Stuart turned and stalked from the library, content to know that his brother would at least be staying in this evening. He wouldn't lose more money, and their mother could rest easily tonight with the knowledge that her second born was safe beneath the same roof.

MEGS FLUFFED up her feathers as Rosamund approached her, blinking silvery eyes that watched her progress. "Megs want pistache."

"Of course you do, darling," Rosamund crooned. "But first, you must behave."

The African grey flapped her wings. "Megs behave, Megs behave."

"I don't believe I've ever heard our Megs behave yet," commented her friend Miranda from across the room.

"True." Rosamund sighed and gave Megs a caress before reaching into the pouch where the parrot's favorite treat was kept and extracting a pistachio. She offered it. "Here you are, my love. No saying anything naughty during Miranda's visit, now."

Megs gleefully accepted the pistachio, her beak working at it.

Rosamund turned back to where Lady Miranda Lenox

awaited her by the tea tray that had just been delivered. "At least she will be preoccupied for a few moments so that we might be able to have our chat."

And a much-needed chat it was.

She had a great deal to tell Miranda, and in truth, she was somewhat afraid to reveal all for fear of what her friend would say, particularly after her revelations to her dear friend Lottie, the widowed Countess of Grenfell, had been met with stern warnings. Understandably so. Lottie's marriage had been a vastly unhappy one. But where Lottie had been in love with her husband, who had proven a wretched philanderer instead of an adoring spouse, Rosamund had no such feelings for Camden. If they were to enter a union, it would be a business arrangement, one that would prove beneficial to her in that she could gain what she wanted—children.

Rosamund seated herself. "Will you pour? You're so much more graceful than I am. I'm forever spilling."

It was true. Miranda was the epitome of grace and elegance. Which was ironic, because most of polite society had turned their backs to her and pretended as if she didn't exist. Not Rosamund. But then, Rosamund wasn't truly considered polite society.

"You are hardly clumsy, my dear," Miranda said kindly.

Because Miranda *was* kind. Sweetly, wonderfully kind. But only to those she cared for, as Rosamund had learned. She was honored to find herself in that rarest of company.

"Show us your bubbies," Megs called into the silence, followed by a whistle.

Mortification had Rosamund's cheeks going hot. Fortunately, Lady Miranda was an old acquaintance, and she wouldn't be chased off by the rapscallion parrot's vulgar vocabulary. Rosamund cast a glower over her shoulder at her beloved African grey, who had become more like a part of her since the two of them had first bonded several years earlier.

"Megs," she chastised sharply, nonetheless horrified. "No more pistachios for you for the rest of the day."

Megs flapped her wings in affront, blinking. "Megs want pistache."

"No," she countered sternly, wagging a disapproving finger at the bird, who eyed her serenely from her perch. "Megs shan't have a pistachio. Megs is a naughty bird."

"Naughty bird, naughty bird," Megs agreed. "Walk the plank."

Miranda's tinkling laughter spared Rosamund from further embarrassment. She turned back to the tea service awaiting them and her lovely friend's unabashedly grinning countenance.

"You needn't be put to the blush on my account," Miranda reassured her. "I find her hilarious."

"Her former owner was, you understand—"

"A sea captain," Miranda finished for her, chuckling. "So you've told me before, and I must say, I'm not surprised one whit. Her vocabulary is delightfully disreputable."

"It is delightfully *something*," Rosamund muttered, casting another stern look in the direction of the African grey. "Not one word out of you, miss."

Megs regarded her, blinking, and then fluffed her feathers as if to offer protest.

Shaking her head, Rosamund turned away. "Now you see why she cannot accompany me in polite circles. One word, and I'd be forever *de trop* in society. Not that I would particularly care much, but Mother would."

And it was, in part, her devotion to her dear mother that guided Rosamund through her days. She couldn't lie to herself; the more she had turned Camden's offer over in her mind, the more she had come to think of how overjoyed Mother would be to see her settled at last, with the potential to have a family. Mother had lamented on many occasions that she feared leaving Rosamund alone in the world one day. It was yet another reason she was even considering Camden's proposal when every modicum of reason she possessed told her she should not.

"We cannot displease your mother," Miranda agreed, expertly pouring tea for the two of them. "You know how much I adore your *maman*."

Rosamund smiled, accepting the cup that her friend had prepared exactly to her liking. "She returns your regard, of course. I do think you're one of her favorites in our little coterie, along with Lottie and Hyacinth."

"How wonderful to hear." Miranda sipped delicately from her own teacup. "Ah, perfection. It's so dreary outside, and I've been to the school all morning, which is utterly exhausting, even if it is rewarding. It was either tea or a nap, and I do so hate waking from naps. My mind always feels as if it's filled with fog when I rise. I'm quite bilious and disagreeable."

It was almost impossible to believe Miranda was anything other than her vivacious, charming self, but Rosamund knew she herself was a veritable bear in the mornings. Particularly when she needed to wake earlier than was her custom. Or when Megs decided to squawk her to waking, which was vexingly more often these days.

"How is your school coming along?" she asked her friend, genuinely curious.

"Quite well, thank you for asking, and despite all Ammondale's determination to destroy it—and me."

The Earl of Ammondale had, until several months ago, been Miranda's husband. Their divorce had not just been acrimonious, it had been the cause of endless society scandal and gossip. Miranda had abandoned the courtesy title,

Countess of Ammondale, in favor of her maiden name and styling, Lady Miranda Lenox.

After making Miranda miserable, Ammondale had sought a divorce when she had flaunted an affair with another man. The truth of the matter was that Miranda hadn't been unfaithful to her husband, whilst he had been nothing but the opposite to her. Miranda's affair had been an elaborate ruse conducted with a close friend, the Marquess of Waring. It was a guarded secret, one that Miranda had only shared with her inner circle and one that Rosamund would loyally defend. The divorce laws did not favor women, and her friend had done what was necessary to gain her freedom from an intolerable union.

It pained Rosamund to hear that the earl was continuing to cause problems for Miranda.

Rosamund frowned. "What has he been about now, the villain?"

"Walk the plank," Megs chirped.

"Oh, Megs, if only I had you to defend me," Miranda said with a small, sad smile.

"You do have Megs, and you have me as well." She settled her tea on the tray before her. "I am wealthy enough to do him some harm, you realize."

"Of course you are, my dear, and I do thank you for offering. But you know I would never ask you to join me in the fray. Nor would I seek to stoop to his levels. It has been punishment enough that you've been frowned upon for maintaining the friendship of a fallen woman."

The mere words—and the public disgrace Miranda yet faced—were enough to set Rosamund's teeth on edge. "You are not a fallen woman. You are true and good and wonderful. What is wrong with this society of ours? A faithful woman must feign faithlessness to escape a lecherous scoundrel because she needs more reason than mere adultery to obtain a divorce, whilst he requires only one."

"It is the law of the land, and we must follow it. I knew that when I married Ammondale." Miranda paused, her gaze drifting to a point over Rosamund's shoulder. "But I didn't have many choices then. Marriage to an earl seemed preferable to looming penury for myself and my sisters."

"Do you regret marrying Ammondale?" Rosamund asked softly, not wanting to pry and yet needing to know the answer.

For two of her dearest friends had experienced vastly unhappy marriages. And she was mad enough to be contemplating consigning herself to the same.

"Many times, I have," Miranda confided, her tone thoughtful. "Other times, I've been certain that I never would have been able to save myself or my sisters, that I wouldn't have been able to fund the school and pursue my own aspirations without having married him. I'm thankful it is over—that is all I can say for certain."

Rosamund took a deep breath, preparing herself to confess all, then exhaled slowly. "What would you say if I were to tell you that I was considering a marriage of convenience?"

Miranda's dark brows rose. "I would say I need more information. Are you truly considering marriage, dearest? And to whom?"

"I am." She took a moment, anticipating her friend's reaction and dreading it. "And it is to the Duke of Camden."

"The Duke of Camden?" Miranda's voice was loud, shocked. Almost shrill.

Rosamund winced. "Yes."

"*Lord Wesley Gilden's* elder brother, the Duke of Camden? The brother of the betrothed who treated you so shabbily that he ought to have been horse-whipped for his sins?"

"The same," she confirmed.

Miranda slumped back in her seat in a most unladylike and undignified pose, proof of her shock. "Rosamund."

"Gormless shite," Megs added suddenly, punctuating her words with a whistle.

"Is Megs referring to you or to the Duke of Camden?" Miranda asked carefully.

She sighed. "To Camden, I'm afraid. She seems to say it whenever he's about or mentioned."

"I cannot say I disagree with our feathered friend," Miranda said. "Rosamund, darling, whatever can you be thinking? First, Camden's reputation is positively dreadful. From the gossip I've heard, he's the worst sort of rake and rogue."

He hadn't seemed particularly rakish or roguish on their recent meetings. But then, no one knew better than Rosamund how easily someone could mask their true personality and intentions. Wesley had taught her that all too well with his betrayal.

"I suppose it wouldn't matter to me, his reputation," she said hesitantly. "Nor how he conducts himself with others. As I said, it would be a marriage of convenience."

"Whose convenience?" Miranda countered shrewdly. "Yours or his? Because I can assure you that marriages with scoundrels are wholly inconvenient for the wife, whilst the husband can do whatever he likes and still be accepted. What if you were to become unhappy in this union of yours? I would hate for you to end as I have, existing on the periphery of polite society, shunned by most."

Her heart gave a pang at the raw emotion in her friend's voice. "I know it has been so very difficult for you, the divorce."

"It is an albatross I gratefully bear. I would have done

anything to escape Ammondale. But enough about me. Why would *you* willingly take on such a burden?"

Here was a subject that was a delicate one indeed, particularly when having a discussion with a woman who hadn't any children of her own. But to omit it felt more and more like a deception.

"I am thirty years old, Miranda," she said gently. "This may well be my last chance to have a family of my own, which I have always dearly longed for. After what happened with Lord Wesley, I didn't dare trust another suitor, knowing my fortune was all every man would be after. But these circumstances are quite unique, and Camden's candor gives me a certain leverage that is appealing."

Her friend's face softened. "I understand that desire all too well, my dear. But you are lovely and witty, and you would make a wonderful wife to any man—one worthy of you. You could find someone other than the Duke of Camden for such a purpose, I have no doubt."

"It is not just the lure of a family that calls to me, I must confess." Rosamund paused, taking a deep breath and exhaling before continuing. "It's also revenge."

It felt petty to admit. Petty to say it aloud. And yet, it was the truth.

And then, somehow, it felt...powerful. It felt tantalizing. She thought of what Camden had asked that night in the moonlit gardens. *Do you deny that the thought of holding the purse strings where my brother is concerned is not appealing?*

"Now, that is indeed a potent lure," Miranda said, solemn understanding ringing in her voice.

She searched her friend's gaze, seeking absolution. "Would it be perfectly dreadful of me to do it, Miranda? Would I be the most foolish woman in all the world? Camden spoke of a marriage contract. I wouldn't accept a union without making certain I'm well protected. I think it possible I could have everything I've ever wanted, without compromising my freedom or my fortune."

"I think, my dear," Miranda said with judicious care, "that you must do what feels best. Seize what you want from life, for you only live it once. It's a lesson I learned during my miserable marriage. And make that bastard pay too."

"Pretty bird," Megs added from her perch. "Megs want pistache."

Miranda laughed at the interjection, and Rosamund joined her, a lightness falling over her that had been missing these last few years. It would seem she had her decision.

She was going to seize what she wanted.

CHAPTER 4

"*Y*our correspondence, Your Grace," intoned Fleetwood, delivering what was undoubtedly yet another stack of bills to Stuart's study.

His gut tightened as he eyed the unwelcome addition to the bills he couldn't pay already lining the polished surface in tidy piles he had arranged and then rearranged according to importance. He was running out of time.

"Thank you, Fleetwood," he said mildly, as if he hadn't a care in the world. "Is Lord Wesley in residence today?"

"Lord Wesley is breakfasting, Your Grace," the butler informed him stoically, as if it wasn't half past one in the afternoon.

"Breakfast," he repeated. "At this hour?"

"I believe his Lordship only recently decamped from his chamber, Your Grace," Fleetwood explained patiently, as if it were perfectly normal for a man to rise at one o'clock in the afternoon and demand breakfast.

It wasn't.

But he also knew that his brother had only arrived home at dawn, drunk and in good spirits after another evening at the green baize, if his cheerful, soused singing had been any indication. Stuart had been awakened by the commotion, half tempted to emerge from his own chamber and plant his wastrel brother a facer.

Violence was not the answer to the ills that plagued him, however.

Marriage, inexplicably, was.

"Fleetwood, would you please inform Lord Wesley that I wish an audience with him when he finishes breaking his fast?" he asked.

"It would be my pleasure, Your Grace," Fleetwood said.

"Thank you." He nodded. "That will be all."

With a heavy sigh, Stuart began wading through the fresh round of missives, surprised when he discovered one bearing unfamiliar, feminine handwriting. There was only one woman who might correspond with him thus, and he tore it open hastily to confirm his hopes. He read quickly.

To His Grace, the Duke of Camden,

After considering your offer of marriage further, I have decided that such a union may be amenable to me if you should agree to a list of conditions, which I have enclosed. If and when you agree to meet these, further discussion of a possible alliance between the two of us will be welcomed. If not, I sincerely wish you the best in all your future endeavors.

Yours truly,

Miss Rosamund Payne

THE NOTE WAS concise and without feminine effusion. There was nary a hint of anything emotional to be found. Nor passion. He wasn't certain what he had expected from her, only that it had not been such impersonal brevity.

Her list of conditions, as he turned to the following sheet of paper, however, was anything but. It was lengthy, detailed, and voluminous. Line after line. Chief amongst them: she wanted to be assured she would maintain control over her fortune and that she would have the option to have children as a result of their union, a decision that would be hers alone.

Children.

Good God. Everything within him turned to ice, for he had no desire to carry on the line. He had always supposed that the rotten legacy of the Dukes of Camden could end with him. Or with Wesley, if his brother outlived him—an unlikely eventuality, given Wesley's propensity for drinking, gambling, and wenching. And yet, the notion of children of Stuart's own was not entirely hateful. And children with Rosamund…

He could put this inconvenient attraction he felt for her to rest. If she was in his bed, he could have his fill of her. As for her fortune, he would need access to the funds. He was marrying her for her money after all.

Further reviewing down the page, he discovered the mention of a dowry, the sum of which was to be settled upon by the two of them. What an odd woman she was, blunt and forthright. But then, in the absence of her father, he supposed she was accustomed to making such negotiations herself.

Without bothering to read the remaining stipulations, he folded the missive and placed it neatly below the stacks of bills awaiting him. Wesley was known to pry into his private affairs without compunction, but if there was one place his brother wouldn't go looking, it would be amidst the endless debts he had a hand in creating.

Stuart rose, deciding an interview with his feckless brother could wait. He needed to speak with Rosamund. To see if they could reach some sort of compromise. Yesterday, if possible.

Her missive couldn't have reached him at a more opportune time. He didn't bother to change from his informal lounge suit, simply found Fleetwood and informed the butler of his change in plans. Within minutes, he was in a carriage he had borrowed from the Duke of Kingham, on his way to Rosamund's address, the London streets slipping torpidly by as he drummed his fingers idly on his thigh.

He had no plan of battle prepared. But then, this wasn't a proper courting. What use was there for subtlety, for flattery, for cozening? He had made clear what he wanted, and so had she. If they could strike a bargain that would be amenable to each of them, that was all that mattered.

Damnation, was that a stain on his trouser leg?

He squinted down at the thing, wondering if he had already reached the advanced age where he required spectacles, and decided that yes, it was indeed a stain and not the result of the light rain that had been spitting when he had exited the town house and entered King's carriage.

Blast.

He ought to have taken the time to change. There was no hope for it now, however. Stuart was going to pay a call upon his prospective bride with the grease from a rasher of bacon upon his trousers.

He extracted a handkerchief as the carriage approached the massive façade of Rosamund's home and scrubbed at the offending stain to no avail. There it remained on the buff-colored wool, a grim testament to the current state of his life.

With a sigh, he tucked his handkerchief away again just in time for the carriage door to swing open.

Stuart alighted and strode up the walk, rapping twice on the door before a servant who was dressed far more impeccably than he answered. He delivered his card as the fellow eyed him as if he were a costermonger with the temerity to knock abovestairs rather than below.

"The Duke of Camden to see Miss Payne," he said with a pained smile.

"Of course, *Your Grace*," the man—presumably her butler —said, his tone suggesting he found Camden's title dubious at best.

"Who is at the door, Wadham?" asked a familiar feminine voice.

The servant turned to address Rosamund, who remained out of Stuart's sight.

"The gentleman caller says that he is the Duke of Camden, Miss Payne."

Stuart clenched his jaw, about to tear a strip off the impudent fellow, when the sound of her footfalls on the marble floor echoed nearer until she had replaced the servant at the door.

"Your Grace," she greeted, dipping into a polite curtsy. "Do come in."

She was wearing a wrap and hat, carrying a reticule, and looked as if she were about to leave on a jaunt. Clearly, she had not been expecting his call. But then, he had hardly anticipated that she would be awaiting him. The tone of her missive had been most impersonal.

As she had said, she was a businesswoman. And all matters between them were to be settled in a similar vein.

Stuart bowed in return and then crossed the threshold, acutely aware of the presence of servants hovering about in the entry as one of them closed the door at his back. "Miss

Payne," he addressed Rosamund formally. "Forgive me for the unexpected nature of my call, but I was hoping you might spare me a few moments of your time."

"I was about to leave, Your Grace."

"I can see. However, I am still hoping you'll allow me fifteen minutes." His neckcloth felt as if it might choke him as he paused, clearing his throat. "It concerns your note."

"I will admit that I hadn't expected your response to be quite so immediate." She raised a brow at him, her dark gaze assessing. "Nor in person."

He gritted his teeth and forced a smile. "Yes, well, I was passing by and thought it would be more efficient to meet in person."

A lie and he knew it. The expression on her lovely face said she knew it too. An impenetrable silence descended, during which Rosamund eyed him as if she were a botanist and he a curious plant she had just uprooted, one for which she had no name.

At last, she nodded, apparently satisfied with whatever it was that she saw. "I can grant you a few minutes."

He felt like a naughty lad caught by his nurse in some manner of mischief. Heat flared up the back of his neck. Christ, what a disgraceful moment, begging an heiress for time so that he might persuade her to marry him and cancel his endless string of debts. When had his life become so beyond his control? And how had he allowed it?

A footman took his hat and gloves then, along with Rosamund's wrap and other garments.

"We can speak more privately in my sitting room," she told him. "This way."

Her town house, which had been her father's before her, was massive. Nary a hint of threadbare carpets or wood in need of waxing. The pictures in the grand entry were all hung in their places with unabashed pride, the green

53

brocatelle wall coverings sharp and bold and fresh. The marble floor gleamed. Everywhere one looked, there were signs of hideous wealth: exotic statues, busts, vases, potted plants, and the shine of gold and gilt. The town house itself had once belonged to the Duke of Wiltenham, though Payne had purchased and refurbished it some years before.

"Is that a Roman piece?" he asked, keeping his voice hushed as they passed an impressive bust of a woman with regal bearing, her hair plaited in intricate braids, the folds of a tunic draped around her elegant neck.

It was a gauche question, he knew, but he was curious. Besides, this was Rosamund. She was known for her eccentricities and refusal to stand on ceremony. On his previous call, he'd been too anxious over the proposition he intended to make her. He hadn't paid much heed to the ostentatious interior of her home.

"Yes, it is," she called. "My father was a collector, and I'll admit that I've found some comfort in taking over the pastime."

He was struggling to pay the few who remained of his domestics, and she was collecting antiquities. No, Rosamund Payne did not need him. But he very much needed her. And he was going to have to be at his most persuasive if he wanted to convince her to ignore all the reasons she should flee in the opposite direction and become his wife instead.

She reached an open door and paused, casting a glance over her shoulder at him. For a moment, he was struck by her. She carried herself with such bold confidence, and the way the light cascading in the nearby window caught in her hair and brought it to life was nothing short of breathtaking. Her locks, swept up in a Grecian braid that allowed riotous curls to frame her face, glinted coppery and gold, an unusual, rich hue that at once seemed to be both blond and red. Her gown, a lovely gray-blue silk adorned with tiered skirts and

54

fringe, emphasized her waist and breasts, and the line of buttons bisecting her prim bodice was an invitation he couldn't help but be tempted by.

Even if he knew that he must not lust after her in this moment, that there would be time aplenty for such matters once they were wed, his stupid cock had other ideas, easily swayed by this intriguing woman.

"Here we are," she said softly, making him belatedly aware that he was standing there like a buffoon, staring at her.

He hastened forward, into a space that was more intimately hers than the drawing room where he'd proposed to her had been, wondering if his ignominy was complete as she preceded him. Within her sitting room, more splendor was on display. Corinthian columns flanked an alcove on one side of the chamber, which was presided over by a massive white marble fireplace with an oval relief above it and a carved mantel holding more Roman busts. The coffered ceiling overhead bore intricate gilt work that complemented the anthemion frieze circling the room. More statues decorated the periphery, whilst a massive Aubusson rug was laden with Louis Quinze settees and chairs.

It felt as if he had walked into a Roman palace. The sole nod to function rather than pageantry was the presence of a writing desk, positioned by a window, laden with papers, brushes, watercolors, and an opened mahogany box bearing trays, all of which had been left open.

Stuart walked toward it, wanting to know if this was where she found herself, painting in the sunshine. For some reason, he was oddly roused by the notion.

"Did you pay an unexpected call upon me so that you could study my dreadful watercolor work?"

Rosamund's voice, behind him, was amused. He had reached the desk by now, and he glanced down to find her current work, which was, despite her words, a skillful rendition of his feathered nemesis.

"She looks so much more innocent in paint," he drawled, turning to find Rosamund approaching him, unsmiling. "Likable, almost."

"Megs *is* likable," Rosamund countered, folding her arms over her chest in a defensive pose. "Quite unlike most people, I might add."

His lips twitched. "Touché. I suppose you are referring to me."

"Actually, I was referring to your brother and a host of others as well, for various reasons. I haven't decided whether I like you or not just yet, Your Grace."

"Ah, excellent." He grinned. "That means there is a chance for me yet."

Slowly, she lowered her arms, her bearing relaxing. "You wish to speak about the note I sent round?"

He clasped his hands behind his back. "Indeed."

And my desperation, he thought with an inward wince.

"You agree to my terms, then?"

"Have I a choice, madam?" he returned, and not without a hint of bitterness, even if it wasn't Rosamund he resented, but the circumstances in which he was trapped.

Trapped by his father.

Trapped by obligation.

Trapped by debts.

Trapped by Mother.

Trapped by his bastard of a brother.

Like a fox with his paw in the snare, it was either nibble it off himself and take a chance at survival, or await his grim fate.

"There is always a choice, is there not?" she asked shrewdly.

"As I've learned, unfortunately, there isn't."

Heaven knew he wouldn't have chosen his present circumstances. He'd done everything in his power to avoid them.

She considered him, her gaze penetrating. "I would remind you that you are the one who came to me with this arrangement, Your Grace."

Arrangement. How polite. What an agreeable way of avoiding the word marriage. Avoiding the fact that he was going to bed her. Give her children. There was nothing polite about a union between them.

He caught the scent of bergamot laced with rose and ambergris and a tantalizing hint of violet, so unique. Much like the enigmatic woman before him.

"I did, indeed. Because it struck me that there is something we both want and need, and that, of all the women in England, none other than you would be as perfectly suited to the task."

A small smile curved her lips. "Pray, do not keep speaking in such a vein, or I'll swoon."

"I'm not offering you flummery, Rosamund. You're far too intelligent for that."

Her mouth twisted. "I wasn't, once."

An unintended reminder. Damn, but he hadn't been thinking of Wesley at all when he had made his observation.

"Even the most intelligent and astute can be manipulated when their hearts are pure," he said quietly.

And indeed, he had no doubt that Rosamund had once loved his brother. He had seen the admiration sparkling in her eyes. Had been, to his shame, envious of the way she had looked at Wesley during their betrothal ball, as if there were no finer man in all the world. Stuart had known then that she hadn't an inkling of who and what his brother truly was. Likely, he ought to have warned her before her heart had been shattered to bits.

Would she have believed him? Heeded his words? It was too late to know—and moot now.

"That is kind of you to say." She moved away from him, crossing the opulent chamber to a window and peering out of it. "I can own my own stupidity, however. I was impossibly naïve, but I've been cured of that now."

He hated the bitterness in her voice. What did she see when she looked out at the world? Was she seeing the St James's street bustling with the fashionable set going about their daily lives, or was she thinking of Wesley?

The very notion of his brother in her mind was suddenly hateful.

He followed her, drawing near at the window, wanting to supplant thoughts of Wesley with himself. Wanting to somehow stake his claim upon her. Foolish, unhinged yearnings, he knew, and yet he could not seem to banish them.

Stuart reached for her, laying his hand gently on her upper arm to jolt her from her reveries. She turned to him, startled. Her warmth seeped into him, and he couldn't deny he liked the way she felt, soft and supple beneath her layers of silk and civility.

"You were neither stupid nor naïve," he said. "You were trusting. There is a difference. Wesley betrayed your trust."

"Yes, he did, but I'm grateful for it, for the lessons I learned. I'll never be so weak again. To think I was almost at his mercy." She shuddered.

Stuart knew he should release his hold on her, and yet he couldn't seem to let her go. "I'm sorry, Rosamund. Sorry for what he did to you. In a way, I feel responsible. I know what he's capable of."

"Thank you." She reached up, her hand covering his. "You aren't to blame, however."

A spark of awareness jolted through him at the connection, her bare skin on his. A tiny touch, scarcely anything at all, and yet desire streaked through him. He wanted to kiss her. To take those lips with his.

Why shouldn't he? They were to be married after all. And he couldn't deny that the attraction he felt for her, long-simmering and yet controlled and ignored, had been steadily growing into a raging fire.

She seemed to sense the change in him, for her lips parted and her eyes widened, those glinting flecks of gold in their warm, brown depths more pronounced. The air between them suddenly crackled with desire.

"Rosamund," he rasped, his voice thick with suppressed yearning. "May I?"

"May you what?" Her tongue flicked over her lower lip, leaving it plump and glistening and so very tempting.

He nearly groaned at the simple, sensual display, one that shouldn't have made his cock so bloody hard and yet did. She would make him say the words. He felt like a young buck, unusually uncertain of himself.

"Kiss you," he elaborated.

She shifted, turning toward him so that they were fully aligned, chest to breasts, her hand still on his—an invitation. "Do you think it wise?"

Sweet God. If he didn't kiss her now, he would die.

"I think it necessary," he forced out, and then cupped her cheek with his free hand.

Her skin was soft and smooth, so vital and warm. A jolt of awareness swept over him. This woman was uniquely beautiful. Intelligent and bold. Vibrant. And she would be his. He shouldn't like it so much, but yet, he did.

Stuart lowered his mouth to hers, painfully aware that she was not a practiced seductress like the lovers he'd grown accustomed to. He needed to proceed with care. To be gentle. Her lips were lush and hot, parting on a small gasp.

That quickly, all the restraint he'd been determined to

show vanished, collapsing under the weight of a rushing wave of possessive lust. His tongue sank inside, tasting her. Tea and bergamot, sweetness, and God, he could not get enough. He was suddenly ravenous, his tongue claiming, his lips moving over hers. And she responded in kind, kissing him back, making a small sound of need that had his prick rock hard.

Somehow, they were moving. Moving as one, and he didn't know which of them had taken the first step, whether it was him or her, but it didn't matter. They didn't stop until she was pressed to the wall, his body against hers, her breasts spilling into him, her soft curves melded to his frame. Her hand had moved, and now she clutched at his shoulders with one whilst the other caressed his nape, her fingers sifting through the ends of his hair. Her tongue played with his, their kisses growing needier, more demanding.

This wasn't what he had intended, and yet it seemed as necessary as air, kissing Rosamund. His hand roamed freely over her, from her nipped waist to her lower back, while the other slipped into her coiffure, her silken hair sleek and cool against his fingers. He longed to pull all the hairpins free, to unleash the beauty of her tresses, to see her mussed instead of perfectly coiffed. He longed for so much, more than he had imagined possible, and it surprised him, the effect she had on him. She was as potent as one of King's elixirs, her enthusiastic response leaving him feeling half drunk.

Dimly, he was aware of a sound. Someone was at the door. He jerked his mouth from hers in time for a new voice to intrude.

"Rosamund, darling?"

The unexpected interruption had him releasing her hastily and stepping away with a guilty start as Mrs. Payne entered the room. She was a short, august lady with snow-white hair and a pleasant, welcoming countenance. He recalled her from their limited interactions during Rosamund and Wesley's betrothal.

He bowed, hoping the elder woman wouldn't know what they'd just been about. "Mrs. Payne, how lovely to see you again."

Rosamund's mother curtseyed, her brow furrowing. "Your Grace?"

Her surprise was evident, leading him to believe that her daughter had neglected to inform her of his proposal. Not a promising sign.

He forced a smile. "Please, call me Camden."

Rosamund bustled past him, leaving a maddening trail of scent in her wake. "Mother! What are you doing? I thought you were resting."

"I decided against it," Mrs. Payne said, beaming in Stuart's direction. "And how fortuitous. I would have hated to have missed such an illustrious caller."

Unlike Rosamund, Mrs. Payne was easily impressed by a title. He recalled that about her now, having quite forgotten. Perhaps this knowledge could be used to his advantage.

His smile deepened. "Fortuitous indeed, Mrs. Payne. Dear Rosamund was just about to ring for a tray of tea, I believe."

Rosamund jerked her head back to him, her eyes narrowed. "I was?"

"You were," he lied smoothly, looking into her gold-flecked eyes. "Just the thing to discuss our betrothal."

"Your betrothal?" Mrs. Payne clasped her hands as if in prayer, mouth agape as she stared from Stuart to Rosamund. "Betrothal? To the Duke of Camden? My darling girl, why did you not say so before now?"

Rosamund continued to glare at him. "Because I've only just found out about it myself, Mother dear."

A bit of maneuvering on his part. Quite badly done of

him, he could acknowledge. But desperate times called for desperate measures.

"Our Rosamund has paid me a great honor," he told Mrs. Payne, who was flustered and wide-eyed at the prospect of having a duke for a son-in-law.

Before him lay the clear and unobstructed path to victory he required.

"BETROTHED." Mother sighed, pressing a hand over her heart. "Truly, Rosamund. What manner of secrets have you been keeping from me?"

Her lips still tingling from those heated, drugging kisses with Camden that had taken her by complete surprise, Rosamund was having a difficult time gathering her wits. The three of them—Camden, Rosamund, and her mother— were seated round the tea tray, Rosamund distracting herself by preparing their cups so that she wouldn't box the Duke of Camden's ears.

Because, regardless of how scorching and wonderful those kisses had been, he had been dancing around the subject of whether he would adhere to her stipulations, leaving her wondering, and then had summarily announced their engagement to her mother.

No doubt about it, he had deliberately sprung this trap, and she meant to make him pay. Just not in front of her dear, kindhearted mother.

Since Father's death, Mother had been brokenhearted. Losing Father had devastated the both of them.

Rosamund blinked hastily against a rush of tears and swallowed a lump of grief that rose in her throat. Despite the time that had passed since losing her father, she could not think of his death and his gaping absence in her and her mother's lives without being moved to tears.

But weeping over tea with the Duke of Camden's sharp blue gaze on her was a humiliation she couldn't bear. Heaven forbid he would think her emotions had been stirred by those passionate, carnal kisses. Which, of course, they had. But no reason to give him any hint of power over her. He may be a duke and she a common miss, but Camden needed her far more than she did him. She was in the position of power in this odd dynamic of theirs, and he would do well to remember it.

"Rosamund darling, are you attending me?" Mother's voice pierced the thick haze of her thoughts, making Rosamund realize she had spent too much time on the Duke of Camden's tea.

"Of course I am, Mother darling. But I can assure you that I have no secrets." She summoned a bright smile for her mother's benefit and extended the cup and saucer to him. "Your tea, Your Grace."

He accepted it from her, their fingers brushing, and the same hated course of awareness swept over her that had when he had touched her earlier by the window. The same that had burst into flame when he had pressed her against the wall and kissed her with such passion that her mind was still muddled and foggy, her body yet humming with desire. She wished she could whisk her hand away from his, yet she could not risk upending his tea, and so she lingered, forcing herself to think of anything but the unsteady way she felt at his touch. Of anything other than his knowing kisses.

The Duke of Camden was more than proficient at kissing. Indeed, he was far better at it than Wesley had been. Wesley's kisses had always been perfectly polite, chaste, and perfunctory. She had believed his reticence had been a sign of respect. Knowing what she did now, she understood that it had been because he hadn't desired her.

Did the Duke of Camden want her? He had certainly kissed her earlier as if he did.

"Thank you, dear Rosamund." He gave her an odious grin now.

One that said he was more than aware of what he was doing.

Well, his brother was a scoundrel as well. It only served that he was one too.

Heat crept up her throat to roost in her cheeks. Did he know what she was thinking about? Did he sense the effect he had upon her? She mustn't think of it, not with Mother as an audience.

"You're most welcome, dearest, darling Camden," she returned, doing her most dramatic impression of a love-sick debutante.

"When did you intend to tell me?" Mother demanded, looking both pleased and flustered. "Had I not happened upon the sitting room when I did, you wouldn't have breathed a word yet, would you? Why, darling? Is it because of what happened the last time?"

Rosamund winced. Her mother was painfully adept at saying the wrong thing at the absolute worst moment. If it was on her mind, it was also on her tongue. Circumspection was not one of her virtues.

"Of course it isn't because of my betrothal with Lord Wesley, Mother," she said, hating the words *betrothal* and *Lord Wesley* in the same sentence. "And I would just as soon never speak of that time again, if you please."

"Oh yes, of course." Mother's expressive countenance was hurt.

Guilt skewered Rosamund. "Forgive me. I didn't mean to

be so harsh. It is merely that the subject is one best forgotten, particularly given the future."

"I ought to have been more delicate," Mother said, frowning. "It is forever a fault of mine, being too bluntly honest when I should not be."

"I find honesty delightful," Camden said smoothly, intervening at the perfect moment.

His interjection earned him another pointed glare from Rosamund, telling him without words that his finding honesty delightful was absurd, given what he had just done.

"It is a rarely appreciated virtue," she said meaningfully.

He continued to grin, unperturbed. "Extra fortunate, then, that I do appreciate it."

"When will the wedding be?" Mother wanted to know.

"We haven't decided just yet," Rosamund told her.

"As soon as possible," Camden said at the same time.

"There is much that needs to be discussed yet," she reminded him through gritted teeth.

"The flowers with which you might decorate the church," he said agreeably. "A gown. I'm certain Mrs. Payne can assist you with all such arrangements."

"I would dearly love to do so," Mother declared.

Oh dear heaven. She had to put an end to this nonsense. His kisses had been lovely—more than lovely, if she were honest— but she required more assurance than his mouth on hers.

"There are some other matters that His Grace and I will need to consider as well," she told her mother.

Such as his intentions. Would he agree to her stipulations? She would have Mr. Watts, her father's man of business and now hers, see that a marriage contract was drafted accordingly by Father's solicitor if so. But if not, then there would be no wedding. She would simply have to disappoint Mother. Even if she dreaded doing so.

The Duke of Camden would not entrap her into marriage any more surely than his brother had. One furtive embrace in a sitting room would not sway her.

"Matters?" Mother settled her teacup in its saucer, frowning. "What do you mean, Rosamund dear?"

"Whether His Grace will sign the marriage contract," she said, angling another sharp look in the duke's direction.

He sat serenely on his chair in an elegant pose, his buff suit complementing his dark hair and startling eyes. "I will sign it, of course."

His pronouncement startled her. She hadn't expected such easy capitulation.

"You will?" she asked warily.

He held her gaze. "Without hesitation."

"Oh, blessed angels," Mother said, pressing a hand to her heart. "My darling daughter, you're to be married."

Rosamund's heart pounded at the finality of it all, the looming change that had been impossible to comprehend even a mere fortnight ago.

"I suppose," she allowed reluctantly.

For it all felt so very real in this moment, sitting here with Camden and Mother. It felt very much like her future instead of a whimsical possibility. And that was beginning to frighten her. She had almost married once. And to this man's brother.

What was she thinking?

How had she even allowed herself to contemplate a match between the two of them after everything that had happened in the past?

It was that same, restless yearning deep within her. The longing for a family she'd never been able to shake. All the wealth she could possibly want or need was in her grasp, and yet there was one thing her fortune could never give her—

children of her own. It would take a penniless duke to give her that.

"When will the announcement be made?" Mother wanted to know.

"The contract," Rosamund said quickly before Camden could offer a response. "After the contract is agreed upon and signed, then we shall move forward with the betrothal."

"I'm paying a call upon my solicitor this very day," he said, his gaze burning into hers.

There was no doubting his sincerity or his intentions. He wanted this marriage, and he wanted it in haste. He was willing to do anything to secure it. Surely she ought to be concerned by this realization.

The Duke of Camden was a desperate man.

Desperate enough to offer for her.

To kiss her.

To wed her.

His kisses hadn't felt desperate, however. They had felt… potent. All-consuming. Decadent. His kisses had felt urgent and earnest, as if he hadn't been able to resist her. And that was the most dangerous realization of all.

"How exciting," Mother was saying to Camden. "I was beginning to fear that dear Rosamund would remain a spinster forever."

Rosamund nearly choked on her tea. Camden turned the full force of his charm upon her mother.

"I consider myself a most fortunate man, Mrs. Payne."

Mother and the duke settled into a pleasant conversation without her, and Rosamund sipped her tea, grateful for the respite. Fearing she had made the second-worst decision of her life.

The first had been to agree to marry the Duke of Camden's coldhearted brother.

And look at where that had left her.

CHAPTER 5

*H*e had to stop thinking about those bloody kisses.

About Rosamund's lush mouth.

About the fiery way she had responded, those seductive sounds of need she'd made with his lips on hers, the way her curves had felt molded against him, beneath his hands.

But how? Ever since they had parted the day before, Stuart had been able to think of precious little else. He had gone to bed with a hard cock and had taken himself in hand to thoughts of lifting her skirts and finding the slit in her drawers, of stroking her sleek, hot cunny to see if she was wet for him. And then he had risen this morning with a prick as hard as marble. He'd had no recourse but to bring himself to release again so that he could proceed with his day sans the poison of lust running through his veins.

It hadn't worked long. He had scarcely made it through breakfast before his mind had wandered back to her. If Rosamund's passionate kisses were any indication, he was going to thoroughly enjoy consummating their marriage and having her in his bed.

DUKE WITH A DEBT

Sighing heavily, Stuart shifted in his chair now, attempting to ease the snug fit of his trousers as a tap sounded at his study door.

"Come," he called, grateful for the interruption.

He had been getting hard again, all over thoughts of the virginal spinster who would have once been his sister-in-law. How fucking depraved could he be?

The door opened to reveal his butler, crossing the room in measured strides.

"For Your Grace," Fleetwood announced, delivering the salver of correspondence this morning as he always did, with the long-suffering look of a domestic who was unfailingly loyal.

Stuart thanked his butler and accepted the latest mountain of debts and other assorted missives. One of the notes bore familiar script, and his gut clenched.

Damn it, he still had time.

He addressed his butler instead, ignoring the sealed note for now. "Is Lord Wesley at home, Fleetwood?"

"His Lordship is not, Your Grace," the butler answered stoically.

Of course he wasn't. He was likely passed out drunk after losing more money Stuart couldn't afford to lose all night long. Something would have to be done with him. Stuart needed to speak with Mother.

"Thank you, Fleetwood," he said. "Has Her Grace breakfasted?"

"Yes, Your Grace."

"Excellent." He nodded. "That will be all."

The butler bowed and disappeared with the empty salver.

Mother often slept late, and Stuart could never be certain of her schedule. Which was rather ironic since she never left her apartments. It wasn't as if she were off paying a bevy of social calls. She had not left the same four walls in years.

And that was another reason Stuart hesitated to visit her there. Her apartments had become her tomb.

Grimly, he seized the latest note from his blackmailer and tore it open, reading.

To His Grace, the Duke of Camden,
Time is waning for the five thousand pounds to be
delivered to Messrs. Dolan and Rowe. A letter has
been prepared for The Times in the event you
forfeit your payment. It will be delivered on the
first of next month by half past ten.

Damn the bastard to hell. Stuart knew precisely how much time was remaining. And the delay in his courtship of Rosamund was making it apparent that he may need to beg for his portion of the funds from the Wicked Dukes Society early if he didn't wed soon. Without Rosamund's dowry, it would be the only way he could afford to pay. He didn't like having to swallow his pride, but he had to keep his blackmailer silent.

Because he couldn't bear to allow the truth to be printed for all London to devour with greedy eyes eager for gossip and scandal. His family would not be the fodder for wagging tongues. Not if he could help it. And thus far, despite his wastrel brother's attempts to thwart him—and despite their father's efforts to drain the family coffers before him—Stuart had managed it.

He crumpled the latest threat and rose from his desk. Crossing the chamber, he tossed it into the fire grate where it belonged, watching it for a moment as it caught flame and burned. Then, he began the miserable climb to his mother's apartments. Up the winding staircase that had formerly been a jewel in the crown of the once-glorious home but was now dull, in need of polish, and covered by a threadbare Axminster carpet that should have been replaced long ago.

But that detail, like the glaring rectangles and squares on the damask, bold and almost new in comparison to the faded wall coverings around them, was something that could not be remedied without securing a wealthy bride. And whilst he believed himself closer to achieving his goal where Rosamund was concerned, he wasn't entirely sure of her just yet.

Oh, she had agreed most reluctantly after he had intentionally revealed the news of their "betrothal" to her good-intentioned mother. However, he didn't fool himself that she was secure in her decision. She could change her mind and throw him over at any moment. He would have no recourse if she did so. And everything he had been struggling to protect these last few years would be consigned to flame just like the letter burning in his study.

But he wouldn't think of that now.

Stuart stopped before his mother's door and gave it a gentle rap. It opened at once to reveal her faithful lady's maid, Norton. With her round-faced visage and her silver-streaked hair, she looked older than his mother, though he suspected that was the result of a life in service rather than her true years.

"Your Grace," she greeted him with a ready, if tentative, smile, dipping into a curtsy.

"Is my mother amenable to receiving a visitor, Norton?" he asked, returning her smile though it pained him.

He took no pleasure in these visits. And even the sight of his mother, once a beloved reassurance, left him in a coil of anxious despair.

"Her Grace is having her tea and was about to sit down with a book, but I am certain she will be pleased to see you,"

Norton reported, opening the door wider to allow him entrance.

He passed her, preparing himself for the familiar, stale scent of the room. All one had to do was cross the threshold to suspect that his mother's apartments were kept closed up and shuttered off from the rest of the household. Thank heavens she allowed a chambermaid in to dust once a week.

His mother was seated at her writing desk, as she often was, and dressed in an elegant navy walking gown quite as if she might descend from her room for a promenade at any moment. Only Stuart knew that she had no intention of doing so.

"Camden," she greeted him with a welcoming smile, making to rise.

He held up a staying hand, knowing that her left hip and knee were dreadfully weak, though they were not the reason for her self-imposed isolation. If anything, they had grown worse for her remaining in this prison of her own making.

"Stay seated, Mother, please," he instructed softly.

She relented, gesturing to a stuffed chair set before the hearth, another favorite spot of hers. "Do sit and stay for a bit. I hope you will."

He rolled his shoulders to ease some of the tension residing there and folded his frame into the indicated seat. Despite the fact that his mother was never far, he didn't allot her the time he ought, and he knew it. Seeing her thus pained him.

"You may send for me at any time," he reminded her.

"Of course I can, but you are so very busy, are you not, my dear son?" Her smile was wistful as she studied him. "And how is my other son this fine day? I've not seen him in even longer than I have last seen you."

Ah, the reason for his call had arrived, and sooner than he had suspected.

"Wesley is…" He paused, casting a glance in Norton's direction. The servant was circumspect to a fault, but there were some conversations a man didn't wish to have before an audience. This was one of them. He forced a smile. "Norton, that will be all for now. When I finish visiting with Her Grace, I'll ring for you."

"Of course, Your Grace." The other woman bobbed a polite curtsy and hastily took her leave.

The door clicked closed on her black woolen skirts.

"That was badly done of you, Camden," Mother chided. "You know that Norton is to be trusted. There is nothing you cannot say before her that you would say to me."

"I beg to differ," he countered gently, ever aware of his mother's fragile constitution. "The matter I'm about to discuss is a delicate one. It involves Wesley, you see."

And whilst the entire household was more than aware of his brother's gambling and drinking and whoring to excess, no one knew—nor could they likely countenance—what he was about to tell Mother.

She frowned, her blue eyes, so like his own, searching his. "You look concerned and tired. A bit thin as well. Have you been eating properly?"

He wanted desperately to remind her that she could join him in the dining room for any meal and ascertain for herself. But past remarks had only caused her further upset and had failed to accomplish their aim of luring her from her apartments.

"If I look concerned and tired, it's because I am," he conceded. "I have done everything in my power to keep all worries from your shoulders. However, I find myself in a position that is both untenable and insupportable for much longer. Wesley has been gambling away everything, down to the last farthing."

"Gambling?" She pressed a hand to her heart. "My Wesley?"

Her shock was understandable. He had not told her of his brother's gambling before. Instead, worried over her growing frailty, he had kept the truth from her in every capacity he could. The fewer concerns weighing upon her, the better, he had thought. Until Wesley had become further wrapped up in his illicit world and the demons that drove him to keep seeking the next false sense of happiness.

"I fear he is as bad as Father," he revealed, "if not worse."

Definitely worse. Wesley had squandered untold sums. Every act Stuart had taken to earn more and settle his brother's debts had only led to Wesley losing more. Now, he very much feared that his desire to protect their mother from the truth had been responsible for enabling Wesley to lead them all to the brink of utter ruin.

"But Wesley never gambled," Mother protested. "His weakness was always light-skirts."

"And so his weakness continues to be," Stuart agreed grimly. "Along with drink and only the Lord knows what other manners of vice. But I do not tell you this so that you can fret over his gambling. I tell you this because I cannot afford to keep him here or to continue funding his profligacy."

She frowned. "But Camden, what does that mean? What do you intend? Wesley is your brother."

"He is no true brother of mine," he said tightly, hurt—even after the years that had passed—by Mother's insistence upon overlooking Wesley's every fault, no matter how grievous. And regardless of the cost to Stuart.

"You are still wounded by that wretched Lady Flora Seaton," Mother observed, shaking her head.

The mention of Lady Flora continued to send a stab of aching betrayal straight through him.

"Do not speak of it," he said, his voice soft.

His mother's spine stiffened. "Her loose morals were her downfall. Did you not see the way she trailed after Wesley? He has a way about him, a certain charm. Has had since he was a very young lad. Why must you blame him for what was clearly that dreadful girl's fault?"

"I blame him because he seduced her," he ground out. "She was my betrothed, curse him, and he seduced her and deceived me."

"If she'd had a care for you, she would never have allowed Wesley to turn her head," Mother said, her voice raised, trembling in her ire.

This was not good for her, he reminded himself sternly. He needed to regain his control over his wayward tongue. This conversation was not about the past, nor was it even about him. Certainly, it was not about Lady Flora. Rather, it was about Wesley. It was about how Stuart's obligations where his brother was concerned had to end.

He had finally been driven to the breaking point.

Ever since Mother's stroke, just after the heated familial argument that had occurred when Stuart had discovered Wesley and his betrothed in a state of dishabille at what was to have been their betrothal ball, Stuart had kept his silence. He had held his tongue for fear of upsetting Mother's precarious condition. Wesley knew it, and he had taken advantage of it at every opportunity.

Stuart realized he was clenching his jaw so damn tightly that it ached.

He forced himself to relax. Mother meant well. She didn't know the extent of what Wesley was capable of. He had intentionally insulated her from his brother's misadventures.

"You are correct that the lady in question didn't care for me," he allowed. "However, that doesn't absolve Wesley of his sins."

"Oh, it hurts my heart, Camden," Mother lamented. "When will you forgive him?"

Never.

He wasn't certain he was capable of it where Wesley was concerned. Not after everything his brother had done to so thoroughly destroy him, and all of it through jealousy. But he couldn't tell Mother that. The doctor had made it explicitly clear that further upset could induce another stroke. She was to be protected at all costs.

"I haven't come here to speak about the past, Mother," he said gently, attempting to right the course of their conversation.

"Of course not." She fidgeted with the gathering of her silk skirt, clearly agitated.

His fault.

And her distress was only about to grow worse when he told her what he had come to say, that he intended to cut his brother off—purse strings, roof over his head, everything.

"What is it that wish to tell me, Camden?" Mother pressed, frowning.

Stuart opened his mouth to tell her that Wesley was a vile infection that needed to be excised so that he wouldn't ruin the lot of them. And he found that he couldn't do it. The words would not come. His heart hammered against his chest, his gut tightening into a sickly knot of dread. These were not words his mother could bear to hear. If she suffered another stroke because of him… No, he couldn't think it.

"I am to be married," he said instead.

Mother's fingers paused. "Married?"

"Yes." He forced a smile, as if the revelation were joyous. "You are the first to hear the news. Our betrothal hasn't been announced in *The Times* yet."

"Oh, Camden." She blinked as her eyes glistened with unshed tears. "I cannot tell you how happy this news makes me. I was beginning to despair over ever having grandchildren. Who is the fortunate lady you have chosen?"

Seeing the unfettered delight on his mother's countenance pleased Stuart. Although marriage was the last institution in which he'd hoped to find himself, he couldn't deny that watching her come to life at the news warmed something inside him. But he knew that when he revealed the woman who would be his wife, the announcement was likely to be met with concern. He hated to chase the cheer from his mother's face, but there was no help for it.

"The lady who has agreed to become my wife is Miss Rosamund Payne," he said.

"Miss Payne?" Mother's eyebrows rose. "The same Miss Rosamund Payne who was betrothed to Wesley before she threw him over?"

He nodded. "I am reasonably certain there is only one."

Mother sighed. "Pray do not tell me this is some manner of misguided attempt to get revenge on Wesley over what happened with Lady Flora."

In part. Guilt tugged at his conscience, but he tamped it down.

"If you don't wish it, then I won't," he said smoothly, aware that his response was more half-truth than outright lie.

"Camden." The disappointment in his mother's voice echoed the expression on her face. "You cannot think to consign yourself or Miss Payne to a union founded on vengeance."

"Miss Payne and I have decided we suit," he said, ignoring her entreaty.

"It is because of her fortune as well, is it not?" Mother asked shrewdly. "I know you asked me not to speak of such matters, but the servants do gossip."

"Norton?" he demanded, surprised to hear it.

The lady's maid turned companion had always seemed above reproach.

"The chambermaid," Mother admitted, a hint of color suffusing her pale cheeks. "If you must know. But I beg of you, don't sack the chit. I'm rather fond of the tales she tells me."

He might have laughed at that were he not left so raw from the continual battle he waged with his brother, his conscience, and the need to protect Mother from it all.

"I'll not sack her," he reassured Mother. "And yes, since you have asked, I took Miss Payne's immense dowry and fortune into consideration before offering for her. You know the circumstances Father's death left me in, and whilst I have been doing my utmost to rectify the estates and refill the coffers, I find myself at a disadvantage on numerous fronts. Marrying her will bring some much-needed funds at a most opportune time."

"It's not a love match, then."

His mother sounded disappointed.

"It is a mutually beneficial union," he said. "I admire Miss Payne in many ways, and I am confident she will make an excellent wife."

"And you, Camden. Will you make her a good husband?" Mother wanted to know. "The marriage I had with your father was not a happy one. I wish for so much more for my sons."

He was more than aware of the enmity that had existed between his sire and his mother. His youth had been a misery of shouts, broken glass, accusations, and rage, steeped in alcohol and adultery. Both his mother and his father had taken lovers, some of whom had flitted about the house as if they belonged. None of whom had made their misery any less.

Still, this was the first Mother had spoken openly of her own discontent.

"I will be as good of a husband to Miss Payne as I am able," he said honestly.

It was the only promise he could make.

"I hope you do, my son, just as I hope you are marrying Miss Payne for the right reasons," Mother said, then smothered a yawn. "Forgive me. I am feeling rather weary today. I'm sure it's the weather."

The weather was gray and misting, as it was most days. But his mother did look tired. He rose and moved to her, bending to place an affectionate kiss on the top of her head. "I'll ring for Norton. You should have a nap."

"Thank you, dear son. I am feeling better today, you know. Perhaps I shall see you at dinner."

He rose, giving her a wistful smile. "Only if you are able, Mother."

They both knew that she wouldn't be joining him. But always when he left her, it was with the tiniest flicker of hope that she might leave her room at last and rejoin the world of the living below. And each time, that hope was inevitably snuffed out like a candle.

Stuart turned to leave her room.

"Camden?"

Mother's call stopped him. He turned back to find her watching him.

"I love you, my dear son."

He swallowed against a rising lump of emotion. "I love you as well, Mother."

He fled her apartments, telling himself that he had made the right decisions. That he had made the only decision. For Mother's sake, he would simply have to endure Wesley's poisonous wrath.

"DRAT. No, no, no. This will not do. Not at all."

Frowning, Rosamund glared at the watercolor before her. Ordinarily, she sought solace in the quiet hours she spent in the town house gardens with her brush, easel, and paint set. But today, despite the weather having improved and the day being relatively mild and the birds singing sweetly as they winged into her charmed square of carefully cultivated flowers and shrubbery, there was no peace to be found.

She had broken the small glass from her watercolor set meant for cleaning brushes, having dropped it on the stone path. And then, she had run out of vermilion and purple lake. Whilst she had sent a footman to fetch her more, the delay had been no less irksome.

"Talking to yourself again, my dear?"

Miranda's amused voice had Rosamund turning with a guilty start to find her smiling friend gliding toward her on the path. The gurgling fountain at Rosamund's side had kept her from hearing her friend's approach.

She rose from the bench, grateful for the distraction. "I always talk to myself when Megs is not about."

The African grey didn't prefer the out-of-doors, whilst Rosamund liked to pursue the pastime in the sunlight, often using garden elements, flowers, and birds as her inspiration for her paintings.

"How is our feathered friend today?" Miranda asked, smiling from beneath the jaunty brim of her hat, a small basket draped over one arm.

She was dressed in a handsome visiting gown of puce silk faille ornamented with satin ribbons and blonde lace, a striped underskirt peeking from beneath a dramatic slit. Her ebony curls had been secured at her nape, with a few left free to frame her face. She was the epitome of the fashionable

London lady. Rosamund, by contrast, wore a plain gown of tan silk trimmed with a hint of red and decorated with splatters of watercolors that had dripped from her palette.

"Megs is as naughty as ever, and she was quite displeased with me for leaving her to paint *en plein air*," Rosamund answered. "Your gown is gorgeous. I'm feeling rather dowdy in my painting frock."

"You could never be dowdy, darling." Miranda ventured nearer to her easel, taking a peek at the watercolor Rosamund had been attempting to distract herself with.

And failing miserably. Both at the painting itself and the distraction.

"I am always dowdy," she countered, "though I do love you for your unfailing loyalty. I'm so pleased to see you this afternoon. It's a pleasant surprise."

"I hope I'm not interrupting," Miranda said.

"Of course not," she hastened to reassure her. "As you can see, I'm merely plodding my way through this watercolor. I've already broken my water glass and run out of colors, so it's just as well that I put an end to my efforts for the day. Shall we take tea inside?"

"You needn't ring for tea on my account. I'm not staying long as I must get back to the school. I wanted to deliver this treat to you, to see what you think."

Her stomach growled as if it had heard the news of Miranda's treat. "I hope it's something edible."

Miranda's treats usually were confections she was working on for her school of cookery. And they were infallibly delicious.

"Of course it is." Miranda smiled as she took the basket from her arm and settled it atop the marble table flanking the bench where Rosamund had been seated. "I've been working on a recipe for *cornets à la Marguerite*, and I think I've finally settled upon one that will do well paired with a cream ice. I was hoping you might try one without the cream ice and give me your thoughts."

Her stomach applauded the opportunity.

"I would love to," Rosamund said.

Miranda's culinary prowess had been one of many sources of contention between herself and Ammondale. He had been horrified that his countess continued to pursue such a bourgeois passion. She had been determined not to surrender her dream of her school of cookery.

Miranda lifted the basket lid to reveal a handful of cornets stacked within, their openings decorated with carmine royal icing and chopped pistachios. The sweet scent of them reached Rosamund.

"They look lovely, Miranda," she praised her friend.

Miranda beamed with pride. "Thank you. Take one and tell me what you think, if you please."

Rosamund reached for one of the delicate cornets, eager to try it. The confection was crisp and delightful, the flavors of almond, sugar, and orange flower water creating the perfection combination. Miranda watched her, eagerly anticipating her response.

Rosamund finished chewing and then swallowed. "These are so delicious that you don't even need to fill them with cream ice."

"Do you think?" Miranda bounced on her toes like a girl, grinning. "Not too much orange flower water?"

"The perfect amount." Rosamund took another delightful bite.

"Would you change anything? What about the pistachios?"

"Megs would approve."

"She was my inspiration for them, if you must know," Miranda revealed with a conspiratorial air. "I've been toying with the recipe for an apple cream ice that I think would pair splendidly with these. When I'm satisfied with it, you and Mrs. Payne must come to tea, and we shall have them for dessert."

"That would be lovely." Rosamund finished the last of her cornet before the sudden realization struck her. "Although soon, I expect I'll not be requiring my mother to accompany me on my social calls."

Miranda gave her a shrewd look. "You've made your final decision, then?"

Swallowing hard against a rush of emotion, Rosamund nodded. "I have."

"Oh, my dear friend." Miranda sighed and laid a comforting hand on her arm. "I trust that congratulations are in order?"

Rosamund smiled weakly. "I suppose."

"And what did His Grace make of the stipulations you presented him with? Do tell."

A bird called overhead, flapping past them and settling in the branches of a nearby tree. Rosamund stared at the happy little bird for a moment, thinking of what Camden had told her.

"He said he agreed with them." She turned back to Miranda. "That he hasn't a choice in the matter."

The admission made a blade of guilt knife through her conscience. She didn't like the notion that his circumstances had essentially forced him into a union, even if it was no fault of hers and he had been the one to seek her out with his unconventional proposal.

"Perhaps we should sit and talk for a few moments," Miranda suggested, sounding concerned. "If you don't mind further interruption of your watercolors, that is?"

"As you can see, I've been rather preoccupied." She gestured to her pitiful attempt at capturing the gardens. "Save me from tormenting myself, please."

Miranda chuckled. "Nonsense. You are extremely talented. I have the fountain painting you made for me hanging in a place of pride in my sitting room."

"And undoubtedly, all your guests cannot help but to wonder why you have such a wretched little thing hanging there," she said wryly.

They settled on the large stone bench, frightening the bird who had been watching them, for it flew from its branch.

"Ha," Miranda said. "You are far too modest, my dear. But let us speak of your impending marriage now. Are you happy, Rosamund?"

"This entire affair has been most unexpected," she confided. "I'm not certain how I feel about it all just yet. Concerned, for certain. It is quite strange to think I'll soon be marrying a man I scarcely know and bearing his children, sharing the marriage bed with him."

Rosamund didn't dare speak of such matters with Mother, despite how much she loved her and the closeness of their relationship. There were certain things she simply could not mention to her mother without boiling in ever-lasting mortification. Thank heavens for the confidence of good friends.

"I was in your shoes when I married Ammondale," Miranda said gently. "Unfortunately, my husband did not take care with me in the marriage bed. I hope for your sake that Camden is a more generous and patient husband than the earl was."

Her friend's words did nothing to assuage the worries that had been gnawing at her ever since the day before, when Camden had formally agreed to her stipulations, with Mother as an audience.

"How will I know?" she asked, feeling woefully uninformed about such matters.

Her knowledge was limited to what she had heard from friends or read, fleetingly, in books. Rosamund had only ever exchanged kisses with suitors, nothing more familiar.

"Have you and the duke kissed?" Miranda asked quietly.

She thought of those heated kisses yesterday, which had come just before a timely interruption, and her cheeks warmed. "Once."

"And was it pleasant?"

Rosamund nodded. "Very much so."

Miranda smiled sadly. "That is a good sign, my dear."

She hated the melancholy in her friend's countenance. And, if she were honest, it also filled her with even more misgiving for the marriage of convenience she had agreed to herself.

"If I may ask, what was it like between you and Ammondale before you wed?"

"He was…painfully polite is the best description. I ascribed his lack of interest in me to a sense of propriety. His mother was a true stickler for every polite society rule, and I believed he had inherited her strict sense of what is right or wrong." She paused, a wry smile curving her lips. "As it happened, he was merely wildly in love with his mistress and was marrying me for the sole purpose of gaining a legitimate heir."

Miranda's story was uncomfortably close to the miserable marriage Rosamund had narrowly avoided with Lord Wesley. Only, Wesley hadn't been marrying her for an heir but her fortune instead, and he had proclaimed his love for her loudly and often. That had been the most egregious betrayal of all, that he had pretended to love her.

"I'm so sorry for all you endured," she told her friend earnestly.

"It is in the past now," Miranda said. "Ammondale and I were never compatible in the way a husband and wife ought to be. It was our downfall, I believe. But enough of that. What concerns me most is *your* future. I want your happiness, my dear."

She wanted happiness too. A family of her own. But she also wanted to be sure that marrying Camden was the right step for her to take. It would seem there was only one way to manage that—discover whether she and the duke were truly compatible, as a husband and wife.

Precisely how she would arrive at that was a question that required pondering.

"Thank you, my friend." She patted Miranda's arm in sisterly fashion. "For now, do you think I might have another cornet?"

Miranda grinned. "You may keep them all. Give some to your mother and let me know what she thinks as well. I should be on my way now. The school is a hive of activity today."

They rose from the bench and exchanged farewells. As Rosamund watched her friend's departing back, she settled upon a plan. Tomorrow, she had a wedding to attend— Viscount Sidmouth and her friend Hyacinth, Lady Southwick, were marrying in the morning. She had no doubt that Camden would be in attendance, for he and the Duke of Brandon were both chums with Sidmouth.

That settled it. She would find Camden at the wedding and speak with him then.

CHAPTER 6

$\mathcal{R}$osamund didn't have the opportunity to speak with Camden until Lord and Lady Sidmouth's wedding breakfast was nearly over. Thankfully, the sheer size of the nuptials had meant that guests were spilling all over the town house, and now that everyone had feasted and the newlyweds were about to depart for their honeymoon, she seized her chance. Separating herself from Mother, she sidled near to Camden, who was looking grim as he stood alone near a potted palm in the hall.

"Weddings are supposed to be a cause for celebration," she told him *sotto voce*.

As if jolted from deep thoughts, he turned to her, his expression shifting—softening a bit. "Rosamund."

Their gazes had met and held more than once over the course of the morning, and each time, she had been reminded of the kisses they had shared. She wondered if he had been thinking of their heated embrace as well, or if he had not been as moved as she had. After all, he was an established rake with a notorious reputation. Her experience, by comparison, was painfully small.

The reminder made her all the more determined to tell him what she must.

"I was hoping I might speak with you for a few minutes," she said.

His pale gaze flicked about, taking in the guests surrounding them. "Now?"

She surveyed the hall as well, hoping no one was paying them any heed; to her relief, their fellow guests all appeared distracted. "It's rather urgent," she told him. "But perhaps this is a conversation best held in private."

He nodded, and his eyes returned to hers, searching. "The library is down the hall to the left. I doubt the other guests are making use of it. I'll go first, and you can join me in a moment."

"Thank you," she murmured.

Camden slipped away from her, blending easily into the crush, though he was a head taller than many of the other gentlemen in attendance. Certainly, he was the most handsome and compelling. Her gaze followed him of its own accord as he disappeared down the hall and slipped into a room that must have been the library. After assuring herself that no one had seen him, nor were they watching her, she made her way to the periphery of the gathered guests. The wine had been flowing swiftly, and from the loud laughter echoing down the hall, it would seem that the guests were all halfway into their cups.

She moved with haste, holding her breath until she had reached the library. She crossed the threshold to find him awaiting her, hands clasped behind his back in a casual pose that made her heart pound. Good heavens, he was so handsome. His lips were unsmiling, and looking at them made her recall, for the hundredth time, how they had felt on hers.

Warm and knowing and skillful. Decadent and intoxicating.

Maybe this was a mistake, her madcap plan to ascertain whether they would suit. What had she been thinking, to even come to him with such a request? He had agreed to her stipulations. She wasn't sure she could find the daring to make such a brazen request of him.

"Come, Rosamund," he said. "Close the door behind you. We'll have privacy here, for a few minutes at least."

Rosamund did as he ordered, the door clicking closed with an ominous, if well-oiled, snick.

"How are you so familiar with the Duke of Arrington's town house?" she blurted nervously into the cavernous room.

Bookshelves lined the walls around them, the comforting scent of leather and paper filling the air. Libraries ordinarily were one of her favorite places—so many possibilities, so many worlds within the quiet spines. And yet, she was not moved to investigate. Camden commanded all her attention.

He inclined his head. "The duchess is a good friend of my mother's. I spent a great deal of time here visiting, getting lost in the halls and finding myself in all manner of trouble as she paid calls when I was a lad."

Strangely, thinking of him as a young boy, filled with an adventurous spirit, exploring the same halls they had just walked, made warmth trickle through her.

She licked her lips, which had gone dry. "I didn't realize that Lord Sidmouth's grandmother was friends with your mother."

During her betrothal to Lord Wesley, Rosamund had never met her. The Duchess of Camden had been ill, her health tenuous at best, and Rosamund suddenly recalled Wesley telling her something about Camden, as the heir, being his mother's favored son. There had been bitterness in his voice, which she had ascribed at the time to hurt feelings. Odd how she had forgotten about that conversation until now, when she couldn't help but see their discussion in a new, troubling light, given what Camden had told her about Lord Wesley.

"The two of them are old bosom bows," Camden said easily, a wistful smile on his lips. "Mother would have dearly loved to attend Sidmouth's wedding today. It's a pity she wasn't able."

"I am sorry that her health didn't permit it," she said, her heart giving a pang at the raw emotion in his voice.

"As am I." They stared at each other in silence, Rosamund's heart beating ever faster as he moved toward her, closing the comfortable distance separating them. "But there is only so much we can control in this life of ours, and as much as I wish she were well, I am simply glad she is with us still."

"Of course," she murmured, feeling even more foolish about her request now that such important matters had been discussed.

As a daughter who had lost her father, she completely understood Camden's emotions. Perhaps they could forget she had requested a private audience and return to the gathering. Surely the time would soon come for Lord and Lady Sidmouth to embark on their honeymoon and for farewells to be exchanged.

She opened her mouth to suggest as much when Camden spoke.

"What is it that you wished to speak with me about?" he asked.

Oh dear.

She was going to have to tell him. How else would she explain convincing him to take the risk of meeting in the Duke of Arrington's library in the midst of a wedding breakfast?

She took a deep breath and then blurted what had been

weighing on her mind ever since her discussion with Miranda. "I've been considering something else. A matter far too delicate to be enumerated in the marriage contract, but one that is important to me, nonetheless."

"You signed the contract," he reminded her.

Rosamund inclined her head, for that formality had indeed been observed between them. "I am aware of that, of course. But as I said, my concern is too sensitive to be bandied about by solicitors, regardless of their oaths and duties."

He considered her, unsmiling, his jaw tense. "Go on."

"Before we marry, I need to know whether we are… compatible," she explained, feeling her cheeks go hot.

"Compatible," he repeated.

One word. His expression was as blank as a new canvas, as if he was completely unaware of what she was intimating.

"Yes. As stated in my stipulations, one of the reasons I am amenable to this match is that it will allow me to have a family of my own," she elaborated. "However, as it stands, I have no notion of whether the two of us would suit."

"Suit?"

She grew impatient. "Are you toying with me, Your Grace?"

"I assure you I am not. I'm merely attempting to make certain I'm clear about what you are saying, Rosamund." He moved toward her with sudden, purposeful strides, and she was so startled that she moved backward in response, until she was neatly trapped, a wall of books at her back and the Duke of Camden hovering over her. He braced his hands on the shelves at either side of her head and leaned close, the heady scent of sandalwood and musk igniting the fires of desire within her. And then he lowered his head, so that she was almost certain he would press his mouth to hers. Kiss her again.

91

But he didn't.

He just stared at her with his pale, impenetrable gaze instead.

Finally, he spoke, his voice low and silken and unbearably intimate. "Because what it sounds like to me is that you are suggesting you want to know how we suit in bed. Is that what you meant?"

In bed. How sinful he made it sound.

Yes, it was what she had meant. But somehow, admitting it to him felt akin to stripping herself of all garments before him. Which, of course, she would need to do one day. But not now. Not yet. Not in the library of the Duke of Arrington's town house in the midst of a wedding breakfast, where, at any moment, someone might walk in and find them.

She licked her lips. "I… Surely it's not such an outrageous requirement. A marriage necessitates a certain closeness, does it not? We haven't courted in the proper sense. I scarcely know you."

"You know me well enough."

"Not that well."

"Are you saying you want me to bed you?"

Was she?

"I…well…I…"

The confirmation wouldn't spill from her lips.

No man had ever spoken to her so bluntly. Was it Camden's proximity, the suggestion in his tone, his decadent scent? His handsome face a scant inch from hers, his mouth so near? She couldn't say, but there was a deep ache inside her. A restless yearning.

Did she want him to bed her? Yes.

Would such a concession be scandalous? Absolutely.

Could she help herself? No.

"Having difficulty finding the words, my dear?" he taunted, a smug smile on his lips.

"Yes," she blurted. "That is what I want."

He stilled, his countenance taking on a harsh yearning she'd never seen from him. It was as if his icy mask had slipped, revealing the man beneath.

"You're certain?" he asked softly.

Here was her chance to tell him *no*. To regain what remained of her sanity.

"Yes," she said.

He straightened abruptly, grasping her hand in his. "Come."

Camden didn't bother to wait for her to reply either. He began striding away, taking her with him.

"Where are we going?"

"Somewhere we can be alone," he said enigmatically. "I came here with the Duke of Brandon. We'll take his carriage."

"Take his carriage without his permission?"

"I have his permission to use it as I please." He cast a hot look over his shoulder at her that stole her breath. "Have you a better plan?"

"Can this…whatever it is…not wait?" she queried, breathless now from the haste with which they were decamping from the library.

They made it to the outer hall, where the voices of the guests filtered from the dining room and ballroom where the breakfast was being held.

"No," he said simply. "It cannot."

He tugged her down the hall and through the entry, where they gathered her wrap, hat, and gloves along with his overcoat, and then into the outdoors. Some of their fellow revelers had flocked to the street where Lord and Lady Sidmouth were preparing to say their farewells and step up into their carriage for their honeymoon. They were all too preoccupied to take note of the Duke of Camden hauling her across the pavements.

"You can't spirit me away with Mother in attendance," she protested, scandalized at the prospect.

She hastened her pace until she was at his side, matching his long-limbed strides.

"I didn't reckon I would bring Mrs. Payne along with us for your debauching," he murmured in her ear as he led her down a line of parked carriages.

Debauching.

Oh dear heaven. She stumbled over her own feet, stepping on her hems. Why did it sound so right and so wrong all at once? She had to put a halt to this sheer madness. They stopped before a gleaming carriage marked with the Duke of Brandon's crest.

"But—"

"No buts, Rosamund," Camden argued sternly. "Get in."

The urgent command in his voice, coupled with the fear that someone would see them entering the carriage together, had her moving. Up into the carriage she went, settling on a Moroccan leather squab.

But to her alarm, he didn't follow her. Instead, he turned away from the carriage.

"Where are you going?" she demanded.

"To tell your mother that you're feeling ill and I'm taking care of you, so she needn't worry. She can take the carriage to your town house on her own, and I will bring you there later."

"Oh," she managed, deflated and rather guilty that she had neglected to think of informing her mother of what was happening in the pell-mell retreat from the wedding breakfast.

He nodded. "I'll be but a moment."

Camden didn't give her an opportunity to respond. He simply stalked in the opposite direction, leaving her to wait. A servant closed the door to the carriage. She sat there staring at the interior of the Duke of Brandon's carriage, telling herself that she should go. That remaining here was a mistake.

She had noticed a sensual shift in Camden that had been nothing short of dangerous in the library. Her heart yet pounded and her nipples were still hard, but their state had nothing to do with the chill in the air and everything to do with the Duke of Camden crowding her into a wall of books and asking her if she was saying she wanted him to bed her.

Bed.

Camden.

These two words together brought sinful thoughts to mind. Thoughts she should not be thinking. But then, wasn't this her idea? Hadn't she been the one who wanted to know whether they would suit each other in the bedchamber?

It had seemed somehow simpler then, when the overwhelming reality of Camden hadn't been before her, around her. When his eyes hadn't been burning into hers with undeniable desire. When his mouth hadn't been a breath away from hers and when she hadn't needed to fret over being whisked from a wedding breakfast in a stolen carriage.

Borrowed, perhaps. He had permission. So he claimed. Oh, what if the Duke of Brandon leapt into his carriage at this very moment and found her here, alone, waiting for Camden to return? Would he raise a cry amongst their fellow guests? Would she be ruined? Perhaps that was Camden's goal. Had she allowed herself to be neatly led into a trap of her own making?

The carriage door swung open, and to her relief, it wasn't Brandon climbing inside but Camden. He settled on the bench opposite her, the servant closed the door once more, and then the duke gave the roof a simple rap, indicating he was ready to take his leave.

All while holding her stare.

Rosamund could scarcely breathe.

Or think.

Yes, that is what you must do, she reminded herself. *Think.*

"Did you find my mother?" she asked as the conveyance lurched into motion.

"Yes." He stretched his legs across the carriage, crossing them at the ankles. In his elegant black suit, he was wonderfully handsome. But she could see wear at the seams. His garments were not new. Indeed, at his left elbow, a clever hand had made an excellent effort at restoring a tear. The only sign was a small pucker, catching Rosamund's gaze for a moment.

She didn't like this evidence of his reduced circumstances. The Duke of Camden was a beautiful man. He should have been dressed in the newest and best fashion, not in a suit slightly faded from laundering, the evidence of repairs everywhere a discerning eye could be cast.

Belatedly, she realized he had offered her nothing beyond that single-word reply.

She jerked her gaze from the flaws in his suit, which seemed somehow magnified in the close quarters of the carriage. "What did you tell her?"

"I told her that a megrim had come upon you and that you needed to rest, but that she ought to proceed home with the carriage the two of you brought."

She closed her eyes for a moment, her stomach twisting into a knot of worry. "What if she tells everyone?"

"I do believe she will hold her tongue."

"But she blurts things sometimes, Camden. She has done for some time now. Inappropriate truths. Something like Megs, now that I think upon it. For all we know, she is announcing to everyone at the wedding breakfast that you have run away with me to assuage my megrim."

He leaned forward, resting his forearms on his thighs as he did so, his regard impossible to avoid. "And if she does?"

She ran her tongue over her bottom lip. "Then I shall be ruined."

"You will also be ruined after I bed you." His tone was conversational despite the sinful nature of his words.

Did nothing move him? Had that naked hunger in the library been naught but her imagination?

"I never said that you should…that we ought to…that…"

Her words trailed away, chased by an acute fit of embarrassment. What she truly meant to say was that even if he did bed her, no one would know. But she kept tripping over *bed*. A three-letter word laden with so many wicked implications.

A slow smile curved the corners of his sensual lips upward. "My goodness, Rosamund. Never say that my brave, fierce, determined woman cannot speak plainly with her future husband."

He was baiting her. But worse, he was enjoying her discomfiture. His unrepentant grin said so. And truly, what was wrong with her that a part of her deep within stirred to the way he had called her *his* woman? How positively primitive.

"If you will recall, I haven't decided you are to be my husband just yet," she reminded him sharply, vexed with herself for being charmed.

For apparently having learned nothing from her disastrous betrothal with this infinitely more dangerous man's brother. She needed to keep her wits about her. To make certain that she made the right decision. She couldn't afford to be swayed.

"Ah," he said, drawing the word out as he straightened, settling back against the squabs. "If you are undecided, then I will have to do my utmost to persuade you. However shall I do it?"

She took a shallow breath. "Camden."

"My given name is Stuart. Perhaps you might try it."

Stuart. She hadn't known. But it suited him. She liked it. She liked the way he was looking at her now as well, as if she were a sweet he intended to devour. Slowly. And with great deliberation.

"Stuart," she repeated, the name feeling foreign.

Intimate. Far too intimate for this confined space when his heated gaze was threatening to send her up in flames.

His smile faded, and he became utterly serious. "There. That was not so difficult, was it?"

"No, I suppose not," she conceded. "However, the rest of it is a mistake. Perhaps I was being hasty in thinking we needed to make certain we're compatible."

"Oh no," he said, his tone smooth. "I think you were absolutely right, my dear. We owe it to ourselves to do so."

"I didn't intend for it to happen today," she blurted, frustrated.

"Rosamund?"

She eyed him warily. "Yes?"

He extended a gloved hand. "Come here."

There was nowhere to go that wouldn't involve being pressed against him. And she didn't trust herself. Or him, as it happened.

"I am perfectly comfortable as I am," she declined primly.

"If you don't come here of your own volition, I'll haul you onto my lap. If that is what you'd prefer, I'm happy to oblige. However, if you would like to sit by my side, then now is the time to do so."

She raised her eyebrows. "Is that a threat?"

The corner of his mouth kicked upward in a half grin. "It's a promise, sweetheart. Now, which will it be?"

She settled her hand in his, and he tugged her across the

carriage, allowing her to seat herself at his side. "There. Are you well pleased now?"

"Pleased enough, if not well pleased."

Rosamund huffed a sigh. "Have you forgotten that I am the one who is truly in control in this situation of ours, Camden?"

The grin faded from his lips. "Of course I haven't. Have you forgotten to call me Stuart?"

His scent was once more wrapped around her, his sinful mouth all she could look at, recalling what his lips felt like, demanding and knowing, moving over hers. Yearning rose within her, the flesh between her legs aching, her breasts feeling heavy and full.

"Stuart," she said again.

"Better," he praised.

And then before she could say anything else, he cupped her nape and angled her head, his mouth descending in the same moment. She tilted her face up, welcoming his kiss with a sigh, feeling as if she might burst if she didn't have his lips on hers. This was new, this sensation that she was unraveling inside, like a tightly wound skein of yarn rolled down a staircase, coming wildly undone. His lips were hot, firm, and demanding, his tongue seeking entry.

She surrendered, opening, giving him what he wanted, forgetting about her hesitation, the wariness fading. This was Stuart, the man she was marrying, the man who kissed her and made the world around them fade. The man who would be her husband, the father of her children.

Did she want that?

Yes.

Their tongues moved together, teasing, tasting, and she found her answer. She very much *did* want that. This was an exercise in futility. Those kisses in the sitting room of her town house had not been an aberration.

The carriage rocked over the road, taking them to their destination, and all her fears vanished. No man had ever kissed her as he did. And she knew somehow that none would. Something unique was burning brightly between them. Something that belonged only to the two of them.

But then, there was more.

His mouth left hers to explore her jaw, to string a thread of kisses all the way to her ear and then lower, traveling down her throat. He stopped at the decolletage of her modest bodice, his mouth lingering there as if he were reveling in the moment, his breath hot through the layers of her gown and undergarments. She suddenly wished that her gown were open, that her chemise and corset were gone. That his mouth was on her bare breasts or the sensitive peaks.

The notion was shocking yet thrilling, and it sent a rush of molten desire to the very center of her, where between her legs she was already damp and aching. He kissed the upper swell of her breast, then the full curve, then finally laid his mouth over her nipple. She gasped, wishing the boning and silk and cotton did not separate her greedy skin from his.

He tipped his head back, slanting a glance upward at her. "Compatible?"

Rosamund swallowed. "Y-yes."

Would he forget this mission of his now that she had shown herself so humiliatingly susceptible to his advances? Likely. He had made his point, had he not?

Apparently not, for he slid from the bench at her side and lowered himself to his knees on the carriage floor. "You sound a bit uncertain, Rosamund. I think I must proceed if I'm to convince you properly."

Holding her gaze, he calmly removed his hat, settling it on the squabs, followed by his gloves. The removal of each finger—slow, deliberate—seemed itself a seduction, even if she had seen and touched his bare hands before.

"What are you doing?" she asked, her voice sounding slightly breathless, which aggrieved her even as she was helpless to stop it. "Why are you on your knees?"

"To test how compatible the two of us are," he said calmly, before reaching for the hem of her gown.

With painstaking care, he raised it a scant amount, to her ankle. Cool air slithered beneath her skirts.

"Stuart," she protested, not certain what she was protesting, only that she should.

"This was your idea, sweetheart," he pointed out, his voice deep and sensual, laden with promise. "I am merely fulfilling your requirement."

He lifted her hems a bit higher, exposing her lower calves.

"You are the one who dragged me from Lord and Lady Sidmouth's wedding breakfast in a stolen carriage."

Stuart wasn't finished, however. Her skirts and petticoats had continued to rise.

"Not stolen," he said calmly. "I had permission. Just as I have permission to do this."

His head dipped, and he pressed a searing kiss to her inner right knee.

She inhaled at the contact, never having imagined that a man's kiss on such an unimportant place might feel so very good.

"What do you think you're…"

Her words trailed away as his mouth flitted over her left inner knee as well. He grasped her skirts in fistfuls of elegant fabric and pushed them into her lap. "Hold this here, won't you?"

"Why?"

"Because I've asked you to," he answered, kissing higher, his lips on her drawers instead of her stockings.

She wanted to press her knees together for modesty's sake, aware that he was growing ever nearer to the split in her drawers, but he had already inserted his broad upper body between her legs. Thankfully, the heavy weight of her gown and undergarments remained pooled, shielding her from his gaze.

"Hold them, Rosamund," he repeated, an edge of ducal authority in his voice that had previously been absent.

Keeping her skirts raised seemed like a dreadful idea. What was it that he intended to do? She failed to see why baring her legs to him would show either of them how compatible they were.

"I don't think this is a good idea," she cautioned, frowning down at him.

Goodness, he was so handsome. So commanding and stern. His hands glided along her outer thighs in caresses that lit something within her, his gaze leaving hers to settle on the sight before him.

"This is what you asked for," he reminded her. "I aim to see how compatible we are."

"But this is a carriage. Should there not be a bed?" Her mind whirled. She was confused. Needy. Wanting. Nothing made sense.

His touch swept higher, beneath her skirts entirely, his hands disappearing, his unusual eyes flicking back to hers. "Rosamund?"

It felt good, his hands on her. Better than good. It made her feel as if she were melting inside in the most delicious, exquisite way.

She caught her breath. "Yes?"

"Hold your skirts and your tongue, darling."

She bit her lip and at last did as he asked. Stuart shocked her by gently nudging her legs apart. But he had told her to hold her tongue, and a raw, potent curiosity came over her. She couldn't look away. Made no effort to stop him. Just what did he intend? She was no naïve miss, but she most certainly had never…

His head dipped beneath the mound of skirts on her lap. Between her legs. And *oh heaven*, there was the brush of his lips over that aching part of her. He kissed her once. Slowly, delicately, in a way he had not kissed her mouth. But she felt it so acutely, because she was so sensitive. There was no question of what he was doing.

"Compatible?" He wanted to know, his lips grazing her folds as he spoke the lone word.

The scoundrel. He was seducing her. Proving a point that he could make her burn with desire.

"Y-yes," she forced out. "You may conclude your…efforts of persuasion."

"Oh, no," he murmured, his voice deep and mellifluous, his breath coasting over her intimate flesh as he spoke. "I've hardly just begun."

Her modesty made her protest. "But—"

He kissed her again, *there*. Her words died. And then his tongue flicked over her, unerringly finding the bundle of flesh that only she had ever touched before. The one that gave her so much secret pleasure in the midnight solitude of her bed. Again and again, his tongue traveled, swirling over her, bringing her flesh to life.

"Oh sweet heavens," she murmured, fingers clasping her skirts in a death grip.

The gray, late-morning light filtered in through the blinds, enveloping the carriage in a cozy, cool glow as they rumbled along, the two of them seemingly the only souls in existence. Wickedly, he played over her, licking and then sucking until her hips jumped from the bench and she cried out before biting her lip hard to stay further noise. It wouldn't do for the Duke of Brandon's coachman to know what they were about in here. Bad enough that Stuart had spirited her away alone. But if anyone were to know...

He licked down her seam, his tongue finding her entrance and sinking inside her, and the last of her coherent thoughts fled. She was a woman ruled by sensation alone. Reason, caution, concern were banished. The Duke of Camden's sinful mouth between her legs was all she knew. All she felt.

Her desire built into a frenzied pinnacle, the pleasure of his lips and tongue sending her into a delirious cloud of pure, unadulterated need. She was going to explode any moment. To come apart beneath his knowing mouth. Right here in a carriage in the midst of the morning, on her way home from a wedding, of all things.

It didn't matter.

Nothing mattered.

He suckled her harder, and it was too much. She lost control, throwing her head back against the squabs and gasping as bliss exploded deep inside her like fireworks in a night sky. But still, he wasn't done. As tremors of her release rippled through her, he lapped at her, making her squirm on the bench, sounds that she scarcely recognized falling from her lips. Another crest hit her suddenly, furiously, and she spasmed again, a strangled moan tearing from her.

So much for remaining quiet and keeping the coachman from hearing. It was too late to care. He ravished her with his tongue as she quaked and trembled, and pleasure washed over her like a warm, welcoming wave from the most beautiful ocean.

Until finally, he relented, withdrawing from beneath her skirts and rocking back on his knees to look up at her.

Her heart was pounding from the force of her release, and she was sagging against the Moroccan leather, her entire body having turned to India rubber, limp and malleable. He caught her gaze, his lips glistening in the light with the evidence of her desire.

"Do you reckon we're compatible, sweetheart?" he asked, still on his knees, his expression desire mixed with smug masculine satisfaction.

It took her a moment to form an answer to his question, for her mind was a jumbled mess. "Er…yes, I do think we are."

He smiled slowly. "Good. Then there are no further obstructions to our marriage, and the announcement can be made in *The Times*."

How final that would be. It was the last step, aside from the nuptials themselves. Could she do this?

The answer was there, in her heart. Yes. She could. And indeed, if she wanted to seize her dream of having a family of her own, she *must*.

"The announcement can be made," she allowed.

He kissed first one knee, then the other, before tenderly taking her hems from her and smoothing out her petticoat and overskirt. As if it were the most ordinary act in the world and he spent every carriage ride beneath a lady's skirts, he rose and seated himself on the bench at her side once more.

But then, for all she knew, he *did* spend every carriage ride beneath a lady's skirts. He was the Duke of Camden, after all, part of a fast set of dukes who were rumored to do very bad things. The thought sent ice chasing after the heat. Rakes were dangerous and devastating. If her doomed betrothal with Wesley had taught her anything, it was that a rake was never to be trusted.

It was no different with his brother, even if the connection between them seemed so much stronger than what she had once known with Wesley.

"I'll see that it's done with all haste," he told her, before pulling at the blinds with one long finger. "It looks as if we've arrived at your town house."

He gave the roof a discreet tap, signaling they were ready to disembark, and her face flamed. The coachman would know what they had been about.

Suddenly, Stuart's words punctured her musings.

They had arrived at *her* town house, he had said. Not his, as she'd assumed.

"Did you have any intention of taking me to bed?" she asked quietly.

He settled his hat back on his head. "I had no wish to ruin you, at least not by taking you completely. I wanted the choice to be yours, rather than forcing your hand."

Or perhaps he had simply been that assured of his abilities when it came to sensual persuasion. Maybe he had known that she would be so moved by what he did to her in the carriage that she would agree to anything.

If so, he hadn't been entirely wrong.

Her chin went up. "What will the neighbors say when I alight from the Duke of Brandon's carriage?" she asked.

"I instructed the driver to deliver us to the mews. Hopefully, no one will be the wiser."

He truly had thought of everything.

She wasn't sure if she should be reassured or alarmed. Either way, one thing was more than clear. Rosamund was going to marry the Duke of Camden.

CHAPTER 7

"You look disgustingly happy, particularly for a man wearing such a dreadful coat," King observed, making a moue of distaste as he passed a glance over Stuart's well-worn lounge suit.

He had been poring over *The Times*, seeking the announcement of his engagement to Rosamund, when his friend, the Duke of Kingham, had sauntered into his study, unannounced, as was often King's preference. King liked the element of surprise, or so he claimed. Now, they were seated before the fire in the hearth on chairs that were likely as threadbare as Stuart's coat was. But he didn't care about his friend's good-natured taunts. For just as King had crossed the room, Stuart had seen the words proclaiming to society that he and Miss Rosamund Payne were to be married. An intense rush of relief had washed over him.

"I thought you found it bourgeois to wake before noon," Stuart offered mildly, impervious to his friend's criticism.

The suit was several years old and undoubtedly outmoded by King's exacting standards. But when one was perilously low on funds, one didn't concern oneself with such trivialities. It was clean and pressed, which was the best Stuart was going to manage until he married. King, by comparison, wore a dark-blue velvet coat with a cobalt cravat, a buff silk waistcoat, and fawn trousers that looked as if they had been sewn onto him that very morning. Nary a stain, a wrinkle, nor a hair out of place atop his head.

"I couldn't sleep," King drawled. "It's the devil of a thing."

"No cure to be found? Not even in one of your potions?"

"I'm rather persuaded that the concoction I enjoyed before bed was the reason I couldn't sleep," his friend admitted wryly.

"And I'm the one you sought out for company this morning?" Stuart pressed a hand to his heart in dramatic fashion. "I'm touched."

"Ha! If you must know, Brandon wasn't at home."

"There goes my poor conceit."

"Also, I read the notice in *The Times*. You're actually marrying her, then, old chap?"

What now seemed a lifetime ago, Stuart and his friends, the fellow founding members of their club, had pledged to see the ignominious legacies of their collective fathers rot. Stuart had meant that wine-soaked vow. He'd never expected to marry. But much had happened to alter the course of his life.

He nodded. "I am indeed."

"First Brandon with all this talk of bloody marriage, and now you." King shuddered. "I can only pray the rest of us remain unscathed."

Stuart chuckled. "You make marriage sound like going to war."

"Both are deadly entrapments," King said, somber, shaking his head.

But Stuart didn't feel the same. For the first time in years, Stuart was at ease. He felt a lightness in his chest that had

been long absent. But more than that, a keen sense of anticipation coiled inside him, tighter than a watch spring. It was
because of her, all of it.

Because of Rosamund, he possessed a sense of palpable
relief that he would soon be able to regain control over his
funds and his brother. That he would be able to spare
Mother and save his family's sordid secrets. And also—he
could not lie to himself—that he would soon have Rosamund
in his bed.

Their marriage may have begun as one of convenience,
but he had been able to think of precious little else ever since
that day in Brandon's carriage when Stuart had buried his
face between her legs and pleasured her until she had come
on his tongue. Her taste, her scent, sweet God, her respon-
siveness… He had intended to prove to her just how compatible they were, and in the end, he had only succeeded in
proving to himself how much he wanted her.

But he had to stop thinking of such things in the
company of his friend. King was too damned perceptive
by far.

He cleared his throat and shifted in his chair, trying to
find a more comfortable position. "As I told you all, I need to
marry."

What he hadn't revealed to his friends was that he was
being blackmailed. He alone knew about the letters that had
come in rapid succession, always demanding more money,
that first shocking missive still making impotent fury rage
through him every time he recalled the words that had been
scrawled in slanted black ink. Words conveying a secret he
had believed no one knew. A secret he couldn't allow to be
revealed.

"Your worthless brother and wastrel father have left you
in straits that dire?" King probed.

"Wesley is doing his damnedest to make certain he bleeds

SCARLETT SCOTT

me dry," he affirmed, guilt slicing through him for not being completely honest, even if he knew he couldn't. "He is hell-bent upon spending every last farthing in my possession."

"Why not cut him off?" King asked. "I know it isn't my business and Wesley is your brother, but good Christ, Cam. No one would blame you for ridding yourself of the plague of a brother determined to whore and gamble his way to oblivion."

"My mother would, however," he said, thinking of the beloved woman he had almost lost. "She is intent upon believing the best of him, and with her infirmity, the doctor has been insistent that she isn't to suffer any upset. It could drive her to her grave. How can I, in good faith, cast her son into the streets knowing this?"

"It's said that a mother's love can see no faults," King drawled. "Having had a mother who didn't give a damn if I lived or died, I never experienced that firsthand."

Stuart sighed. "I'm sorry for that."

"*She* wasn't." King raised a brow. "She was more concerned with her lovers, I fear. But never mind my sordid upbringing. Let us discuss the most pressing matter, your arsehole brother. I do know some enterprising fellows, Cam. For the proper motivation, it would only require one shove in front of a carriage or a bit of arsenic in his soup…"

"King."

"Right." His friend shrugged. "You can't fault a chap for asking."

"Murder feels a trifle worse than merely cutting him off and casting him to the streets," Stuart pointed out dryly.

"Such a strong, hideous word, that," King said. "I prefer to think of it as an unfortunate mishap facilitated by a helpful criminal."

"Jesus," he muttered, scrubbing a hand over his chin.

110

"Please don't tell me you've employed such tactics in the past."

King held his gaze. "I've never employed such tactics in the past," he said with an innocent air that Stuart couldn't be entirely certain was genuine. "Feel better now, Cam?"

"No," Stuart answered with blunt honesty. "I bloody well don't."

"Perhaps a drink would assuage your conscience," King suggested.

"Impossible. I'm afraid my brother has drained the household dry of every last drop of spirits."

King extracted a small bottle from within his coat. "Fortunately for you, I come prepared."

Stuart eyed the offering with a raised brow. "A new potion of yours?"

King was known in their circle for his delight in crafting concoctions that were both mysterious and potent. His skill certainly pleased the other members of their club, particularly at the house parties they hosted.

"It is indeed." King grinned.

"Dare I inquire what it is?" Stuart asked, although he already knew the answer.

"Don't spoil my fun," his friend chastised, offering him the bottle. "Have a sip and tell me what you think."

He extended the bottle to him, and Stuart accepted it. "I'm about to have a very unpleasant conversation with my arsehole of a brother soon, so I'll need all the fortification I can beg, borrow, or steal."

Stuart unscrewed the cap on the bottle and brought the slim, tapered neck to his lips. The liquid hit his tongue, smooth and mellow with a hint of sweetness. It was rather good, actually. But that was hardly surprising. King's potions were infallibly delicious; it was the aftereffects that varied.

"What manner of unpleasant conversation, if I dare ask?" King queried.

Stuart winced, recalling the task awaiting him, one which he had been dreading. "I need to tell him that I'm marrying his former betrothed."

His friend whistled. "You haven't told him yet?"

He shook his head. "Theirs was not a love match. At least, it wasn't on Wesley's part. I don't believe him capable of loving anyone, not even himself. But as you can imagine, the circumstances are a trifle unconventional."

"Ah, damn it all. You had better drink up, my friend," King advised.

And he thought his friend was not wrong about that. Grimly, Stuart took another pull from the bottle. Warmth coursed through him, the potion already having an effect upon him.

"But not too much," his friend added. "This potion is decidedly a strong one."

"Am I going to hallucinate a mermaid and convince myself I'm a fish?" he asked wryly, recalling a past incident concerning one of King's brews and a particularly inebriated club member.

"God." King chuckled. "I had forgotten about poor old Lord Roderick. As long as you stay away from water, table legs, and marble statuary, you'll be fine. But whatever you do, don't sneeze, walk in a circle, or eat cheese for the next few hours."

Stuart was mid-sip when his friend issued the alarming— if confusing—instructions. "Are you jesting?"

King grinned. "Of course I am."

Stuart took another swig.

His evil friend raised a brow. "Or am I?"

"Bastard," he said without heat, threading the cap back on

the bottle and returning it to King. "Here you are. I thank you for the calm before the storm."

"Any time, old chap," King said. "I aim to serve." He tucked the bottle back inside his coat. "I suppose I should be on my way. But do think on what I said. Just a bit of arsenic in the soup ought to do it. All one need do is soak some flypapers."

They both rose from their chairs, King smoothing every wrinkle from his velvet coat and brushing the sleeves for any hint of lint.

"I'm not sure if I ought to be concerned you possess intimate knowledge on the means of obtaining arsenic for poisoning someone or impressed."

"Do be impressed." King winked. "I can assure you that, were I in the mood to murder anyone, you would never be in danger. I cannot, however, say the same for everyone in my acquaintance."

Bloody hell.

Only King.

His spirits further lifted with the aid of his friend's latest potion, Stuart saw King off. But when he inquired with Fleetwood about Wesley's whereabouts, it was to discover that his brother had already skulked from the town house, likely off to lose more money Stuart didn't have.

Informing Wesley about his impending nuptials would have to wait for another day. He would pay a call on his future duchess instead. They needed to arrange the details of their wedding, and he simply needed to see her again.

CHAPTER 8

*R*osamund was frowning over her watercolors when a servant informed her that she had an unexpected caller—His Grace, the Duke of Camden.

Her *betrothed*, she thought for a breathless moment as her paintbrush hovered over her canvas before she settled it in the glass water basin on her writing desk. Because it was official now. The notice in *The Times* had stared back at Rosamund when she had opened the paper earlier that morning.

"See him in, if you please," she said, trying to tamp down the frenzied rush of excitement that lit within her, rather like a flame igniting into a roaring fire.

If only she could stop thinking about what had happened in the Duke of Brandon's carriage. Her cheeks were flushed, and the same, aching hunger that had refused to abate since their wild ride through Mayfair pulsed deep within her. Even her nipples were hard and pebbled beneath her corset. She squeezed her thighs together to stave off the yearning, but the action only seemed to heighten her affliction.

He strode into her sitting room unannounced, jolting her

from her musings, which was just as well. She rose from her seat.

"Your Grace."

"We agreed that you would call me Stuart," he reminded her, stopping within reach and executing an elegant bow.

His scent wafted over her, and for a heady moment, she longed to throw herself into his arms. A most unexpected reaction, even given what had happened between them before they had parted last.

"Stuart," she murmured, feeling suddenly, unaccountably shy.

This man was to be her husband. Now was decidedly not the time to allow the memory of all the shocking intimacies they had shared in Brandon's carriage to resurface. No, she had to maintain her composure.

He took her hand in his, bringing it to his lips for a chaste kiss that sent a frisson down her spine before he examined her fingers, smiling. "Purple lake, vermilion, and chrome yellow."

Rosamund smiled. "You forgot gamboge."

He gave her a sinful grin that made something low in her belly flutter. "I hope I'm to be forgiven. The shades of chrome yellow and gamboge are so similar, I find. You were painting again. Have I interrupted?"

Good heavens, he was a handsome man. She had known this, of course, in the sense that one knows the sun is in the sky above. However, she had not admired him, for he was a force she had not dared to stare at overly long, also like the sun. He had been forbidden to her. Beyond her reach. But he was within reach now, and the contact of his bare skin on hers was enough to make her melt inside. A sudden longing to paint him rose. The lines of his face—striking jaw, high cheekbones, proud nose, and high forehead—were made for being captured on canvas. If only she were talented enough to paint him. She would preserve his image forever as he looked now, his lips curved upward, his eyes shining, his wavy, dark hair perfectly tousled, the sunlight filtering in the windows casting him in a gilded air.

Belatedly, she realized she was staring at him. What was wrong with her? She had seen handsome men before, even if none of them had kissed her so passionately. Or in such intriguing places.

"Your call is welcome," she said, realizing it was the truth and not merely a forced polite response.

She…*liked* the Duke of Camden. Indeed, she enjoyed his company, even beyond his searing kisses and skilled caresses. It was a sobering revelation.

"Thank you." He released her hand, still regarding her warmly, his gaze never leaving hers. "What are you working on today? I'm guessing it is no longer my feathered nemesis's portrait?"

"I'm having a dreadful time with it, but you may look if you like," she said, thinking of how she had been struggling to capture a vase of fresh flowers she had arranged on a table by the window. "The shadow cast on the rosebuds is giving me difficulty. I may just surrender and begin a new piece."

"I would love to see your painting," he told her easily. "If it pleases you, of course."

"You truly wish to see it?" She raised a brow. "I must warn you that flowers are not exactly my forte."

"I'm sure you're being modest." His smile gentled, becoming intimate, just for her.

She swallowed hard against an unexpected rush of longing. No man had ever looked at her thus, with such tenderness. As if she were of the utmost importance to him and everything she said and all she did were sources of immense fascination to him. Which was surely a skill he had acquired during his tenure as a rake.

The reminder of his past served as a tart rebuke. What was she thinking? She was a rational, reasonable, intelligent woman. One who'd had her heart broken by a cad before. She must not, above all, read too much into Camden's concern for her. He needed her fortune, and she wanted a family, and those were the only two reasons they were marrying. The reasons they stood together now in this very room. She would do well to remember it.

Rosamund stiffened her spine and renewed her determination to remain thoroughly immune to this man's charms. "I am only modest where it is due," she said, moving toward her writing desk, where she kept her watercolor set in its polished mahogany box.

The drawers were presently open in disarray, her brush where she had abandoned it in a sea of purple-red water. Her porcelain palette was already drying. She would need fresh water to bring the paints back to life.

She gestured to her painting, which was only partially completed, frowning at the rosebuds. "The intricacy of the furled petals always escapes me as well, as you can see."

He had trailed closely in her wake and stood at her side, gazing down at her effort with what appeared to be genuine interest. "This is fine work, Rosamund. When you finish it, we shall have it framed and hang it on the wall in the salon in my town house."

The mentioning of his town house jolted her from her musings. "Why would you wish to hang one of my watercolors in your salon?"

"Because it is yours and because you are immensely talented, even if you insist otherwise." He turned the full force of his unusual gaze back upon her. "And because the salon shall be yours after we wed."

Her lips parted, her mind hanging upon his mentioning of the salon at his town house rather than his praise for her talent. "That won't be necessary. I have my sitting room here, which I have decorated to my liking."

He smiled, the corners of his eyes crinkling in a way she couldn't help but to find appealing. "Yes, but you'll not be living here any longer after we marry, my dear."

The pronouncement left her gaping at him.

"Don't be silly. Of course I shall live here. This town house is my home. It is where all my father's antiquities are. It is where I have always lived."

He cocked his head at her, his smile fading. "But you are to be my duchess. Your place will be at my side, in my home, in my bed."

Somehow, in all her logical, extensive plans for what a marriage between them would require, she had not thought of this. Nor was it spelled out in any of the conditions he had agreed to as part of their marriage contract. She reeled with the implications, feeling dizzied. Surely she could dissuade him from this course.

"I cannot live in your town house with you, Camden," she said. "You must know that."

For many reasons. She was an independent woman of means. She liked the carefully crafted world she had built around herself.

"I know nothing of the sort," he said, clasping his hands behind his back and regarding her in a censorious fashion.

"Don't look at me that way," she snapped.

"What way, my dear?" He was calm, unsmiling, so very patient.

Rosamund did not like it, because her heart had been fairly galloping ever since he had crossed her threshold. She did not like the effect he had upon her. She did not like how handsome he was. And she *did not* like the idea of living in his town house.

"As if I am a costermonger with the absolute daring to knock upon your front door."

He frowned. "Poor as I am, I still never answer my own door, especially not to costermongers."

"You're being obtuse." She was wringing her hands before her whilst he remained the picture of serenity, and yet she could not collect herself. "I cannot live with you. I *will not* live with you. This is where I live."

"Am I to schedule appointments with you to do my marital duties? Do you truly intend me to pay a call upon you so that I may shag my own wife?"

Her cheeks went hot at his vulgar words. "You mustn't speak that way."

"Mustn't I?" At last, he had lost his polished veneer, his hands no longer clasped behind his back as he reached for her, pulling her against his hard form. "Tell me, sweetheart, how should I speak? Should I remind you of how much you liked my tongue on your—"

"Stop," she gasped, hands fluttering wildly before they landed on the lapels of his coat. "Are you trying to shame me?"

But it wasn't shame she felt just now, making her drawers go damp and her sex pulse with yearning. Rather, it was the opposite. He made her want to be wanton, and therein lay the danger.

"I would never seek to shame you." He dipped his head and pressed a fervent kiss to the corner of her jaw, near her ear, his breath falling like hot silk over her skin. "I'm merely trying to make you remember that there is passion between us, that I've more than proven how compatible we are as man and woman." He kissed the shell of her ear, his lips grazing her as he continued. "That there is no bloody way I am going to agree to your living in a different house as if we are polite strangers when I fully intend to spend every night pleasuring you senseless."

Her knees threatened to give out. She'd thought she was more resilient, that she could remain impervious to all rakish attempts at seduction. But he had proven her wrong.

What was she to say to such an outrageous, sinful proclamation?

She wetted her lips, trying to gather her wits. "You can do that here."

He kissed along her throat. "This isn't my home."

"And yours is not mine."

His hands swept over the small of her back, pressing her more firmly against him. "This is a battle you'll not win, sweetheart." He kissed the hollow at the base of her throat, his tongue flitting out, as if he were tasting her madly thumping pulse.

"You're being unnecessarily stubborn," she managed. "We can each remain in our homes and meet where we wish, when it suits us."

He lifted his head, his gaze searing hers. "There is only one place where it suits me to have you, and that is my bed."

He meant it. And she couldn't deny that the effect those words and the sensual promise in his expression had upon her was tremendous.

"I'm not selling this house," she said, feeling her resistance crumbling.

"Nor do I expect you to. It is your mother's home as well as yours. What other objections can you have? Tell me."

"I am accustomed to the running of this household."

"I'm sure your mother will run it as smoothly in your absence," he reassured her easily.

But Rosamund wasn't as confident of that. Mother was getting on in years, and since Father's death, she had come to rely upon Rosamund so much.

"She needs me."

He cupped her cheek. "Of course she does, but as your husband, I will need you more."

He was speaking of the physical. Of sexual congress. Sharing a bed. Perhaps even thinking of his masculine pride, which likely could not bear for society to know that he and his duchess were keeping separate residences. But the way he was touching her now, the way he looked at her, was clouding her judgment. Making her weak.

"Yes, but I am all she has left," she protested softly.

His thumb stroked gently over her skin. "You may visit whenever you wish. Meet with the housekeeper. Polish the bloody silver whilst you're here. All I ask is that you come back home to me, that you live with me, as you are meant to do, as my wife."

"I don't know what to say. This is most unexpected."

"Unexpected?" His lips quirked into a half smile, as if he were amused. "Did you not think about what would happen after we wed?"

She bit her lip, not wanting to admit the depths of her foolishness. "What about your brother?" she asked instead of answering his question directly.

He stiffened at the mentioning of Lord Wesley, his jaw hardening. "What of Wesley? He has nothing to do with us."

Us. Was it wrong of her to like the way that sounded so much, for it to glide over her like warm honey? Likely, yes, it was. Wrong for her ability to resist him, certainly.

"Of course not," she said, trying not to stare at his lips. "But I'm not sure I should like to see him every day or share the same roof."

He frowned, his thumb stilling on her cheek. "Do you still have feelings for him?"

"No," she answered instantly.

Truthfully.

He held her gaze, unrelenting. "You're sure?"

"Certain."

Camden—Stuart, as she must think of him now—stared at her another long moment. And then slowly, giving her time to object should she wish it, he lowered his head. She didn't object. Instead, Rosamund slid her hands up his coat to his shoulders, drawing him nearer as she rose on her toes. Their mouths met in a whisper-soft kiss. A tender collision followed by the tantalizing brush of his lips over hers. It was too soft. Too teasing. Not enough.

Making a sound of frustrated desire, she twined her arms around his neck, pressing herself shamelessly to his strong, lean form, increasing the pressure of their kiss. With a growl, he angled his mouth over hers, his tongue seeking entry as he took command. She surrendered willingly, lips parting for the slick, hot invasion. He ravished her with potent, drugging kisses and possessive thrusts of his tongue.

He tasted unusual, like anise with a hint of sweetness, and she never wanted their kisses to end. The longer he kissed her, the more need flowed through her, leaving her aching. She moved against him, seeking relief and finding none. As if he sensed what she wanted, Stuart guided her backward until the hard surface of her writing desk met her bottom through the layers of her gown and petticoats.

If they didn't take care, they would upend her water and paints and send all cascading to the floor in a jumbled sea of color and paintbrushes. But then he slid a long leg between her parted thighs, and she forgot to fret over spilled watercolors. Instead, the most delicious sensation radiated from her center as he pressed his leg between hers. Instinctively, she writhed on him, seeking and finding more pressure. More of what she wanted. She was swollen and wet below, the sensuous glide of his tongue in her mouth mirroring the rhythm of his thigh thrusting between hers.

But it wasn't sufficient. There were too many layers separating them. She ground herself mercilessly against his thigh, and yet she couldn't achieve the stimulation she craved, like when his tongue had flicked over her sensitive bud in the carriage. Curse her skirts. Pleasure was building within her, her breath coming faster, everything within her heightened to the point of acute awareness.

Her senses were intense—the rasp of his coat against her hands as she gripped him to her, the bristle of his shaved whiskers against her cheeks as he kissed her, his decadent scent of sandalwood and musk, his tongue gliding into her mouth, his lips firm and hot as they coaxed her response, their breaths mingling, each thrust of his thigh dragging her cotton undergarments over her sex. It was there, so close, her release, taunting her, and yet she couldn't find it.

Stuart knew.

He fisted one of his hands in her skirts, dragging her hems upward. The sound of paintbrushes rolling to the floor and landing in soft thumps on the Axminster didn't serve as a deterrent for either of them. Even if her replacement water bowl went next, she wouldn't care. His hand found her inner thigh, the cotton of her drawers impeding the contact of bare skin on bare skin. Still kissing her, he slid his hand higher at the same moment as she arched her back and scooted her bottom toward him. He dipped his fingers into her folds, his touch sending an electric pulse of desire radiating outward from her core.

He stroked her, gently at first, and then when she moaned and sucked on his tongue, he circled her pearl. Once, twice. It was agony and ecstasy. He strummed around where she wanted him most, teasing, tempting. Breaking down all her resistance. If he asked her to move to the moon with him in the next breath, she would gratefully agree to it.

But still, he would not give her what she wanted. Not quite. Frustrated, she broke the kiss, her head falling back.

"Stuart," she breathed. "Please."

He drew another tantalizing circle around her swollen bud. "It's not enough, is it?"

"No," she ground out, thrusting her hips toward him shamelessly, beyond caring now.

He had driven her to the edge of reason. Lust clouded her mind. She was an aching bundle of need, seeking what only he could give her.

"This is what it would be like if you lived here instead of with me, where you belong," he murmured. "You would be all alone in your bed at night, longing for me to bring you to completion."

Oh, the wicked man. He was tormenting her with sensual pleasure and all so he could emphasize his point.

"Are you…" Her words trailed off, her mind going blank as a new page when he grazed the sensitive underside of her pearl. "Are you trying to seduce me into agreeing to live with you, Camden?"

"Perhaps." His smile turned sinful as he drew another circle around her flesh beneath her skirts. "Is it working?"

It was, but she was too stubborn to admit it. So instead, she released her grip on his shoulder and slid her own hand beneath the layers of petticoats and silk. "I can bring myself to completion as well, you know."

"You beautiful, naughty thing." He cupped her mound, keeping her from pleasuring herself as she had been intent upon doing. "What do you think about when you touch yourself? Do you think about what happened in the carriage between us?"

Heat crept over her cheeks as she pressed his hand over her, seeking friction. "Perhaps. Move your hand, you rogue.

I'll not be persuaded to live in your town house under duress."

"Your cunny doesn't feel like it's under duress to me," he said, his voice low and dark. "It feels hot and wet and desperate for more."

The air whooshed from her lungs. "No one has ever said something so bold to me before."

He rotated his palm, and she gasped, her hips jumping to do his bidding. "And you like it, don't you? Just think of all the pleasure I can give you when you're in my bed every night."

To emphasize his words, he released his hold on her and gave her what she'd been seeking these last few torturous minutes—a delicious stroke over her pearl, then another. She grasped his wrist but made no move to replace his fingers with hers. His touch felt ever so much better than hers in that moment.

"I thought the intention was to...*oh*..." He swirled the pads of two fingers over her, sending hot sparks skittering in his wake. "To have relations with each other so that you... *ah*..." More firm, knowing strokes interrupted her words as she gasped before corralling her thoughts again. "So that you could have your heirs and I...*uh*." His fingers were moving faster now, firmly rubbing over her aching bud.

She gave up on finishing her sentences. Words? What were words anyway? She was mindless. Hips chasing his fingers, heart racing in a steady thrum, closer, closer, closer. She was almost there, ready for the wave of bliss to break over her. Just a little bit more. His lips found hers again and he kissed her passionately, and she was nearly there...

"Rosamund? What in heaven's name is going on?"

They broke apart as one at the shocked voice of her mother echoing through the room. But his hand was still beneath her skirts, and so was hers. Their ragged breaths coasted over each other's kiss-swollen mouths. They'd been caught.

Thank heavens for Stuart's tall frame before her, blocking what was happening under her dress from her mother's view. But she couldn't hide the stockinged leg that was wrapped around his hip, the heel of her embroidered boot digging into Stuart's right buttock.

Rosamund slowly peered over his shoulder, all too aware of his stilled hand, yet pressed against her most intimate place. Her mother stood near the door to the sitting room, which was thankfully closed. Dressed in her preferred gray silk, her eyes were wide, mouth agape as she stared at the undoubtedly shocking vignette before her.

"Mother," she said faintly, unhooking her leg from Stuart's hip and discreetly disentangling herself from him, shaking out her skirts. "It isn't what you think. Camden and I were discussing our plans for the wedding."

That was rather a nonsensical explanation, and she knew it.

"It looks to me as if you were discussing your plans for *after* the wedding," Mother said pointedly.

Stuart turned and offered her mother an elegant bow. "Mrs. Payne, I must humbly beg your forgiveness for my lack of control where my betrothed is concerned. I promise it shan't happen again."

"I shall see that it doesn't," her mother returned, frowning. "I know the two of you are eager for your marriage, but you must cling to your restraint. I am sorry I was so belated in joining the two of you—I had been out visiting friends myself. I came as soon as I returned home and learned that you were paying a call, Your Grace. It would seem that I arrived just in time."

Rosamund was too mortified to speak, her cheeks scalding.

"Indeed you did, madam," Stuart said, his countenance serious. "The fault is all mine. I am but a weak and sinful man."

"I will take you at your word that such a lapse in propriety won't happen again," Mother said sternly before slanting a meaningful look in Rosamund's direction. "It is more than clear that you ought not to be alone together before you are married, and that further, we must have this wedding happen as imminently as possible."

Mother had never cared much for society's edicts. Even during Rosamund's betrothal with Wesley, she had often allowed the two of them unprecedented time alone together. Now with her father gone, Rosamund had rather become the ruler of the household, with her mother happy to follow her lead. But it would seem she had finally pushed her mother too far.

"Of course, Mother," she said humbly. "We will make certain to marry as quickly as we are able."

"I will obtain a registrar's license today," Stuart said politely, nary a hint of the deeply passionate man who had seduced her on her writing desk to be found. "We will be married in two days' time."

"That is best, Your Grace," Mother agreed, nodding.

But his smooth response had Rosamund's suspicion rising. Had he intended for them to be caught? She couldn't help but to wonder. Mother's intrusion and her having spied them in a torrid embrace left them with no alternative other than to marry in haste. Not that they ran the risk of scandal if they did not, but Rosamund would sooner throw herself from a window than be the cause of her mother's disappointment or embarrassment.

It would seem he had not only cozened her into marriage, but into living beneath his roof and wedding him in haste. No doubt about it, the Duke of Camden was a clever man, a seasoned seducer, and a worthy opponent.

And in just a matter of days, he would also be her husband.

CHAPTER 9

"*I*s Lord Wesley at home, Fleetwood?" Stuart asked his long-suffering butler, just narrowly refraining from adding *because if he isn't, I'm going to hunt him down and throttle him myself.*

"I do believe that his Lordship is at home and yet abed," Fleetwood confirmed.

"Excellent." He nodded. "Thank you, that will be all."

Stuart moved from his study in his butler's wake, on a mission to roll his arsehole brother out of bed if necessary. Because he was running out of time to have a discussion with Wesley about his impending marriage.

One more day until he was a married man. And he could scarcely wait. Not for the marriage itself, but for the consummation of the wedding. For Rosamund in his bed, in his arms. For the chance to finish what they had begun in Brandon's carriage and carried into Rosamund's sitting room at her cavernous town house.

He hadn't intended to trap Rosamund into a hasty wedding. But as it happened, the timing was nothing short of providential. He would have the funds to pay his blackmailer, and he wouldn't have to go to his friends and beg them to loan him funds. His pride was spared. His secret would remain a secret. And perhaps—just perhaps—he could move forward with his life.

His life with Rosamund.

The notion filled him—still—with a deep and abiding sense of ease. A rightness that had been conspicuously absent from his life for far too long. A rightness that faded somewhat as he ascended the stairs to his brother's bedroom. Like it or not—and he wasn't entirely sure he had finished persuading Rosamund before her mother's untimely interruption—she was going to live with him here at his town house. Which meant he needed to at last have the conversation he had been dreading with Wesley.

He stopped before his brother's door and rapped on it. No answer. Stuart knocked again, more firmly this time. An inhuman-sounding groan, muffled and scarcely audible, greeted him.

"Wesley," he tried, knocking more insistently. "It's your brother."

"Go to hell, brother. I'm trying to sleep."

His patience grew thin, so he opened the door and stalked into the darkened room. It was damned difficult to see in the dim light with the curtains pulled tightly over the windows. Stuart tripped over something soft—likely garments his brother had shed when he had arrived from his latest round of vices.

"What are you doing in my bedroom?" Wesley growled.

The room smelled of spirits, smoke, and clothes in wont of laundering, tinged with sweat. Stuart had to swallow to keep from gagging and remember to breathe through his mouth.

"I need to speak with you."

"Speak with me when I've finished sleeping," his brother complained.

Stuart ignored him, stalking across the room to throw open the curtains and allow some much-needed light to stream into the chamber, illuminating its sad state. Garments were strewn everywhere—trousers thrown haphazardly about, stained shirts crumpled on the floor. Bottles, some empty and others partially full, cluttered nearly every surface. There was a bottle of laudanum at his brother's bedside, which caught Stuart's attention.

"Now I see why you haven't allowed the chambermaid entrance," he muttered, glaring at his brother, who was lying unrepentantly in his mussed bed, his eyes bloodshot and his hair standing on end. "Laudanum now, Wesley?"

He plucked the bottle from the table at his brother's bedside, sickened at the evidence all around him of Wesley's excesses, but most particularly troubled by the laudanum.

"It is my medicine," his brother snapped. "Give that back to me. I need it."

"What you need is to get your arse out of bed so that I can have a conversation with you."

"I don't want to talk to you. Get out of my room."

His brother's expression was mulish.

"I'm not going anywhere," Stuart told him calmly in return, narrowly resisting the urge to toss the bottle of laudanum headlong into the fire at the opposite end of the room.

"Fine, then." Wesley waved a hand dismissively. "At least make yourself useful and fetch me the chamber pot. I need to take a piss."

That was it. Stuart's tentative grip on his patience snapped. He tossed the laudanum into the fire grate, gratified as it smashed to bits on the bricks, making the remnants of the evening's fire crackle and hiss as it rained down on the coals.

"Get out of the fucking bed," he ordered his brother.

"I paid for that bloody laudanum only yesterday," Wesley complained. "You owe me a new bottle."

"Get out," Stuart gritted through clenched teeth. "Of. The. God. Damned. Bed."

"Jesus," Wesley grumbled, throwing back the bedclothes and rising, still clad in last night's trousers, judging by the wine stain marring the buff fabric. "I'm out of the bed. Stop throwing things like a child having a tantrum."

"Get dressed," he clipped out.

"I *am* dressed." Wesley rubbed his bare chest then yawned loudly. "Say your piece and get the hell out of my room."

Stuart took in the sight his brother presented, thinking that if he'd been a painting, it would have been titled *Dissipation, Portrait of a Drunken Wastrel.*

"This is my house," he reminded him sharply. "I own everything in it."

Wesley sneered. "But not every*one* in it, and you would do well to remember it."

"Damn you, Wesley, you have been warned," he growled, infuriated. "There is a matter of some import which we need to discuss."

The scent of spirits grew stronger as his brother shuffled listlessly toward him. *Dear God*, Stuart realized, he was still soused from the night before.

"Do you need some blunt, brother dearest?" Wesley smirked. "I'm flush in funds at the moment."

How it was that Stuart continued to regard his brother calmly rather than smashing a fist into his nose was a mystery of the universe that he suspected would never be solved.

"Hardly that. You reek of spirits. I'm likely to get drunk on the fumes you're emitting."

"I'm not in my cups at all," Wesley said and then hiccupped. "I won two thousand pounds again just the other night, y'know. I suppose whispers have made their way to you, and you're going to demand it all so you can pay some bloody creditor of yours."

Stuart clenched his jaw. "Your contribution to the extensive debts you've created would be appreciated. However, it isn't funds or debts that I wish to speak with you about."

His brother staggered to the left and nearly tripped over the side of a wing chair piled with more clothing before righting himself, scowling. "What the hell is it? I don't appreciate being summoned from my bed like this, you know. A man needs his damned rest."

"Perhaps you would have more rest if you didn't go to sleep at half past eight in the morning," he pointed out, trying to tamp down his resentment and failing miserably.

Wesley's lip curled. "Are you having the household spy on me now, brother?"

He raised a brow. "Hardly. The domestics all have far more important tasks than watching my scapegrace younger brother. Now, are you finished being insolent? Because if so, perhaps you ought to have a seat so we can speak like gentlemen."

But Wesley gave him no quarter, scoffing as he retrieved a discarded shirt and slipped it on, doing up the buttons. "I'm not a gentleman, and I don't want to sit."

"As you wish. The news I wished to discuss with you is my impending marriage."

Wesley blinked. "Marriage?"

"Yes."

"*Marriage*," Wesley repeated.

"As I said. Twice."

"Who is the fortunate lady?" Wesley sneered. "Dare I ask?"

"The lady is one you are acquainted with," he said with great care, some deep, previously unknown part of him feeling irrationally possessive and protective of Rosamund. He didn't want her near Wesley. Didn't even want to speak her name to his brother. And yet, there was no other recourse. He had to do it. They were marrying tomorrow. She would be living in this house.

"Just how *well* am I acquainted with her?" Wesley asked, grinning before he issued another hiccup.

"She was your betrothed," he said, unable to keep the bitterness from his voice.

His brother was silent, apparently rendered speechless. A rarity.

Finally, he gathered his wits and spoke. "You're marrying Rosamund Payne?"

Wesley laughed then, as if Stuart had just relayed the finest joke.

"You do not have leave to speak of her so familiarly," he bit out, hating her given name on his brother's lips.

She was going to be *his wife*, damn it.

Wesley's laughter faded. "You're not afraid she's still in love with me, are you, brother dearest? That she is marrying you so she can be closer to me? Because it would be a grave concern of mine if I were you."

"No," he snapped. "She harbors no tender feelings where you're concerned. Of that, I have no doubt."

Wesley swaggered forward with an exaggerated air, giving him a smug grin. "I would not be so certain if I were you. She was desperately in love with me, you know. It crushed her spirit when she discovered Madeleine was carrying my bastard. I've never heard a woman weep so pathetically."

Stuart clenched his hands at his sides, knowing Wesley

was soused and taunting him to provoke a reaction and determined to deny him the pleasure. "You are a heartless cad."

Evidence: he had cast off his French mistress before the child had even been born, leaving her penniless and without a roof over her head. Stuart had given her as much as he had been able to see that she wouldn't be without food or a home. The last he'd heard, she had returned to the Continent with Wesley's child, having married a wealthy merchant. The two were certainly better off beyond Wesley's venomous reach.

"I always thought she was a bit plain, her nose rather overly large, but maybe I'll seduce her just for sport," Wesley continued. "What do you think of that, another woman you care for on her knees, my cock in her mouth?"

Despite his every intention to remain unmoved, Stuart's reaction was instant and uncontrollable. He rushed forward, slamming his brother into the barren damask wall, grasping a handful of his shirt with one hand and holding his opposite forearm to Wesley's throat.

"Don't you fucking touch her!" he roared in Wesley's face, fury overtaking him.

But Wesley was unmoved, still smirking. "I'd like to see you stop me, brother. We both know that I'm the better-looking of the two of us. You may be the duke, but when they have the choice between the two of us, they always choose me."

"That was before you were a drunken ruin," Stuart snarled. "What woman would want you now? You haven't a farthing to your name, Christ knows when you last had any of your clothes washed, your eyes are bloodshot, and you reek of whisky, smoke, and stale piss. Not a pleasant combination designed to lure the ladies, to be sure."

Stuart was being brutal, and he knew it. Part of him understood that Wesley couldn't help the monsters within him. He was driven by jealousy and greed, and his love of drink had made him even more selfishly cruel than he had been before. But damn it, thoughts of Wesley even entering the same room as Rosamund made Stuart want to tear down the goddamned walls.

She was *his*, damn it.

Not Wesley's.

Never Wesley's.

His brother was laughing again. "Nothing a bath and a shave won't cure. Mark my words, brother. I'll have your plain little spinster. When I'm through, she'll be wishing she married me after all instead of you."

Stuart pressed his forearm against Wesley's neck. "If you so much as look at her in an impolite manner, I'll toss you out of here on your arse and cut you off."

"You can't cut me off," Wesley rasped, struggling a bit to catch his breath from the force Stuart applied to his neck. "Mother would never allow it."

He didn't relent. "Mother has no notion of what you've become. It would kill her if she knew. But her protection of you is not infinite."

"Just as it would…kill her…if you cut me off," Wesley panted.

Curse him to hell. Mother was ever Stuart's weakness. He had to think of her. To put her fragile health first. He couldn't bear to lose her because of his own stupid rage over his brother's antics.

With another curse, he released Wesley, pushing away from the wall. "You will not speak of my duchess with anything less than respect from this moment forward. And if you dare anything with her, there will be consequences. Don't think that my love for Mother will save you from everything. I have powerful friends."

"Tell yourself that if it makes you feel better," Wesley said, still grinning.

"Go to hell, Wesley."

"Only if you join me."

Stuart stalked from the room to the sound of his brother's drunken laughter.

"WHAT ELSE DO you have for me, Mr. Watts?" Rosamund asked her father's man of business—now hers—as they were seated at Father's desk in his office.

The room still smelled of him. Cigars and leather, blended with that mysterious scent so many pieces bore after they had been passed down for centuries, rather as if they had been confined to the rafters of an old attic. The office was also untouched. Nothing had changed after Father's death—Rosamund had seen to it. The shelves were still lined with hundreds of books he had amassed over the years. It was cluttered with Roman statuary, with priceless paintings, with oddities he had collected: ancient swords and vases, ferns that she had kept living, and even a taxidermy of his favorite hound, Dash. His ledger book remained where he had preferred to keep it in the corner of his desk, and she proudly continued to make use of his pen and inkwell.

"I believe that is the last of the latest reports, Miss Payne," Mr. Watts said, pushing his spectacles up on the bridge of his nose.

A kind, balding man with a round face and ruddy cheeks, Mr. Watts had been her father's most-trusted man. And he had proven his loyalty and dependability to Rosamund again and again during the time she had taken over her father's affairs and she had been swept up in grief over the sudden loss of her hero and greatest champion.

When Father's death had been new and as painful as an open wound, she had sat here at his desk on many occasions, counting back in her mind each day that passed, pretending that at any moment, he might come thumping through the door with his cane in hand. At first, it had been just yesterday he was alive. Then two days ago, and three, until finally, it had been a sennight, then a fortnight, and longer. The world had carried on relentlessly, blissfully unaware of her father's absence. So, too, had her responsibilities.

Her father had owned a tremendous number of businesses. Shipping, textile factories, a hotel in London and another in Paris, mines, and more. He had taken her under his wing when she had been quite young, preparing her to be his only heir. To his credit, he had never made her feel inadequate for having been born a female rather than a male.

He had bequeathed everything to her in his will, with the provision that she look after her mother, seeing to her every comfort. Rosamund had done so with ease and without hesitation, assuming the mantle of business owner initially as a means of distracting herself from her grief and soon enough because she had found she possessed an interest in it.

Fortunately, she had the keen eye and sharp mind of Mr. Watts to aid her, steering her back on course if ever she drifted astray. She rather considered him to be a second father, for he had certainly cast himself in Father's mold.

She settled her father's pen back in its holder. "And you have pored over the marriage contract again, Mr. Watts, have you not?"

"I have, as has Mr. Trumbull," Mr. Watts reassured her, referencing her solicitor. "You are uniquely protected, thanks to the provisions Mr. Trumbull enumerated in the contract. The duke cannot lay claim to your business interests, and the control of your fortune will remain yours, aside from the generous sum allotted as your dowry by your father in the hope you would marry. His Grace is to receive the full amount, his to dispense with as he sees fit."

Her greatest fear was that she had somehow overlooked something, made an error somewhere in the marriage contract, particularly after Stuart had all but demanded that she live with him instead of remaining at her own town house.

She nodded now, forming a tremulous smile. "Thank you, Mr. Watts. I am indebted to you, as always. I cannot think of where I would be without your trusted counsel."

Mr. Watts gave her a benevolent, fatherly smile in return. "You need not thank me, Miss Payne. You know that I owe your father everything I have. If he had not believed in my potential many years ago, I shudder to think where I would be now. It is my great honor to offer you any paternal advice and protection that I am able in the absence of such a great man."

The fondness in his voice, coupled with the references to her dear father, brought tears forth to sting Rosamund's eyes. It never seemed to matter how much time had intervened between when she had whispered her last farewell to him when he'd lain there on the bed, so still and pale, and the present day. There would not cease to be a day when his loss would not loom large in her heart, a wound that could never fully heal.

"Do you think he would have been happy to see me married?" she asked Mr. Watts, her voice gone thick with her effort to stay her tears and keep from weeping.

"Of course he would have," Mr. Watts reassured her. "Your father wanted nothing more than for you to have all the happiness you could find in this hard, cold, cruel world of ours."

She bit her lip, trying to distract herself, but her nose was tickling and her vision had become indistinct. "I know I cannot change the past, but sometimes…oh, sometimes, I wish he were still here."

He extracted a handkerchief from his coat and offered it to her. "As do I, my dear."

She accepted it gratefully, using the scrap of fabric to dab at her eyes before forcing her thoughts back to where they belonged, where her father would have wanted them—to business. "Will you accompany me to see the new shipments, Mr. Watts?"

"I would be delighted to do so," he said. "I think you'll be well pleased by the latest statuary that has arrived from the Continent."

Rosamund forced a smile for both their benefits. "I'm sure I will be."

With another look around Father's office for comfort, she rose to her feet, hoping she wasn't about to make a grave mistake in marrying the Duke of Camden.

ON THE MORNING of his wedding day—the same day Stuart was meant to have his payment delivered, per the edict from his blackmailer—another letter arrived. He read it as he stood at the window of his bedroom, dressed in the suit King had lent him for the purpose of *not looking like a beggar before his new bride*, as his friend had helpfully explained. King had also opined that Stuart's existing wardrobe ought to be sold for rags. Stuart had ignored him.

But he couldn't ignore the seed of worry, burrowing deep in his gut, as he opened the missive that had been delivered to him on a salver by Sharpe and cast his eye over the by-now-familiar slanted script.

*To His Grace, the Duke of Camden,
Felicitations on your impending nuptials to the
heiress Miss Rosamund Payne. Accordingly, our
price has increased. The sum of ten thousand
pounds shall now be delivered to Messrs. Dolan
and Rowe, or, as previously specified, a letter will
be delivered to The Times.*

DAMN THE BASTARD TO HELL.

Stuart crumpled the letter and tossed it into the grate, watching it burn.

The seed took root and sprouted, along with the fear that this menace would never be done.

CHAPTER 10

*I*mpossible as it was to believe, Rosamund was a married woman.

Not just any married woman.

She was now the Duchess of Camden.

No longer Miss Payne. No longer a spinster. What a whirlwind of change after so many years.

The morning had been a personification of the past few weeks—a mad rush of indecision followed by an inevitable, final choice. Rosamund had decided upon a different gown for the ceremony at the last minute, resulting in her lady's maid having to help her remove the gown she had initially selected with all its myriad buttons and hooks, then to frantically dress her in a new gown. As there hadn't been sufficient time to have a gown made for the occasion, Rosamund had chosen a striking red silk ornamented with blonde lace and velvet bows, forgoing a more subdued morning gown of ecru silk from the same Regent Street dressmaker.

Her decision had been worth the frenzied struggle to don a new gown when she had joined her husband in the church and his gaze had all but devoured her. She had felt, for the first time in as long as she could recall, as if she were truly beautiful. As if she were capable of commanding the admiring gazes of every man who had joined them.

They had spoken their vows in what seemed a dream for how quickly it had passed, before pews filled with their closest friends and family members. And now, she was seated at her husband's side at their wedding breakfast. As a point of pride, they were holding the affair at Stuart's town house. Evidence of his reduced means was the hallmark of the once-grand edifice. She had not dared to call attention to the threadbare carpets, the faded wall coverings bereft of pictures, or the alarming lack of domestics. These matters would need to be addressed, however, now that she was the mistress of the house.

"You aren't eating the *Poulets gras au Cresson*," her new husband observed softly at her side. "Is it not to your liking?"

The food was excellent, and that was thanks to Stuart's willingness to allow her own chef to aid his cook in the preparation of the morning's many courses.

"It is delightful," she murmured, making a show of cutting off a bite-sized piece.

The problem was not the quality of the offerings. Already, there had been decadent asparagus soup, lamb cutlets, lobster salad, and an assortment of meats in aspics.

To emphasize her response, she brought the forkful of meat to her lips.

His gaze settled on her mouth, and all the misgiving that had been churning in her stomach since she had risen that morning was banished by an instant spark of awareness.

The way he was looking at her. *Good heavens*, it was positively sinful.

At least the consummation of their marriage would come soon enough. It was a wicked thought to entertain before all their happily chattering and eating guests, and she hoped none of them would spy the flush she felt creeping over her cheeks.

She swallowed the chicken and watercress cream, then licked her lips.

His gaze jerked back to hers. "We have a journey ahead of us. I don't want you to be hungry."

"Yes, of course." She shifted on her chair, trying to ignore the liquid heat pooling between her thighs by distracting herself.

Tomorrow, they were off on a honeymoon in Hertfordshire at Stuart's country seat, Gilden Hall. It had been a surprise, but a welcome one. She would have an additional fortnight to prepare herself for living under the same roof as her former betrothed. Stuart had warned her that the house was not in its finest form, but given his lack of funds, that was to be expected. Rosamund was eager to explore the land and house.

Best of all, the general proximity of Gilden Hall to London meant that she and Stuart could travel by carriage instead of train, and Megs could accompany them. Rosamund had made the mistake of bringing her beloved parrot with her in a private train car once, and she would never repeat the error. Poor Megs had been terrified of all the sounds and bumps and swaying. She had scarcely spoken for days after their return, having spent the entirety of the journey huddling in a corner of her cage.

"Is something amiss?" Stuart asked her, his voice hushed, his hand settling on her lap beneath the table.

The heavy fall of his hand on her upper thigh had her inhaling sharply. Her entire body was so acutely attuned to his. She'd spent the morning not far from his side, breathing in his heady scent, admiring the breadth of his shoulders in his elegant coat, the lean lines of his long, muscular legs in his trousers, admiring how very handsome he was. More than once, she had caught herself wondering how this beautiful man had come to be hers.

It seemed an impossibility. Her old feelings of never being sufficient had returned with relentless determination, telling her she was not pretty enough, not smart enough, not interesting enough. That, aside from her fortune, there was nothing truly outstanding about her.

That Stuart was only marrying her for her wealth.

She tamped down such thoughts yet again to answer him.

"Nothing is wrong," she said. "I am merely weary after all the preparations for today."

True, there had not been as many preparations as most society weddings would have possessed. Their nuptials had been hasty. Rosamund didn't fret over details such as flowers or the wedding breakfast menu. Mother had quite thankfully commandeered those tasks. Stuart's mother, meanwhile, had been notably absent from all planning and the wedding itself. Nor was she at the breakfast. Stuart had explained that she was feeling too ill to join them. Rosamund had decided she would pay a visit to her new mother-in-law's quarters when she was strong enough for companionship. How lonely it must be to spend life as an invalid, confined to a chamber. Rosamund didn't think she could bear it, not even with Megs to entertain her.

"Has my brother caused you any trouble?" Stuart asked quietly next.

It had been very strange to see Lord Wesley again, sitting in the pews at her nuptials to his brother. Not, to be certain, the wedding day she had once imagined for herself. But she was wholeheartedly glad that she had not married Wesley, that she had discovered what manner of man he truly was before she had been tied to him for life.

"He hasn't spoken a word to me," she reassured Stuart,

SCARLETT SCOTT

taking note of the tension in his bearing, in the tight clench of his jaw.

She had known that there was no love lost between the brothers. Stuart had been candid about Wesley seducing the woman he had loved and intended to wed, about the vicious jealousy that ruled his brother. But there was more, she suspected, behind Stuart's apprehension. She wondered now if the brothers had exchanged words.

Over her?

Surely not, she thought. That was fanciful musings on her part.

"Good." Stuart nodded, reaching for a glass of wine and looking unaccountably grim. "See that he doesn't. I don't want him bothering you. Should he do so, come to me, if you please."

He spoke with quiet care, making certain that his words didn't carry beyond the two of them at their private table.

"Has he done or said something to make you think he would?" she asked, searching her husband's expression.

Husband.

Yes, he was that now.

How little she knew of him. There would be much to learn.

"We can discuss it later, my dear," he told her calmly. "I should hate to ruin the meal by lingering on such an unpleasant subject."

"Of course," she agreed, subtly removing her hand from above the table and placing it upon his on her lap.

She had meant the gesture as one of wifely comfort. But the moment their bare hands touched, awareness swept over her. Stuart's expression suggested he had felt the same potent response. She laced her fingers through his, feeling a curious sense of tenderness rushing up from deep within her, melding with the desire.

146

But just as quickly as she felt it, she banished it, removing her hand and turning her attention back to her plate. She mustn't make the mistake of allowing herself to become too vulnerable. Today was the first day of the rest of their lives, and she would need to become more adept at guarding her heart if she was to make the most of this marriage of convenience.

She wanted a family, she reminded herself. Children of her own. She *did not* want to lose her heart to a man who was a notorious rake and had only married her to save his estates from ruinous debt. All she had to do was remember that.

Needing a moment of quiet, she excused herself from the table and rose, slipping from the wedding breakfast, in search of the lady's withdrawing room. But she had scarcely made it into the hall before Lord Wesley waylaid her, quite as if he had followed her from the room.

At such proximity, the signs of three years' worth of dissipation were evident. He was yet handsome, as she had remembered, but there were notable changes in him now. His face was thinner, his cheekbones slashing in stark relief beneath his eyes, where dark half-moons and lines marred his formerly youthful skin. His blond hair was too long, and his suit—not nearly as elegant as Stuart's—hung on his tall frame.

Her reaction to him was one of visceral contempt.

She eyed him warily. "What is it that you want, Lord Wesley?"

He gave her a slow smile, his gaze raking down her body in a way she did not like. "I think you know what I want, Rosamund. What I've been starving for."

Surely he was not suggesting what she thought he was. What manner of man would accost his newly wed sister-in-law in the hall outside her wedding breakfast and make an amorous overture to her? Lord Wesley Gilden, it would seem.

She forced a cool smile. "There is ample food at the wedding breakfast. If you are hungry, I suggest you begin there."

He laughed. But where once she would have thought the sound so very charming and irresistible, she now knew it was not genuine.

"I don't think I'll find what I want within the ballroom when you've run out here into the hall," he said, stepping closer.

The scent of wine emanated from him. The reason for the glassy look to his eyes, she thought, and moved to put more distance between them.

"I have no notion what you're speaking about, my lord," she told him, frowning to discourage his further unwanted attentions.

"I think you do, Rosamund." He started forward.

"And I think you are soused, Lord Wesley," she told him sharply. "I will be generous and forget this exchange ever happened."

When she made to skirt around him, he placed a hand on her forearm, staying her. "I'm not so drunk that I don't know what I want. And you want it too. You always have, have you not? I do recall your pretty words of love and all the tears you later shed over me quite well, Rosamund."

She shook free of his hold. "You do not have leave to speak with me so freely, Lord Wesley. In future, I suggest you exercise restraint and hold your tongue. Excuse me."

Without bothering with the pretense of manners, she whirled away from him, seeking refuge in the lady's with-drawing room, her stomach knotted. Little wonder Stuart possessed such disdain for his brother. Lord Wesley had just propositioned his sister-in-law on her wedding day. Thank heavens she had thrown him over years ago. He would have made her life an utter misery.

She could only hope her life with Stuart would turn out far, far differently.

IT WAS late afternoon by the time the last of their guests had departed and Stuart had performed the customary introduction of Rosamund to his domestics. Mother would have to wait as she had been napping when they had stopped together at her room. Now, their tour of his dilapidated town house had at last brought them to the room that would henceforth be hers. He almost dreaded the presentation of the room, which had gone unused for the better part of a decade after Mother had chosen to take a different chamber upon his father's death. It was in as dreadful a state as the rest of the town house. But together, they would rectify that.

He opened the door for Rosamund, allowing her to precede him into the chamber, which had been aired out and thoroughly cleaned, if not decorated in proper style, in preparation for her arrival. "After you, my dear."

"Thank you."

Rosamund crossed the threshold in her magnificent red gown, the one that had been taunting him all morning and afternoon long. The brilliant color brought out the sparks of fiery cinnamon in her hair, and the way it hugged her waist and emphasized her breasts was nothing short of criminal.

He followed in her wake, the intricate train of her gown necessitating more distance between them than he preferred. But never mind that. He couldn't very well shag her the moment he had her alone in a bedroom.

Could he?

His conscience warred with his desire for her.

As he closed the door behind them, a familiar voice cooled the lust in his veins considerably, siding with his conscience.

"Gormless shite."

Fucking hell. The bloody parrot.

"Megs," Rosamund chided, gliding across the chamber to where her damned feathered beast preened on its perch.

"We meet again," he drawled, pinning the nettlesome creature with his sternest ducal glare.

Megs stared at him, unperturbed, those silvery eyes unwavering. "Walk the plank. What a good bird."

"Megs, you truly must learn to get along with the duke," Rosamund said, taking up a small velvet pouch that was near the bird's perch and shaking a pistachio into the palm of her opposite hand.

"Megs want pistache," the bird declared, fluffing her feathers.

"Somehow, I hadn't thought she would be finding her new home in your bedroom," he said dryly.

"She has always slept in my bedroom from the time she first came to me," Rosamund told him as she offered the undeserving bird a nut.

Megs took the pistachio in her beak, nibbling on it while continuing to glare at him.

He turned to his new wife, who had just declared that an African grey parrot who despised him would be an omnipresent fixture in her bedroom. "Perhaps she would be more comfortable in the adjoining sitting room. With the door closed."

And locked, he thought uncharitably. Better yet, back in Rosamund's town house, keeping her mother company. The solution seemed an excellent one.

"I'm not sure if she will settle there," Rosamund said, turning back to him.

And with the full force of her gaze on him, it was almost impossible to recall there was a parrot in the room at all. Rosamund stole his entire attention. She was nothing short of stunning in her regal gown, rubies and diamonds at her throat and ears, red silk roses tucked into her elaborate coiffure. Every man in attendance today had been unable to look away from her, including his bastard of a brother.

But Stuart didn't want to think about Wesley now. He could only hope his brother had gone in search of his usual amusements and that he wouldn't return until after Stuart and Rosamund left for their honeymoon tomorrow morning.

"Perhaps it wouldn't hurt for her to try spending the evening elsewhere," he suggested, trying to keep his rampant cock under control.

It wouldn't do to ravish his new wife at the first opportunity. And particularly not before a damned bird.

"Megs can be rather noisy when she's distressed." Rosamund was busy fretting, nibbling on her lower lip. "She has already had the upheaval of new surroundings. I fear she'll be distraught if she isn't with me as she is accustomed."

Was there a polite way to tell one's wife that one wanted to fuck her senseless without an audience? To explain that licking her cunny whilst her pet bird watched on was decidedly unappealing?

Not for the first time, it occurred to Stuart how woefully inept he was at being a husband. A proper man. Not a lover, not a rake carrying on with his mistress or whatever experienced woman had tempted him for the night. No, this was different. A whole new world. One in which he had never existed before, nor dreamed he would.

He scrubbed a hand over his jaw, still searching for a means of conveying his opinion without causing her insult or distress. "Rosamund."

She was fussing over the parrot now, cooing at her and

rubbing the bird's head with her thumb. Was it wrong to be jealous of the feathered menace? Because he was, just now. He wanted to be the sole recipient of his glorious wife's attention. He wanted her to be desperate with desire for him, throwing her arms around his neck, kissing him wildly. He didn't want her to be caressing her parrot.

"Rosamund," he said again, his tone intentionally firmer this time.

She turned to look at him over her shoulder, still stroking the African grey. "What is it?"

He felt foolish. He felt as if he were bursting with raw, feverish lust. He felt as if he had waited a lifetime for this moment without previously realizing it, only to be standing there now like a dolt in a borrowed suit, second to a parrot.

He stared at her, unable to think of a single way he might convey the whirlwind of emotion and passion writhing within him. "I don't think the bird likes me," he said stupidly instead.

This earned him a tinkling laugh from his new wife, and that didn't help to assuage his hardening cock one whit. Rosamund's laugh was husky and beautiful. He wanted to kiss her while she was smiling, to drink the joy from her lips. He wanted...so much that it frightened him.

"Come here," Rosamund invited, extending a hand to him, smiling softly.

He settled his palm in hers, their fingers entwining, and he felt the connection deep within. There was a feeling of rightness, of possession, of his body recognizing that this was his woman. The future mother of his children. The thought made his prick thicken, much to his dismay. When had the notion of having a babe ever made him randy?

What was happening to him?

The answer appeared in the next second. He was allowing his new wife to pull him to her pet bird, and he was essentially no better than the feathered nuisance, adoring her, preening for her, desperate for her slightest touch. They stood side by side, their fingers still linked, and then she raised their hands as one.

"You must introduce yourself to Megs properly," Rosamund said, "and show her some affection. Show her that you mean no harm."

"Gormless shite," the bloody parrot announced.

He gave Rosamund a meaningful look. "As I said, the thing doesn't like me."

"I cannot blame her at the moment." Rosamund frowned, looking adorably cross with him. "*She* is Megs, not a thing and not a bird. She is my companion, and for years now, she has been my steadfast champion, in times of grief and times of pain, just as in times of happiness and joy."

He wondered what had caused her happiness and joy, having an inkling of what had caused her grief and pain. This revelation was not helping to abate the ridiculous jealousy he felt toward the feathered thorn in his paw.

Stuart cleared his throat. "My apologies. I know she is your companion and that you love her. Clearly, she returns your feelings."

The parrot was currently bending her head sideways in a ridiculous fashion, just so that she could receive the touch of Rosamund's free thumb beneath her neck. Damned bird.

Megs straightened and stared at him, unblinking. "Feelings, feelings. What a pretty bird."

Excellent. The little intruder was taunting him now.

"I'll help you to pet her," Rosamund said, bringing their linked hands to hover over the parrot.

He half expected the creature to peck him.

"I don't know if I ought to…"

"Nonsense," she countered. "All you need to do is be

gentle. Use one finger or your thumb, and stroke her feathers as I've done. She will adore you in no time."

Surprisingly, Megs held herself still as Rosamund guided his hand to the feathers atop her head. Using his forefinger, he lightly stroked the bird as Rosamund had demonstrated. She released her hold on him, and then he was petting the dratted parrot himself. And the bird was looking into his eyes with her silvery gaze, and for a moment, he thought they'd formed a truce.

Until Megs chirped, "Gormless shite."

He withdrew his finger and turned to Rosamund. "You see? I made an effort to call pax, and she threw it in my face."

His wife was clearly struggling to contain a smile. "Perhaps she needs to grow more accustomed to you. The only gentlemen she has known thus far during her time with me are my butler and some of the footmen. You are new to her."

"She may have all the time she requires," he said reasonably. "In the adjoining sitting room."

"But she sleeps in my room."

"That was before you had a husband."

She drew back her shoulders, her eyes narrowing. "Are you saying that since I have married you, you now have the right to issue an edict on where Megs shall sleep?"

This woman.

He wanted to kiss her. To get her out of that dress. To taste every inch of her luscious form.

"Put to point," he drawled, "I don't recall the many stipulations in the marriage contract discussing where the feathered menace would sleep. But that's not why I'm objecting to her presence in your bedroom, Rosamund."

She planted her hands on her waist in a defensive pose, a woman ready to go into battle. "Why, then?"

"Because I don't want to make love to you with an audience," he told her, holding her gaze.

Her lips parted. "Oh."

"Yes, *oh*." He reached for her hands and pulled them from their positions on her waist, then used them to tug her against him. "I want you all to myself. No interruptions. No *gormless shites*."

"Gormless shite," Megs chirped, fluttering her wings.

He raised a brow. "The feathered demon simply cannot behave herself."

"You might have simply said so," Rosamund countered, her voice low. "I thought you were being overbearing. Although calling Megs a demon is rather a bit much…"

He ignored the last. Because the bird was nothing if not demonic, at least in his estimation.

"I have no intention of being overbearing with you." He lowered his head, nuzzling her ear and inhaling the sweet scent of her deeply into his lungs. "But I do intend to be *inside* you. As soon as I'm able."

He kissed her throat, absorbing the ripple as she swallowed hard at his words.

"That is…you are…"

Stuart smiled against her silken skin. How he adored when she grew flustered and couldn't complete her sentences. Ordinarily, Rosamund was so composed and capable and buttoned-up, almost to the point of frostiness. But he knew the heated passion burning hotly beneath her prim exterior. And her complete lack of control made his cock hard.

"We can leave Megs as she is for now," he murmured. "Come to my room."

To emphasize his invitation, he placed a series of open-mouthed kisses down her neck, sucking gently, tasting some of the floral essence she must have dabbed there when she dressed that morning. Sweet, she was so sweet. And after waiting what had felt like an eternity to make her his wife and then go through the formalities of their wedding day, he had her alone at last.

Well, save the bloody bird. But he'd improvised.

Rosamund made a low sound in her throat, tilting her head back to grant him greater access. "I…we…yes."

He kissed her neck again, holding her to him, his eyes closing as he savored the moment, the feeling of her in his arms. He hadn't expected to be so moved, to want her so much. Stuart straightened and, still holding one of her hands in his, drew her to the door adjoining their chambers. The parrot fluffed her feathers on her perch but didn't offer further objection.

Which was just as well, because he would have ignored it.

He crossed the threshold into his bedroom, drawing Rosamund into his territory, and shut the door firmly at her back. They would have no audience here. No interruptions. And by God, he couldn't wait to make her his wife in deed as well as in name.

CHAPTER 11

*R*osamund's heart was pounding furiously.

Stuart intended to consummate their marriage. Here in his room. Now, in the midst of the afternoon. Somehow, she hadn't expected him to be so eager. She had thought they would carry on with the formalities of the day before returning to their rooms to rest and change in preparation for dinner. Instead, he wanted to seduce her.

And she planned to enjoy every second of it.

She had a moment to glance around the room. It was as sparsely furnished as the rest of the town house, the Axminster also in need of replacement. There were no pictures adorning the walls. The ridiculous thought occurred to her that she might paint him some watercolors to liven up his space. How wifely of her. Everything felt new and strange and exciting.

"This is your bedroom, then," she said stupidly, feeling nervous and shy even though she had been alone with Stuart many times.

Because never had she been his wife, about to share his bed.

SCARLETT SCOTT

He wanted to be *inside* her, he had said. And although she was no hen wit and knew the mechanisms of sexual congress, those words still made her feel faint, as if her knees might buckle, sending a streak of something wonderful straight to her core.

"This is my bedroom." He flashed her a wry grin, looking unfairly handsome, stubble already shadowing his strong jaw from the morning's shave. "Such as it is. I have no Roman statuary or priceless antiquities to adorn it, but it has sufficed."

She wanted to kiss him, she thought as she studied his sensual lips. Did she dare? She took a step toward him, closing the small distance separating them, and flattened her palms on his chest. There. That felt nice. He was a wall of lean muscle, and she wondered how he accomplished such a fine form. Likely, he engaged in fencing or some other gentlemanly manner of sport.

"Did you…mean what you said?" she ventured, feeling her cheeks go hot.

"God yes." He leaned his forehead against hers. "Ever since I saw you this morning in that red gown, I've been able to think of nothing other than peeling it off you."

Hyperbole, she was sure. But Rosamund smiled, nonetheless. "You make me sound like a banana. I don't believe my lady's maid has ever peeled a gown off me."

"Then she is doing it all wrong," he said, punctuating his words with a slow, albeit chaste, kiss. "I would be more than happy to demonstrate."

Molten heat settled between her thighs. "Would you?"

She couldn't keep the breathlessness from her voice.

"Of course." He raised his head and took a step back. "Turn, my dear."

She mourned the loss of his warmth and strength burning

into her, but she did as he asked, spinning to present him with her back and the row of buttons her lady's maid, Bayneham, had swiftly fastened that morning.

His lips grazed her nape, and she lowered her chin instinctively, giving him full leave to kiss her wherever he liked. Which, as it happened, was along the curve of each nearly bared shoulder, until he reached her spine. His fingers found the fastenings, and she felt buttons beginning to come undone, slowly and surely. He continued kissing her as he went, even when her chemise and corset impeded him from kissing her bare skin. Pluck, pluck, pluck went each button. Kiss, kiss, kiss went her husband's mouth until he reached the last in the long line, and her bodice loosened, gaping.

She held the silk to her, knowing a moment of foolish modesty. But Stuart rounded her skirts to stand before her again, his light-blue gaze smoldering with undisguised desire. He reached for her right sleeve first, his fingertips glancing over her bare skin and making her shiver with suppressed longing. He bent forward then, his lips kissing a trail down her arm as he slowly dragged her cap sleeve down until he pulled it free. Without hesitation, he moved to her left sleeve, doing the same.

The silence in the chamber was only broken by the whisper of her velvet-and-silk bodice gliding down her skin, Stuart's kisses, and her own ragged breath. How could the act of removing her bodice—whilst she was still trussed in so many layers and so much boning—drown her in lust? She was thirty years old, and she had disrobed thousands of times before. But never had it felt so laden with sin, like the decadent prelude to something impossibly wonderful.

He draped her bodice over a nearby chair and moved behind her again, finding the tapes of her skirts and undoing them with ease. The red silk and accompanying train cascaded to the threadbare floor in a sinful susurrus. She stood before him in her favorite pair of boots, her petticoats, chemise, corset, stockings, and drawers, and although she was covered sufficiently, she felt as if she were nude.

"Perhaps…I… Ah…" she stammered, nervousness overtaking Rosamund as he moved to her topmost petticoat, unfastening it and sending it to join her overskirts.

He knelt before her on her skirts, and although she had a wardrobe positively overflowing with gowns, her instinct was to remind him to take care with her precious silk. But then he looked up at her, and he was so wonderfully handsome with the light playing over his face that she forgot to care.

"Give me your boot, sweetheart," he said, offering his hands, palms up.

She decided on the right boot first, hoping she wouldn't crumple to the floor as she balanced on one leg. His long, elegant fingers went to work on the laces, undoing the tie and then loosening them before he slid the leather from her foot.

He pressed a kiss to her instep. "Your servant, Duchess."

Oh good heavens. What was it about this man on his knees for her, tending to her, kissing her foot, that made her want to swoon?

"You needn't," she protested weakly.

But he ignored her, gently placing her stockinged foot on the carpet and then wordlessly requesting her left boot. She gave it to him, grasping the back of a chair to steady herself as she watched him work. When the second piece of footwear was removed, he kissed her instep again, then placed her foot on the floor.

"Now your corset." He rose and spun her again, his nimble fingers making short work of her lacings.

A few more tugs and her aching nipples were set free. The

undergarment loosened, and she hauled in a great, deep breath, her heart thudding madly, as if she had just run up and down all the steps in her town house thrice over. This was what he did to her. And he planned to do far more before he was finished.

Hands landed on her waist in a possessive grasp, and then he spun her again so that she faced him. Holding her stare, he unhooked the corset's busk. Her breasts spilled free, only barely contained by her thin silk chemise.

"My God, you're beautiful, Rosamund," he murmured, such awe and reverence in his voice that she believed him.

She, who had forever been trapped in the shadow of her father's enormous wealth, at long last felt not just attractive, but desirable in her own right. There was no denying the way her new husband looked at her.

"No one has told me so before you," she managed.

"Fools," he said and bent his head to adorn the tops of her breasts with more kisses through her chemise. "You're bloody glorious, Rosamund. I don't think my cock has ever been so hard."

His praise, mingled with such shocking vulgarity, took her breath. And then he groaned, almost as if he were in agony, and sucked the peak of her breast through the silk covering it. Glorious. He thought she was glorious. And she made his...*cock* hard.

"Mmm," she managed, her hand fluttering to his shoulder, another to his head. She didn't know where to place them.

All she knew was that she wanted to touch him everywhere.

And she wanted him to touch her everywhere too.

His mouth was hot, drawing on her nipple, but she wished the boundary of cloth separating her bare skin from him was gone. She also wished he were not wearing so many articles of clothing. He was still fully dressed. This seemed a dreadful injustice she needed to help rectify. But how? He was intent upon devouring her through her chemise, taking her other nipple into his mouth and leaving a wet mark over the one he had just abandoned.

"So sweet," he murmured against her breast. "I'm going to peel this off you now, just like I promised."

Sweet heaven.

He made good on his words by pulling the sleeves of her chemise down her shoulders, to her arms. Another slow, firm tug, and he drew the undergarment around her elbows, her breasts popping free in the cool evening air.

"Perfection," he praised, giving the chemise another jerk until it was pooled around her waist.

And then he cupped her breasts. She arched her back into his touch, wanting more. It felt so good, his bare hands on her skin, his thumbs rolling over her aching nipples simultaneously. Lowering his head, he feasted on her, licking, sucking, nipping with his teeth. He lavished attention on her breasts until she could scarcely bear more, and she was threading her fingers through his hair, holding him to her, needing something that was beyond her reach.

Needing what had happened in the carriage.

"Stuart," she managed breathlessly, writhing against him, twisting her body so that it was in contact with his. "Please."

"Damn." He released a nipple and kissed a hot trail along her collarbone. "If I don't take care, I'll come in my trousers, and King will never forgive me."

Dimly, some part of her mind recognized the difference in today's elegant suit: it had been borrowed from the Duke of Kingham. She hated that his circumstances had been so reduced but held her tongue, not wanting to hurt his pride. Instead, she helped him to pull her chemise past her hips, sending it to the floor with the rest of her garments.

Together, they removed what remained: drawers, stockings, red silk garters.

His lips found hers, and they kissed deeply, her hands tearing at his clothes so that he would be revealed to her as she was to him. His coat fell away, and her fingers fumbled next with the buttons on his waistcoat until he chuckled into her mouth and helped her. Next came the buttons on his shirt, which were smaller and even more difficult for her trembling hands to manage whilst he kissed her witless. Somehow, they came undone, and the crisp white linen was whisked away to reveal hot, taut skin beneath her questing fingertips.

Touching was not sufficient, however. Rosamund wanted to see him.

She stepped back, breaking the endless kiss, and drank in the sight of him, so potently male, stripped to the waist. He had called her glorious, but here was proof that he was far more so. Her gaze traveled over the breadth of his shoulders, his strong upper arms, the wall of his chest and his stomach, where a line of dark hair disappeared beneath his waistband. The prominent bulge in the placket of his trousers sent a jolt of liquid desire to her center.

Her new husband took note of the direction her eyes had fallen.

"See how much I want you?" he asked, his voice velvet-soft and sinfully deep, laden with sensual promise.

To emphasize his words, he stroked a hand over the front of his trousers, smoothing the buff fabric over the outline of his rigid length. She had seen many a marble male member on the various statues in her father's collection and, later, in her own collection as she had taken up where he had left off. But the statues were so very small in comparison to what appeared to lie beneath the fall of Stuart's trousers.

"Oh my," she whispered, biting her lip as she jerked her

stare back up to his, intrigued and roused. "That does not appear to be anything like the Roman statuary I've seen."

He grinned at her. "My wicked wife. Have you been ogling the ancient marbles in your collection?"

Embarrassed heat suffused her face. "I wouldn't call it ogling. More like studying."

His smile deepened, revealing a lone groove in his right cheek that she couldn't help but find magnetically attractive. "No need to study cold marble any longer, sweetheart. You have your own flesh and blood example right here."

Cupping her cheek, he brought his lips down on hers again, kissing her soundly, his tongue gliding against hers until she was drowning in desire, banishing the last traces of mortification from her. By the time he withdrew, she was breathless again, clinging to him like a vine.

"Explore if you like," he told her, reaching for her hand and bringing it between their bodies, to the front of his trousers. "I'm yours."

Oh, how she liked those words, the notion that this beautiful man was hers. It filled her with potent power. She worked at the buttons, pulling one free from its mooring, then another. The placket loosened. She glanced down, watching as she completely undid the fall of his trousers, putting his hardness—barely encased in a pair of cotton drawers—on crude display.

"Touch me," he invited. "Please, Rosamund. I need to feel you."

Tentatively, she did as he asked, laying her hand over that sinful bulge, feeling the warm strength of him through the thin layer of fabric that acted as barrier. The arc of pure, molten desire it sent through her made her knees go weak.

"Ah, God," he growled, taking her hand in his and urging it over him with greater pressure. "That's it. Take me out of my drawers now."

She found the slit in the front of his undergarment, not unlike hers, and she parted it, allowing his cock to spring outward, erect and decidedly larger and different from the statues in every possible way.

"May I?" she asked, hand hovering over him, longing to touch. To stroke, to tease and caress and bring him pleasure as he had done for her.

"Please," he said simply.

It was all the invitation she required. Rosamund gently touched him, amazed by the feeling—he was hard yet his skin was so distinctly soft, and beneath her caress, to her utter amazement, he grew even larger.

"It's growing," she murmured.

"You have that effect on me, love."

"I had no idea such a thing was possible." She stroked him tentatively at first and then with growing confidence, liking the way his body responded. "How much bigger does it get?"

He choked out a laugh. "Sweet Jesus, woman. You're going to kill me."

"You don't like it?" Rosamund asked, her hand hovering over the thick column. "Shall I stop?"

"I bloody love it," he said on a groan. "I want more of it. But I also want to last."

He caught her hand in his and brought it to his lips for a lingering, tender kiss before releasing her and pulling his trousers and drawers down in one fluid motion, leaving him as naked as she was. She had only a moment to admire the rest of his form before he was guiding her to his bed. The sturdy tester was large and tall, and she needed his help to settle into it, in the absence of a piece of furniture to boost her.

"I'll have a stool brought in," he said, as if reading her thoughts, caressing her hips as he aided her.

She lay on her back, watching him as he joined her on the

bed without any issue, his taller frame allowing him to climb in with ease. She knew a moment of nervousness as she spied his large cock, standing prominently between his horseman's thighs. This monstrous thing was meant to fit inside her, and such a feat seemed a sheer impossibility.

As if he sensed her concern, Stuart began dropping kisses on her body, caressing her skin in soothing motions at the same time. "Relax, sweetheart. We will go as slowly as I can manage. Pleasure is meant to be savored."

He kissed her breasts, her belly, and then lower, his lips feathering over her hip bone, as she melted into the bed. She needed no prompting to part her thighs for him, and he took her silent invitation, his dark head lowering until his mouth brushed over her sex, taking his time as he had promised, his tongue darting over her folds, gliding up and down her seam as if he were drinking her up before flicking her pearl. She inhaled, her hips jumping toward him as pleasure streaked through her body.

His fingers glided as he feasted on her, slicking her own moisture down her swollen folds as she undulated beneath him, helpless to do anything other than surrender to the mindless bliss awaiting her. She felt a bit of pressure at her entrance and then the delicious sensation of his finger inside her, shallowly at first and then deeper as he lashed her pearl with determined strokes.

The invasion was unexpected and foreign, and yet her body instinctively knew she wanted more. Flattening her feet on the mattress, she arched upward, bringing his finger deeper. He growled his approval into her throbbing sex, still intent upon pleasuring her mercilessly with his mouth. Then his finger began to move, ever so slowly at first, pumping in and out of her with gentle, measured motions, drawing the tension within her to a crescendo. It was heavenly, the way he tongued her as he worked his finger in and out of her, her inner muscles clenching at him, wanting to keep him there. It was so much better than what had happened in the carriage because now the aching emptiness inside her was being filled by him. He was inside her, and the knowledge and sensation coupled together made her cry out with helpless need.

"That's it, sweetheart," he praised. "You're so, so wet. Come for me. I want your cream dripping down my wrist."

"Oh, Stuart," she cried out, body bowing as pleasure exploded deep inside her, making her toes curl into the bedclothes while wave after wave of white-hot bliss washed through her.

"Yes," he crooned, withdrawing his finger and then replacing it with his mouth at her entrance, lapping her up as if he couldn't get enough of her essence. "You taste so bloody sweet."

He licked her as the last of her pinnacle roared through her and then ebbed away, leaving her boneless and sated until he began kissing his way back up her body again and the heaviness of him between her legs filled her with renewed longing. He sucked her nipple, his mouth wet from her, glistening, the scent of them both wrapping her in a sensual haze. Reaching between them, he gripped his cock, guiding it over her sensitive flesh, slicking the head up and down her slit.

Stuart moved to her other breast, suckling her as he notched himself against her. Oh heavens, the pressure was intense and wonderful all at once, like his finger yet so much larger.

"I don't…think…you can possibly…fit," she managed breathlessly.

He lifted his head, casting an amused look up at her. "Trust me, sweetheart."

He gently guided her leg over his hip, opening her to him, the position easing his entrance. His head dipped, and he sucked her nipple hard again as he pushed forward, the tip of his cock breaching her.

She gasped, arching into him, the intensity of the connection beyond anything she had ever imagined. "Stuart."

He rocked into her, filling her with more of him, the stretch of her inner walls exquisitely sensitive, on the border of pain. There was a heaviness deep within her, mingling with need. Another shallow thrust of his hips, and he gave her more of himself.

She moaned, clinging to him as if she feared he would slip away when the fullness within her and the weight of his body pressing her into the bed proved there was no fear of that happening. He released her breast and hovered over her, his countenance taut with worry and desire as he leveraged himself on his forearms.

"You feel so good, love," he murmured. "So tight and wet on my cock."

His naughty words made her relax, something within her softening. Another flex of his hips, and he was seated within her, his hips aligned with hers, and she was full of him, his cock somehow buried deep.

The breath fled her, her fingers tightening on his shoulders. There was such a strange blend within her, of desire and discomfort, of need and uncertainty.

"Breathe, sweetheart." Stuart cupped her face with one hand and lowered his lips to hers, kissing her softly, tenderly. "Breathe and relax. Let me make you feel good."

He kissed her again and began moving, his length slipping almost completely from her and then sliding in again. She tasted herself on his lips as she opened for his questing tongue. He began a steady rhythm, thrusting into her, then withdrawing, increasing his pace a little as his hand moved between their bodies.

His fingers sought and found her swollen bud with expert

ease, and the combination of his touch on that sensitive place and his cock dragging in and out of her was almost too much. It chased the lingering sharpness, the slight pinch as her body grew accustomed to his and replaced it instead with pleasure so potent that she could do nothing but cry out into his mouth and hold him to her.

She was so close to coming apart again. His fingers worked her into a frenzy, each stroke of his cock inside her making that delicious tension wind ever tighter. She was acutely aware of everything—the heat of his body blazing into hers, the weight of him, the hardness of his muscled form, the barely leashed strength. The gentleness, too, the way he kissed her with such reverent care, even, the relentless strumming of his fingers over her pearl, the glide of him in and out, in and out, the sounds of need emerging from low in his chest, the breathy cries she couldn't contain. The scent of the two of them combined, the coolness of the bedclothes beneath her, the softness of the pillow, the scrape of his whiskers on her chin, the rake of her nails down his back as he claimed her.

She never wanted this moment to end. Never wanted him to be anywhere other than where he was, atop her, inside her, making her his. He moved faster, his body tensing, his cock surging inside her, and the dam broke. Bliss surged from her core, spiraling outward, and she stiffened beneath him, shuddering at the force of her climax.

He broke the kiss, rising over her to drive into her body with frenzied pumps of his hips, his breathing as ragged as hers, his muscles flexing with each movement. "Rosamund. Fuck. I'm going to fill your sweet pussy. Fill you and fill you until I give you a babe."

For some inexplicable reason, her body reacted to those words, to that promise. Her cunny fluttered around him as she splintered apart yet again. He sank deep, his cock hard and insistent and just where she wanted him, where she had to have him—or so it seemed—lest she expire from want.

"Yes," she gasped out, beyond all rational thought. "Please, Stuart. I need you."

He thrust into her again once, twice, and then the hot rush of his spend flooded her as she clutched him tightly, holding him to her, never wanting to let go.

CHAPTER 12

*S*tuart returned to the town house later than planned that evening.

"Dinner is awaiting you, Your Grace," Fleetwood informed him as Stuart handed off his coat, hat, and gloves.

"Where is my wife?" he asked, hoping Rosamund wouldn't be cross with him over his disappearance.

"Her Grace is awaiting you in the gold salon, Your Grace," the butler informed him.

The gold salon hadn't been used since Mother had been well. It was a small chamber, lined with some *bric-à-brac* Mother had collected over the years—family paintings, pictures, some sketches. The paintings that had been worth anything had long since been sold, as had a great deal of the furniture. Stuart thought the space sad and preferred to keep to his study rather than dwell among the ghosts of the past.

"Did she choose the salon herself, Fleetwood, or was it a recommendation made to her?" he asked curiously.

"I do believe that she inquired with Mrs. Wadham," the butler told him, referring to the housekeeper, who had been jubilant at the prospect of having a mistress to oversee the menus once again.

Like many roles Mother now eschewed, household management had fallen to the housekeeper. The fewer demands made upon his mother, the better.

He nodded. "I see. Might I ask how long she has been awaiting me?"

"Dinner has been held for the last hour," his butler told him, his face an expressionless mask.

Blast. Rosamund had spent the last hour in the gold salon, likely wondering where he was. It wasn't how he had intended to begin their marriage. But there had been no help for the delivery of the funds. One more day, and he ran the risk of his blackmailer revealing all.

He thanked the unsmiling Fleetwood and hastened in the direction of that forlorn room, hoping he wouldn't find a wife who was outraged by his absence. They had made love for the better portion of the afternoon, and he must have fallen into a deep and sated asleep afterward. He had awoken in a panic, having recalled that he was due to deliver the funds to the solicitor's office so that his blackmailer could hopefully slink away into whatever hell he had emerged from. The small fortune in return for that bastard's silence was a sum he would pay again and again if it meant protecting his mother, however.

Taking great care not to awaken Rosamund, he had slid from the inviting warmth of his bed and her arms, dressing with silent haste to make his grim delivery. As luck would have it, he had been waylaid by a snarl of carriage traffic, and now he had returned, an unpunctual arse on his own wedding day. All he could hope was that this damned business of blackmail was finally at an end, that all family secrets in danger of being revealed would be forever kept, and that he could begin to move forward with his life.

Whatever the hell that meant.

At the moment, he couldn't be certain. He hadn't expected to marry at all, let alone to feel the depth of emotion he had earlier when he'd made love to Rosamund. He couldn't lie to himself—although he was no innocent and he'd earned his reputation as a rake, he had never in all his days experienced what he had with her earlier.

It was exhilarating and terrifying all at once.

As he approached the gold salon, he heard voices. Rosamund's soft tones coupled with a familiar—and damned infuriating—baritone.

Stuart didn't bother to knock, striding across the threshold of the room, fury igniting something deep within him. Rosamund was by the lone window, frowning at Wesley, who was standing entirely too bloody near to her. Stuart had a moment to appreciate her luscious figure molded in a cream brocade gown *à la polonaise*, adorned with blonde lace at the cuffs and decolletage, the entire affair accented with a vivid floral embroidery. He had to swallow hard against a rush of desire and force himself to concentrate on the tableau before him rather than merely upon his wife.

"What the hell are you doing here?" he asked his brother without preamble.

Wesley turned to him with a smug grin that he longed to wipe off his face with his fist. "What am I doing here? Lovely to see you this evening as well, brother. I was merely keeping my new sister company. After all, she was left alone, and on her wedding day."

Stuart clenched his fists at his sides. "You never take dinner here."

"This is not an ordinary day," Wesley said, waving a hand dismissively. "Besides, it has been so long since I have been able to spend time with dear Rosamund. I missed her, and I daresay she missed me as well."

The pointed reminder of the past was enough to have Stuart clenching his jaw so hard that it would be a miracle if he didn't crack a bloody molar. "You aren't welcome here, Wesley."

"But this is my home." His brother was smiling and still far too close to Rosamund for Stuart's liking.

His new wife was watching the verbal parrying between himself and Wesley with a frown, and he didn't know if the look was meant for him, for his brother, or for the both of them.

"Was he troubling you?" Stuart demanded of Rosamund.

"Lord Wesley only just joined me whilst I awaited your return," Rosamund said quietly.

There was something in her countenance that gave him pause. He turned back to his brother. "If you insist upon dining here this evening, then you may as well go to the dining room ahead of us. I would like a moment alone with *my wife*."

If he placed emphasis upon the last phrase, it couldn't be helped. He was still thinking about what had happened with Lady Flora. About Wesley's claims that he would have Rosamund as well. After the intensity of the passion they had shared earlier, he was feeling raw and possessive.

Wesley would touch Rosamund again over his lifeless corpse, by God.

"But surely there's no need—" Wesley began smoothly.

"There is every need," Stuart interrupted harshly. "You will go to the goddamned dining room because that is what I told you to do and because your presence in this very household is dependent upon my goodwill. Is that clear?"

Wesley's mask of sham civility slipped for a moment, his lip curling into a sneer. "Perfectly, brother. I shall see the two of you at dinner."

With an elegant bow that was far more for Rosamund's

benefit than his, Wesley took his leave of the gold salon, stalking out of the room like a petulant child and slamming the door in his wake with more force than necessary. Had there been any paintings yet adorning the walls, they likely would have gone toppling to the threadbare Axminster.

Stuart blew out a breath of frustration and raked his hand through his hair. "Forgive me for my tardiness, Rosamund," he said. "And for the presence of my villainous brother as well. I had no notion that he intended to join us for dinner. If I had, I would have told him in no uncertain terms that he was to spend the evening elsewhere."

And Wesley bloody well knew it, the devious miscreant.

Rosamund moved toward him, still unsmiling. "Where were you? When I woke, you had left, and no one in the household seemed to know where you had gone. Either they didn't know, or they refused to tell me. I'm still not certain which it was."

He didn't want to lie to her, and yet he could not confide the truth in her either. It was a truth that wasn't his to reveal. Either way, this was decidedly not how he had planned to return home to her after the time they had spent in his bed that afternoon. Those hours had been so much more than he had dared to hope, and they had changed everything for him. There was no denying the *compatibility* they shared, as she had so maddeningly called it.

"I had a few small business matters requiring my attention," he explained instead, taking her hand and bringing it to his lips for a reverent kiss. "You look every bit as beautiful in this gown as you did in that sinful red creation. Are you hungry? I must beg your forgiveness—there was a snarl of carriages that couldn't be avoided on my return. It cost me an extra half an hour, if not more."

He was aware that he was babbling and that it was most unlike him. But then, he had also never had a wife before.

And he was deceiving her on the first day of their marriage, which he most assuredly regretted. Guilt hung heavy in his gut as her gaze searched his.

"What matters so distracted you on your wedding day?" she asked quietly. "I didn't think you were a man of business."

Hellfire. He wasn't. Of course he wasn't—at least, not beyond the club he ran with his friends.

"It was something I couldn't help," he said noncommittally.

"Your mistress." Her voice was hushed and yet laden with raw hurt.

"I don't have a mistress," he hastened to reassure her.

But she was already moving past him in her elegant gown, the lamplight catching in her red-gold hair to reveal the burnished glints hiding in her silken tresses. She looked every inch the duchess this evening, utterly beautiful and entirely formidable. He wanted to take her in his arms and beg her forgiveness, but he had a suspicion she wouldn't allow it just now.

"You don't have one any longer, I suppose," she said, a tremble in her voice that hit him like a slap to the face.

He moved swiftly, blocking her from the door and making her draw to a halt, her voluminous gown swaying from the sudden cessation of motion.

"My business did not concern a mistress, Rosamund," he said softly, hoping she would believe him without requiring him to offer more.

Her chin went up. "So, you dashed away without telling me, in the middle of our wedding day and after you had consummated our marriage, leaving me to be awakened by a strange man, for some reason other than to give your mistress the congé?"

His mind caught on one part of her sentence in particular. "A strange man woke you?"

DUKE WITH A DEBT

Pink color blossomed on her cheeks as she pinned him with a glare. "Your valet, I believe," she said with icy sangfroid.

"Sharpe," he provided. "Damn it. I apologize, Rosamund. I ought to have sent word to him that you weren't to be disturbed before I left."

"It is understandable, I suppose. You were likely too preoccupied with the unpleasant nature of the conversation awaiting you." Her voice was sharp and pointed as any blade.

"Christ." He scrubbed a hand over his jaw, feeling the full prickle of his whiskers in desperate need of a shave and realizing the sight he must present, bedraggled from the rain, unshaven, and back in his old favorite lounge suit. "Listen to me, sweetheart. I didn't leave your side so that I could cut ties with my mistress. I hadn't a mistress when I first came to you with my proposal, and I most assuredly don't have one now."

"Then why would you leave me after…after…" she stammered, her flush deepening.

Fuck, she was adorable. He couldn't restrain himself a moment longer. Stuart reached for her, hands settling on her cinched waist, and pulled her gently into him, her decadent scent in his lungs and her softness filling him with fire.

"The truth is," he began, looking down into her upturned face, "that I had no intention of bedding my glorious wife in the midst of the afternoon. I had wanted to woo you properly. But then I brought you to your chamber, and we were alone at last, and I couldn't wait a moment more to have you naked beneath me."

"You expect me to believe that? I fear you think me every bit the fool that your brother did."

"Don't," he bit out.

"Don't what?" she asked, her gaze crackling with defiance.

"Don't compare me to him," he ground out. "I am nothing like him, Rosamund. *Nothing*."

"You are brothers, are you not?"

"To my everlasting regret." He took a deep breath, trying to calm himself and dispel the inevitable rage that rose within him when he discussed Wesley. "What did he say to you when you were alone? Did he try to do anything untoward? If he did, by God, I will beat him to a bloody fucking husk."

Rosamund's hands had settled on his chest as lightly as butterflies, a pale comparison to the way she had scraped her nails down his back earlier. "I don't wish for violence. Regardless of how terrible he is, he is your brother. He had only just joined me here in the salon when you arrived. You needn't be concerned that anything happened. But neither have you offered an explanation as to why you were gone this afternoon, if not to throw your mistress over."

He closed his eyes for a moment, inhaling and gathering the calm that was fast fleeing him before opening his eyes and meeting her brown gaze. "I swear to you, Rosamund, that I was not throwing my mistress over, that I had no mistress. I'll not lie. I did not come to our marriage bed without a complicated past. But I can assure you that I intend to honor my vows to you."

Her brow furrowed, a sheen of tears glistening in her eyes. "Then tell me where you were, Stuart. I beg of you."

He knew a moment of painful indecision as he warred against himself. Could he tell her? And reveal the secret that wasn't his? Was there another way to convince her? Could he confide just enough and keep the rest enshrouded in mystery, all the better to protect Mother?

"Very well," he relented. "I will tell you what I can. But you must first promise to me that you will not carry this secret beyond these four walls. Can you do that?"

She frowned. "Stuart—"

He flexed his fingers on her waist, interrupting her. "Rosamund, promise me."

"Very well, if that is what you need from me." She nodded, unsmiling. "I promise not to carry your secret from this room."

"I'm being blackmailed," he blurted.

Her lips parted, and she stared at him in shock. "Blackmailed?"

The mere admission had his inner rage boiling to the surface again. He hated that he was at the mercy of some unknown foe, hated feeling so powerless and vulnerable.

With a heavy sigh, he nodded. "Yes. I fell asleep after we made love, and when I woke, I realized I had reached the designated day for the funds to be delivered. I hadn't the ability to pay the bastard until our marriage was complete. That's where I was, Rosamund. Not throwing over a mistress. Not seeing another woman. I was arranging for the payment to be made."

"My goodness, why did you not tell me this before?" she asked.

"Because I wanted to handle it without causing you any undue worry," he admitted. "Also, it is a point of pride, I suppose. I hate that I've been reduced to paying an unknown foe for secrecy."

"What secrecy? Why are you being blackmailed? Help me to understand, Stuart."

"That is what I cannot tell you. The reason for the blackmail is…a family matter."

Her brows rose. "Concerning you?"

He might have known that she would not simply accept his explanation. Rosamund's agile mind was busy churning. Wondering.

"Not directly," he relented.

"Your brother, then?" she guessed next.

"Do not ask of me what I cannot give you."

"But, Stuart—"

He interrupted her protest with a kiss, pressing his mouth to hers. It didn't take long for the kiss to deepen. She parted for him with a soft, needy sound that had his cock twitching to attention, making him forget all about blackmailers, his troublesome brother, and family secrets. He gave her his tongue, tasting her—sweetness and passion and Rosamund.

His Rosamund.

By the time he raised his head, they were both breathless. He held her stare, unwavering. "The secret I protect is not my own. Either way, this business is done. The debt has been paid, and I don't expect to hear anything more of this."

His gut clenched at his words, because he wasn't as certain of that as he would like to be. His blackmailer could become greedy. There was every chance that Stuart hadn't heard the last of him.

"Very well," Rosamund said. "I'll not ask you to unburden yourself further. But this has reminded me of another stipulation I neglected to include in the marriage contract."

He flattened his palm over the small of her back, caressing her there. "Oh? And what is that?"

"Fidelity. Do you intend to take lovers, Stuart?"

He stared down into her upturned face and realized suddenly that the thought of any woman other than Rosamund in his bed was foreign and hateful. When the hell had this happened? He had become besotted with his wife of less than one day. He wanted to be *faithful* to her.

Good sweet God.

How?

Why?

He reeled, the discovery taking him by complete surprise. Rosamund stiffened in his arms, misunderstanding his silence. "No need to answer. I shouldn't have asked. This is a marriage of convenience, of course."

But he wouldn't allow her to push away, instead tightening his hold to keep her anchored to him, their bodies aligned.

"There is only one woman I want in my bed," he told her honestly, "and that is you."

But she wasn't persuaded, flattening her hands on his chest and pushing. "Please, Stuart. Don't lie to protect my feelings. I understand that this is a business arrangement and nothing more. You get your coffers replenished, and I get the children I've longed for. I'm not expecting anything else. But I do hope that you'll at least wait until—"

He kissed her again, halting her words for the second time. It seemed a most efficient means of silencing her, and he couldn't resist the potent lure of her lush mouth. She responded for a moment before jerking her head back and pinning him with a hard look.

"You can't just kiss me to keep me from speaking, you know."

She was even more adorable when she was vexed. What was wrong with him? Where was all this tenderness coming from?

"I can't help myself." He grinned down at her. "You've cast some manner of spell on me."

She pursed her lips. "You're trying to distract me now."

"No, I'm trying to tell you that I intend to have you in my bed every night." He cupped her cheek gently, stroking the elegant curvature with his thumb as he fell into her gold-brown gaze. "I'm going to pleasure you every way I know how. And I'm going to be faithful, Rosamund. I expect the same from you. If, at some point in the future, something should change, we will decide upon a mutually agreeable course."

"If you grow bored of only bedding your wife, you mean."

He didn't know what he meant, only that the notion of cleaving to one woman forever was vaguely terrifying.

"Perhaps you shall grow bored of me," he pointed out, hating the notion even as he spoke it.

He would kill any man who dared to touch her. The vehemence of his reaction—guttural and instinctive—again took Stuart by surprise. He would tear any bastard who dared to attempt to seduce her away limb from limb.

She searched his gaze for a long moment, and he wondered what her clever mind was thinking. "I don't think there is any danger of that for now."

For now.

He kissed her again, not stopping until she had softened against him, her tongue gliding eagerly against his. Reluctantly, he withdrew, pleased at the sight of her mouth, swollen and dark with his kisses.

"Good," he said. "Now, I suppose we ought to go to dinner. I've delayed it long enough."

Stuart straightened, offering her his arm. Rosamund settled her hand in the crook of his elbow, and together, they proceeded to the dining room.

DINNER WAS FAST PROVING NOT ONLY TRYING but dreadful. The unwanted presence of Lord Wesley at the table left both Rosamund and Stuart in a heightened state of discomfort. Wesley's nettlesome insistence upon interjecting his conversation didn't help.

"I am so pleased to have you here at our table with us, sister," he said with ebullient enthusiasm.

Rosamund summoned every bit of kindness she had and forced a smile at Lord Wesley for the benefit of the servants working on the next course. "I am happy to be here."

In truth, she wished she were back in the haven of Stuart's bed. That he had never left and neither had she. It troubled her anew to think of someone blackmailing him over a mysterious secret he refused to reveal to her. She didn't like the notion of anyone knowing something about him that would cause sufficient harm that he would pay to keep the truth from being revealed.

She also didn't like that he was keeping whatever it was from her. But that was a matter for another day. This was the first of many they would share together, and there was time aplenty to learn more about her new husband along the way.

An awkward silence fell as the servants completed their task. Stuart's glare was murderous, aimed in Wesley's direction. His brother, meanwhile, was on his third glass of wine. The pair of footmen were newly hired, and they took their time, whisking away the soup course and laying out the mutton pie *à la Perigord* and *asperge à la sauce vinaigrette*. Rosamund had scarcely tasted the *potage à la Prince* before it and had only managed a few spoonsful.

The footmen excused themselves and disappeared, leaving Rosamund, Stuart, and Wesley to the course, which was laid out beautifully on the table. The silver epergne at the table's center was one that Rosamund had brought with her, but the serving dishes were Gilden family relics, some of which were flawed with hairline cracks and chips. The preparations for her move to Stuart's town house had been frenzied, but she fully intended to see the home and household restored to its former glory.

The three of them tucked into the mutton pie and asparagus, Stuart continuing to glower at his brother. *Heavens*, to think how he would look at Wesley if he knew what had happened earlier at the wedding breakfast. Rosamund had been torn between telling Stuart and simply ignoring it. If anything, Wesley's cloying cheer at dinner this evening persuaded her that she should tell her husband. She wanted honesty between them at all costs.

And she would have it, too. He couldn't keep his secrets from her forever.

Could he?

"My, but this mutton is tender and delicious," Wesley drawled, his gaze pinned on Rosamund. "It's so moist that it practically falls apart in one's mouth."

There was an insinuation in his words that set Rosamund on edge. Apparently, Stuart felt the same way.

"I'll not countenance any of your antics today, Wesley," he warned his brother coldly. "It is purely out of deference to my wife's charity that you are joining us at this table at all. Don't think I won't have you hauled out of this room like a petty thief at the first opportunity if I must."

His words were harsh, and so too was the expression on his face. Gone was the gentleness he had shown her that afternoon in his bedroom. The icy duke had returned.

Wesley, however, appeared unperturbed by his brother's ire, lifting his wineglass instead with such haste and lack of care that some of it sloshed over the rim of the crystal and splashed on the back of his hand. "To dear Rosamund's charity. I, for one, am terribly thankful that it is so… generous."

His gaze dropped to Rosamund's breasts in a pointed leer. She straightened her spine, barely suppressing the childish urge to launch a fork of mutton at his face from across the table.

"Take care, brother," Stuart warned. "You are treading very dangerously."

"Or what shall happen?" Wesley laughed, then took a lengthy draught of his wine. "I rather doubt you would deign to have me removed from dinner before your bride and new domestics. Only think of how the tongues shall wag."

Wesley was not wrong about that. Gossip traveled quickly through polite society, like fire burning up dry kindling.

"You will conduct yourself as a gentleman at this dinner, damn you," Stuart seethed.

"There is also the matter of how dear, sweet Rosamund was once my betrothed," Wesley said snidely. "Only think of what the scandal broth shall be. Everyone will think you've turned me out of my own home because Rosamund prefers me and the jealousy is eating you alive. It wouldn't be the first time such a thing has come to pass. I daresay they'll all swallow it down like mother's milk."

"You do not have leave to refer to my wife by her given name," Stuart snapped, pounding his fist on the table for emphasis and making the dishes rattle in the process.

"I threw you over, if you will recall," Rosamund interjected with as much calm as she could muster. "I sincerely doubt anyone would believe that I would prefer a drunkard second son I've already rejected over the handsome, mighty Duke of Camden."

Her biting words hit their mark. Wesley cast a dark look in her direction and reached for his wine. "Cheers, *sister*. You seem to have already learned my brother's ability for cutting family down as if we were enemy soldiers."

"I am merely speaking plainly," she pointed out, unmoved by his attempt to cast himself as innocent.

He was toying with both her and Stuart, just as he had toyed with her earlier at the wedding breakfast. She wanted nothing to do with his games. It made her sick to think that she had once been so foolish that she had believed in his silver tongue, his pretty words and lies. He had only ever been manipulating her and using her to gain what he'd wanted most—her fortune. And now that it would never be his, he wanted something else instead. But she was not about to betray her husband with anyone, let alone with a venomous snake such as Lord Wesley.

"Leave her out of this," Stuart warned him. "My wife is no concern of yours."

"Oh? Is that so?" Wesley asked lightly. "Strange, that. I thought the reason you wanted to marry her was so that you could throw her fortune in my face. Perhaps I was wrong. My mistake."

The insincerity in his voice couldn't be denied.

"Shut up, Wesley," Stuart commanded.

"Why should I when I'm only stating the obvious? Everyone at the wedding breakfast knew why you'd married the great heiress Miss Rosamund Payne," Wesley sneered. "What other reason could you possibly have to want her other than that she was mine first and she's hideously wealthy?"

Rosamund's stomach twisted in a knot. It wasn't as if what Wesley said came as a surprise. She knew precisely why Stuart had married her. Rather, it was having the truth thrown so viciously in her face after everything she and Stuart had shared hours earlier. She felt raw and uncertain and perilously close to the heartbroken woman who had thrown over Wesley after she'd learned the truth.

Stuart shot from his seat, his expression harder than granite as he faced his brother. "You will never speak of my wife so callously again. Get out of this dining room at once. You are no longer welcome here. Indeed, you never were welcome, but it was the duchess's good graces that enabled you to remain."

"I haven't finished eating my dinner yet," Wesley said with a careless shrug. "Besides, what are you going to do if I don't leave? Order Mother to come down from her room so she can listen to your tantrums? We both know she hasn't left her chamber in years."

Rosamund's gaze went from her husband to Wesley, then back as she tried to dissect the anger and the accusations the two men were hurling at each other. The dowager's absence from today's wedding ceremony and breakfast suddenly made sense if what Lord Wesley had just said was true. Stuart was livid—she had never seen him so furious.

"Leave," he insisted with quiet menace.

Wesley at last stood as well, staggering a bit as he reached for his wineglass, sending the freshly poured crystal tipping over, a blot of fine French wine seeping into the snowy table linen and spreading quickly. "I seem to have lost my appetite," he snarled, and then he snagged the bottle with more force than necessary.

Without another word, he stormed from the dining room, slamming the door at his back. When he had gone, the tension instantly began to leach from her. Her shoulders sagged, and she exhaled the breath she hadn't realized she had been holding.

"Damn him," Stuart growled, scrubbing a hand over his jaw before raking his fingers through his hair.

He looked extraordinarily weary in that moment, as if the burden of so much obligation were upon his shoulders. And indeed, given what she had learned today, and after seeing what his relationship with his brother was like, it was clear that he did have a great deal weighing him down. Although she loathed the notion of causing him any further unease, she knew she needed to tell him about her interaction with his brother at the wedding breakfast.

His gaze went to her. "Forgive me, Rosamund. This wasn't how I intended to spend our first dinner together as husband and wife."

"You need not apologize. You aren't responsible for your

brother's actions. However, there is something I must tell you about Lord Wesley, and I ought to have done so before now, but I…"

She allowed her words to trail away, uncertain of how she should proceed.

Stuart tensed anew, his jaw on edge, a muscle twitching in his cheek as he clenched the back of his chair in a death grip. "What of him?"

Somehow, he looked even more rigid, emanating icy fury. Rosamund bit her lip, considering what she would say next with great care. "He seems to have forgotten the manner in which our betrothal ended. I, however, have not."

"What do you mean, he seems to have forgotten?" he asked, his voice and gaze taking on an urgency that quite unnerved her. "Were you lying to me earlier when you said he wasn't untoward with you? Did he touch you?"

She thought of the familiar way Wesley had touched her arm that morning, how he had stood in impolite proximity to her. Thought of the blatant innuendo in his smile and eyes. These things, taken apart, could not be deemed untoward. Moreover, she had no wish to kindle further discord between the brothers.

"He laid a hand on my arm this morning when I left the wedding breakfast for the lady's withdrawing room," she conceded. "Nothing more. I can assure you that you need not concern yourself that I have any interest in his…attentions. I wasn't certain if it was worth noting, and I didn't wish to cause a row on our first day as husband and wife."

"Of course it was worth noting." Stuart strode toward her, their plates cooling and forgotten in the aftermath of his brother's antics. "You should have told me at once."

"As I said, I didn't want to be the cause of any upset. I handled him myself."

He pulled her to her feet and into his arms, taking her by

surprise, embracing her quickly and firmly, his chin resting atop her crown. "I've no doubt you did, but I should be the one to handle him. He's my brother. You needn't suffer him."

She wanted to ask how she wouldn't have to suffer him when he lived beneath the same roof, but she also didn't want to push Stuart further than he'd already been shoved. Rosamund wrapped her arms around his waist, breathing in his clean, heady scent, listening to the steady, reassuring thump of his heart.

"I assure you," she told him quietly, "I'm more than capable of seeing to myself. I have done for these last thirty years."

"He intends to seduce you, just as he did my former betrothed," Stuart said. "You may as well know it. He has told me as much himself."

His words shocked her. She jerked her head back, searching her husband's handsome face, which was still stony, his jaw tense.

"But he made his disdain for me more than clear three years ago when I threw him over, and then again this evening," she protested. "I cannot imagine why he would take an interest in me now that my fortune is no longer available for him to seize."

"You are beautiful and you are my wife, and Wesley has always coveted everything that is mine. He'll stop at nothing to get what he wants."

"He will stop at me," she said, old rage she'd thought long cooled burning back to life. "He cannot have me, and my loyalty is to you, Stuart. You know how I feel about him after the way he treated me."

She hoped that her new husband knew how she felt about him as well. But her pride was too strong, prevailing over her tongue, and these were words she could not make herself speak. Not now. Not yet.

Stuart inhaled sharply, then slowly exhaled. "Thank you. I am sorry to mention such ugliness to you, let alone force you to witness what you did at this table, but I felt you were better warned. My brother is devious and manipulative. He isn't to be trusted."

Had their conversation not been so serious and earnest, she might have laughed. "I am more than aware that he isn't trustworthy. I learned that on my own."

"Of course you did. Jesus, what am I thinking?" He raked long fingers through his hair, looking suddenly weary. "He makes me half-mad."

"You have many burdens and obligations resting on you, I think." She reached up to cup his jaw, unthinking, needing to offer comfort. "I hope you can share them with me. Let me take on some of them for you. We are husband and wife now."

Rosamund settled her other hand on his shoulder blade, gently rubbing in a circular motion. Beneath her hand, he was all lean, muscled strength. She couldn't help but admire the way he felt, so masculine and powerful. And much to her shame, although she was meant to be offering solace and understanding in this moment, she was also thinking about his body beneath the trappings of civility. Of how it had felt to be naked with him in his bed, his mouth between her thighs, his cock deep inside her.

Longing sliced through her. What a wanton she was proving to be.

He stared down at her, unspeaking, and then slowly, as if they weren't in the midst of an interrupted dinner with footmen about to arrive at any second, he lowered his head toward hers. Their lips met, his soft yet insistent, hot and tasting of the sweetness of the wine he'd consumed with dinner thus far. He groaned, crushing her nearer to him, as if he intended to never let her go.

She returned his kiss, trying to show him without words where her loyalty lay, to tell him how much he had somehow come to mean to her. Because she had grown to care for him. There was so much more to Stuart than she had initially supposed. More than she had ever been privy to previously. He kissed her passionately but tenderly, demonstrating with actions rather than words how he felt for her.

And she was grateful for that. She didn't feel unwanted. Lord Wesley's cruel words fell away as Stuart's lips moved over hers with aching skill and care. She held him close, her body already attuned to his, heat pooling at the apex of her thighs. Shamelessly, she rubbed her breasts against his chest, seeking all the contact with him she could have. Still, it wasn't enough. With Stuart, she always wanted more. And more and more and more.

Lucidity returned to her in the form of the dining room door opening, followed by the hushed footsteps of footmen retreating with the next course, serving ware clinking, the floor creaking. The reminder was necessary. She couldn't have that just now, not in the dining hall, of all places.

He lifted his head abruptly. "I fear we've mortified the footmen," he said, grinning down at her.

She smiled back at him, his lack of concern infectious. "Do you think they will return with the next course?"

"It depends if I order it." He kissed the bridge of her nose. "Are you hungry, sweetheart?"

Was he implying what she thought he was? Did he intend to skip the rest of the meal so that they might entertain themselves by other means? Her heart pounded harder.

"I think I've had my fill of this dinner," she answered honestly.

Because all she wanted was more Stuart. She wanted to be alone with him. Naked with him. In his bed with him. Was it wrong to say such sinful things aloud to one's husband?

She wasn't sure, so she held her tongue. This was all yet so very new.

"Excellent." He kissed her swiftly before releasing her mouth to stare down at her, his gaze dark with sensual intent. "So have I. But I haven't yet had my fill of you. Indeed, I don't think it's possible to."

"I feel the same."

His mouth found hers yet again for a deep, drugging kiss that had her swaying on her feet before it was done. "I reckon we should leave this dining room before I make a feast of you here on this bloody table. Then we would truly scandalize the servants."

She held his gaze, feeling bold and powerful and desired. "I'm not certain I would mind if we scandalized them."

"Sweet God, woman. What you do to me." Taking her hand in his, he led her from the dining room, the remnants of dinner abandoned on the table linens and the chipped Gilden family porcelain.

CHAPTER 13

*T*he procession of carriages—one borrowed from the Duke of Brandon and one a new purchase, thanks to the influx of funds from Rosamund's dowry— rumbled up the rutted approach to the sprawling seventeenth-century brick façade. Stuart opened the Venetian blinds completely as the carriage turned and jolted to a halt before the rounded oak double doors.

He hadn't been inside his country seat in some time. The large edifice needed repair in its older wings, and he preferred to be in London. When he did venture to the country, it was usually to Wingfield Hall, where the Wicked Dukes Society held their infamous house parties. He had always preferred to leave the estate in the hands of his steward, who sent him regular reports. But he had wanted to spirit Rosamund away for a honeymoon, and that need had been underscored last evening when Wesley had caused mayhem at dinner.

Rosamund was seated opposite him, a covered cage containing her parrot on the floor between them.

"Welcome to Gilden Hall, my dear," he said. "Such as it is."

"Gormless shite," Megs announced from beneath her covering.

She had been relatively quiet for most of the journey, so he supposed he ought to feel grateful for that small mercy.

"Megs," Rosamund chastised softly. "You are meant to behave."

"What a pretty bird," Megs chirped. "Megs want pistache."

"And you shall have one when we are inside," she promised.

"Have you ever considered gifting the feathered menace to a friend?" he asked.

"Of course not." His wife shot him an indignant look. "Megs is my companion."

And the thorn in his side.

He said nothing as Rosamund's eyes narrowed on him. "You *are* joking, are you not?"

Only partially.

Stuart smiled. "Quite. How could I possibly live to see another day were I not insulted by a bird every other hour?"

"Perhaps she believes it's a term of endearment," Rosamund suggested. "Have you ever thought of that?"

"I applaud your attempt to make me believe the plumed pest secretly adores me," he drawled. "But I've seen the way she looks at me. It's a death glare, rather as if she were plotting my demise."

"Megs does *not* give you a death glare."

He raised a brow. "She most certainly does."

"Gormless shite," Megs chirruped happily from her cage.

"Ever so much more talkative now that we've come to a halt," he grumbled.

The carriage door swung open, bringing with it sunlight and fresh country air. Stuart descended from the conveyance first, landing on the stone drive, and turned to offer his hand to Rosamund. In typical Rosamund fashion, however, she was fretting over her bloody parrot and attempting to carry the cage herself.

"Leave it, my dear," he commanded. "One of the servants will carry the cage inside."

"But what if someone drops her?" she worried.

He recalled the anxious manner with which she had presided over the delivery of Megs to the carriage early that morning. She had fluttered about the pair of strapping footmen, wringing her hands as she worried one of them might lose control of the cage and cause her precious bird injury or distress.

"Would it make you feel more at ease if I were to carry the cage?" he offered.

She turned to him, indecision written on her countenance. "Would you?"

"Anything for you," he promised with ease, realizing the veracity of his words as they left him.

He would indeed do anything Rosamund required of him, whether it was carting her insult-spewing parrot about or bringing her to this moldering family estate so that she might have some semblance of a honeymoon. Or giving her children. His prick twitched at the thought of that. There was something about getting her with child, filling her with his seed again and again until his mission was accomplished, that made him ridiculously randy. He was going to have to think of something else now just so he could walk through the great hall bearing the damned parrot.

"Thank you," Rosamund said softly, apparently having made her decision as she took his extended hand and allowed him to help her alight from the carriage.

Her perfume wrapped around him, mingling with the fresh scent of country grass and trees and damp earth. She was wearing a cool gray gown accented with brown lace and ruffles that was far too alluring to be a travel gown for the way it clung deliciously to her curves. Her hat was a jaunty gray with an upturned brim and satin ribbon. Not for the first time, he noted the lack of feather ornamentation on her millinery—curious, for many women were perpetually festooned in so many feathers they could well be mistaken for avian themselves.

By God, she was beautiful, bathed in warm afternoon sun and surrounded by the verdant beauty of the country.

And his wife.

"Is something wrong with my hat?" she wanted to know, her nose crinkling as she looked up at him.

Christ, he'd been standing there mooning over her like a love-sick swain.

"Not a thing," he told her smoothly. "I was merely wondering at the lack of feathers in your hats."

"I don't wear feathers," she told him firmly. "Have you any notion how many poor, innocent, lovely birds are murdered each year for the sake of adorning hats?"

No, but he had a feeling she was going to tell him.

"Millions," she proclaimed, shaking her head. "It is a horrid practice, and I shan't add to it. Silk flowers and satin ribbons suffice."

He might have known his generous-hearted wife couldn't bear to wear feathers when she doted over her African grey as if she were a child.

"Of course," he agreed, inclining his head toward the doors, which had opened to reveal the servants anticipating their arrival. "We ought to make our way inside so that the carriages can be unpacked. I'll fetch the feathered one."

Rosamund glided elegantly toward the entrance to Gilden Hall, and Stuart dutifully clambered back into the carriage to extract the bane of his existence.

"Gormless shite," the parrot chirped as he carried her heavy cage into the front hall.

If the butler, housekeeper, and assorted maids and footmen awaiting them heard, they gave no indication. Now that he was within the ancient edifice, he was once more reminded of just how dilapidated it was. And damned drafty too, even on a warm day like this one. He settled the cage on the floor and performed a formal introduction to the domestics after he and Rosamund had handed off their hats and gloves along with her wrap.

"I present to you Her Grace, the new Duchess of Camden."

Beneath the covering on her cage, Megs made kissing sounds. He inwardly sent up a prayer that the winged demon would hold her beak.

Rosamund smiled brightly, and he forgot about the outlandish parrot. She was lovely on any occasion, but when she exuded genuine happiness, she was nothing short of breathtaking. How had he ever seen her as anything less than blindingly beautiful?

He cleared his throat, realizing he had yet to finish his obligation, and gestured to the elderly butler, whose white hair had noticeably thinned since Stuart's most recent visit. "This is Mr. Fitzsimmons."

A few old family retainers had remained here at Gilden Hall, but many of the faces greeting them were new, having been hired in anticipation of his nuptials. Yet another sign of how Rosamund's dowry was already at work.

The butler bowed stiffly. "Your Grace."

"The housekeeper," Stuart went on, "Mrs. Lumley."

Mrs. Lumley had been the housekeeper for the last twenty years at least. Streaks of silver shot through her dark hair, yet another reminder of how long it had been since Stuart had come to Gilden Hall.

The housekeeper curtseyed, her chatelaine jingling. "I

would be more than happy to see Her Grace to the blue chamber, which we have readied at Your Grace's request."

The blue chamber adjoined the ducal apartments. It was located in the newer wing of Gilden Hall, less prone to drafts and leaks. As its name implied, all the furnishings and wall coverings were shades of blue.

"That would be most appreciated, Mrs. Lumley," Rosamund told the housekeeper with a warm smile. "After all this travel, I find myself quite fatigued."

"One of the footmen might carry the birdcage for you," Mrs. Lumley suggested. "Where would you have it placed, Your Grace?"

"Oh, that won't be necessary," Rosamund said brightly. "His Grace will carry Megs for me. She is partial to him, you understand."

"Of course, Your Grace," the housekeeper relented instantly, as if it weren't just a bit unusual for the master of the house to be carrying a birdcage about like a servant.

Dutifully, Stuart took up the cage and followed in the wake of his housekeeper and his wife.

"Gormless shite," Megs announced as they ascended the grand stairs.

So much for his prayer the feathered devil would behave herself. But Mrs. Lumley, to her credit, didn't hesitate. She simply carried on as if Stuart hadn't just been insulted by the bird he was transporting. Grimly, he turned his attention to the mesmerizing sight Rosamund presented as she glided up the staircase in her gray silk. Her hips gently swayed, her glorious hair plaited into a braid and then coiled over her nape. He longed to press his lips to that tantalizing swath of skin, to inhale deeply of her scent, to feel her soft warmth beneath his mouth.

He wondered how weary she was from their travels. A gentleman would allow her to rest. Perhaps a nap and a bath.

Certainly some sustenance. But there was nothing gentle-manly at all about what he was feeling toward his wife at the moment. He wanted nothing more than to tear that demure silk from her tempting curves and to suck her nipples and stroke her pretty cunny until she came all over his fingers.

The only sustenance he wanted was her. Her pussy on his face, her cream on his tongue. He wanted to devour her until she was limp and sated, and then he wanted to sink his cock deep inside her and fuck her until they were both crying out and he pumped his hot seed within her.

Damnation, these thoughts had to stop. His cock was pressed uncomfortably to the placket of his trousers, and each step dragged the linen of his drawers against his aching erection, which was already leaking. He made a sound in his throat, gripping the cage more tightly in an effort to distract himself.

The noise didn't go unnoticed by Rosamund, who glanced back at him over her shoulder. "Is something amiss?"

Yes, something was amiss. His brain had clearly rotted, because he was carrying his wife's parrot and all he wanted to do was shag her all day and all night long. They had made love again last night, and in the early hours of the morning, he'd been forced to take himself in hand, concerned he would make her sore. And still, he could think of nothing other than making her spend and then filling her with his cock.

He gritted his teeth. "Nothing at all, my dear."

She frowned, still paused on the stairs. "Is the cage too heavy for you? I'm sure the footmen could manage quite well."

Did she think him a puling whelp?

"The cage scarcely weighs anything," he countered for the sake of his pride.

It was an exaggeration, but never mind that. He wasn't

about to have the footmen take over now, and particularly not when he required the cage to shield his erection from any watchful gazes.

With a thoughtful look, Rosamund nodded, and they resumed their climb. Thank God there were separate dressing rooms and sitting rooms off the blue chamber. His feathered nemesis was going to find her temporary home in one of those spaces, on the other side of a closed door, as quickly as possible.

After what seemed an eternity, they reached the blue chamber, and Stuart dutifully deposited the cage on a table near a window that overlooked the gardens. He excused himself to give Rosamund a moment alone with Mrs. Lumley so that she might discuss whatever it was that the lady of the house spoke about with her housekeeper.

He needed to take a long walk.

And perhaps a swim in the cold Gilden Hall lake to cool himself.

ROSAMUND WAS at last settled in to what would be her temporary bedroom during her honeymoon with Stuart. Bayneham had finished unpacking and putting away all the garments, boots, books, and watercolors she had brought with her for the next fortnight. So much upheaval in so few days, coupled with travel and a wedding, had left Rosamund unusually weary. She stood at the mullioned windows in her chamber now, looking down at the overgrown garden of Gilden Hall.

Like most other parts of the estate—and Stuart's town house too—the garden would require a great deal of work and rejuvenation. It was plain to see, even with the most casual observation, that the Dukes of Camden had been cursed with meager funds for many years. The burden had not been brought on by Stuart, but he had inherited it, much like his title.

During her betrothal to Wesley, she had never visited Gilden Hall. The London town house, however, had been in far better form than it was presently. There had been no denying the shabby, though genteel furnishings, worn carpets, and faded wall hangings. However, the stark absence of pictures on the walls, when three years ago there had been many, was a clear indication, like the state of Gilden Hall itself, that the straits in which Stuart found himself had recently grown worse.

She thought about his troubling revelation the day before, that he was being blackmailed, and wondered if that was the cause for the further devastation of his coffers. Whose secret was Stuart so intent upon keeping, if not his own? Who would he want to protect so much that he would pay any price for his blackmailer's silence?

Rosamund had been turning the matter over in her mind during the journey to Hertfordshire and as she and Bayneham had overseen the unpacking. And there was only one reasonable conclusion for her to reach.

He was protecting his mother.

But why? And what could the dowager duchess's secret be?

A slight knock at the door adjoining her bedroom to Stuart's interrupted her musings. She turned away from the gardens. "Come."

The door swung open to reveal him on the threshold, still dressed as he had been earlier for travel, and so unfairly handsome that she had to remind herself of her need to maintain her restraint. It wouldn't do to become too fond of him already.

"I hope I'm not interrupting," he said, casting a glance around the room as if he were looking for someone.

Bayneham, she realized.

"Of course not." She smiled, and it was genuine. "Do come in."

She was pleased to see him. More alarming, however, was the realization that she had missed him. *Good heavens, Rosamund*, she chastised herself inwardly. *It has only been a few hours. You must gather yourself and stop acting like a hen wit.*

"Your lady's maid has finished the unpacking?" he asked, crossing the room to her.

"She has."

He stopped before her, taking her hands in his and bringing them to his lips for an ardent kiss that sent heat flooding between her thighs. "And the feathered she-devil? Has she been settled as well?"

"If you mean Megs," she said pointedly, "she is comfortably settled in the dressing room. Traveling here has left her tired, I believe. I haven't heard a sound from her."

"Excellent." He tugged her gently forward, into his embrace, and she went willingly. "I've missed you, these last few hours."

She placed her hands on his shoulders, trying not to admire their breadth and strength and failing. "Has it been a few hours? I hadn't noticed."

She was being wretched and she knew it. But she couldn't allow him to charm her. He was too dangerous to her heart. Rosamund refused to allow herself to have tender feelings for a man who had married her for her fortune. They had a contract, she reminded herself sternly. This was a business arrangement between them, nothing more.

"My pride is wounded," he said softly, his head dipping toward hers. "It requires the sweet balm of your lips to restore it."

Their mouths connected in a chaste kiss that was somehow gentle and seductive all at once. She promptly forgot all the reasons she must guard herself. All the reasons she must not allow herself to be vulnerable, as malleable as bread dough in his knowing hands.

Because his tongue glided along the seam of her lips, and nothing else mattered. She opened for him, giving him her tongue as well. He tasted like tea, and she supposed she must as well. A tray had been sent up for her by Mrs. Lumley. One must have also been provided to him. She pressed nearer to him, her nipples hardening in her corset, aching for his touch. All the exhaustion that had been gathering within her was dispersed by a potent rush of desire so strong and furious that it made her knees tremble.

How could she want him so much? How could he feel as necessary as the air she breathed, as water? This was dangerous territory indeed, and yet she was helpless, hopelessly in his thrall.

He tore his lips from hers to drag them down her throat, leaving hot, openmouthed kisses in his wake. "Tell me you haven't missed me just a bit," he murmured against her skin. "I cannot be alone in this all-consuming desire."

She licked her lips, tasting him, and tipped her head back. "You're not. I… Oh heavens, that is…"

He had sucked on her throat and then nipped her with his teeth, and a molten bolt of need had gone straight to her core.

"God, I love it when you get flustered," he murmured, his lips finding their way to her ear now. "It makes my cock hard as marble."

He licked the hollow behind her ear, and she couldn't contain her moan of pure, unadulterated need. Every swipe of his tongue tightened her nipples, as if he were sucking them.

"It…it does?" she managed breathlessly.

He hummed against her ear, his breath hot and humid. "Would you like to feel?"

Here was an invitation that her inner wanton could not refuse. She liked touching him. Liked knowing the effect she had on him. Heavens, who was she fooling? She loved that she, a previously untried virgin, could wield so much power over a wicked rake.

"Yes," she whispered. "Show me."

She was still too hesitant to touch him so intimately without his direction, and he seemed to understand this, taking her hand in his and lowering it between their bodies, settling it over his rigid length.

"Feel what you do to me. I've been thinking of making love to you again ever since I woke this morning. Sitting in that carriage with you was pure agony. All I wanted to do was toss up your skirts and lick your sweet cunny until you spent and then fill you with my seed."

Her sex throbbed at his forbidden words, the description of what he had wanted to do to her as vivid in her mind as if it had happened. Because she had been thinking of it too.

She stroked him through his trousers, growing bolder as he sucked her earlobe. "Why did you not do it, then?"

"Because the feathered menace was taking up half the bloody carriage," he growled.

She laughed at the thwarted desire in his voice and continued her exploration of him below. "I suppose it was prudent of me to make a place for her in the dressing room, then."

"God yes," he groaned, jutting his hips forward, pressing himself into her hand. "How are you feeling? Please don't tell me you're tired and sore. I'll die if you do."

She had been tired until he had appeared, making her

want him so desperately. As for soreness, her body was tender in new places, but that didn't prohibit her from needing him. Smiling, she rubbed her cheek along his, enjoying the rasp of the whiskers shadowing his jaw against her skin.

"I'm feeling like I want you to peel me out of this dress."

"I'll die another day, then." His lips sought hers, eager and demanding, and she lost herself in his kiss.

Working as one, they tore at each other's clothes. This was no slow and steady seduction. It was a frenzied need to be naked. Buttons came undone. Laces were untied. Silk and cotton and linen fell to the floor. By the time they were lying together on her bed, they were both breathless. The bed was stiff and unforgiving beneath her, but the bedclothes were soft enough, and when Stuart buried his face between her legs, the mattress beneath her and everything else in the room—in the world, even—ceased to exist.

Parting her swollen folds, he licked her, his tongue gliding over her aching flesh in long, relentless swipes. She tangled her fingers in his thick, dark hair, holding him to her as her hips undulated beneath him, and he devoured her. He groaned into her as if she were the most delicious thing he had ever tasted, the vibration echoing in her pearl, and then he rubbed his face against her sex. His stubble teased her highly sensitive flesh, making her gasp with pleasure as his tongue swirled over the bud of her sex. With another low sound of desire, he latched on to her pearl and sucked hard, simultaneously slipping a finger deep into her channel.

It was exquisite, his long finger finding a place inside her that made wild bursts of pleasure rocket through her. But he didn't relent, suckling and adding another finger, thrusting in and out of her until she could withstand the sensual torment no more. With a cry, she came violently, shuddering ʋeneath him as the force of her pinnacle roared through her like a train bustling down the tracks.

She scarcely had enough time to recover before he was rolling her onto her stomach, his big hands palming her bottom, giving both cheeks a gentle squeeze. Still breathless, her body pulsing with the aftermath of her release, she looked over her shoulder.

"What are you doing?"

"Enjoying your beautiful arse." He lowered his head and kissed the indentation of her spine.

She liked that. Liked it very much, in fact. And she also liked the gentle massage he was giving to her rump. It felt forbidden, however.

"Are you certain you're meant to...to...do such a thing?" she ventured. "It seems quite wrong."

He gave her a smoldering look that melted her insides. "I can assure you that I am, and that there is nothing at all wrong with admiring my beautiful wife's equally lovely bottom."

He kissed her left cheek, then gently bit, and she arched her back instinctively.

"Oh," was all she could manage.

"Rise up a bit, sweetheart," he urged, gently guiding her. "Onto your knees. Yes, just like that."

"How will this work?" she wondered.

And then he astonished her by licking into her from behind.

"Oh sweet heavens," she gasped helplessly as desire flooded her.

"A bit like this," he said and then sank his tongue deep again while he found her pearl and stroked, his fingers firmly swirling over her. "Mmm, and like this."

She panted, needing more, about to lose control again.

Desire was a coiled spring, ready to fly apart at the slightest provocation. But then, he withdrew from her, and she felt a different sensation at her entrance as the blunt tip of his cock pushed through her wetness. He stroked himself up and down her seam, the slippery sounds of her desire joining her ragged breaths in the silence of the room.

"Surely you cannot…from behind," she managed.

"Of course I can." He worked his length over her faster, with more insistence, his voice strained. "With this angle, I can go deeper inside you and bring you greater pleasure. And I can watch my cock sinking inside your sweet pussy."

Dear God. She was incapable of speech. Perhaps for the rest of her life.

All she could do was moan and present herself to him, lifting her back end higher.

"You like that, don't you, my filthy girl?" he asked, his voice low and dark and decadent as velvet. "You like that I'm going to watch as I fuck you, and then I'm going to fill your pussy when I come. I'm going to give you so much."

As he spoke, he had aligned himself with her perfectly. One thrust, and he sank inside her, and she was so needy from his words that the sensation of him stretching her was enough to make her spend again. A tremor shook through her, and she cried out with her release, her walls clenching on him.

"I knew it," he said, withdrawing from her only to thrust deep again. "You were made for me, sweetheart. Your cunny is so fucking perfect. So tight and wet and hot. You feel so good."

Heaven help her, but she *liked* when he described that part of herself. Liked hearing how she felt. It was wicked, she knew. But she didn't care. She began to move with him, meeting him thrust for thrust.

"Yes, sweetheart," he ground out. "That's it. I love watching your pretty pink pussy take every inch of me. Come on my cock. I want you to coat me with your cream."

She felt dangerously near to doing so. Her body had never been so unbearably stimulated. It was as if every part of her was intensely aware, her nipples tight points that abraded the bedclothes with every thrust, her bottom connecting with his thighs, his cock impaling her. It was beyond anything she could have imagined. Closing her eyes, she surrendered to sensation, becoming one with him. His fingers delved between her thighs again, stroking her pearl, and that was all it took.

She flew apart, pleasure arching through her, her cry throaty and animalistic, torn from some primitive place within her that she hadn't known existed. He moved faster, groaning low, pumping in and out until he sank deep and then the hot rush of his seed flooded her. Her heart pounded as he collapsed, his chest a hot wall at her back, his lips brushing over her nape, her shoulder, his cock still filling her.

"That was incredible," he said raggedly, dropping another kiss on the side of her throat before he withdrew from her body. "The way we are together, it's madness."

He rolled to his back at her side, his skin flushed from his exertion, so masculine and beautiful. She was too sated to move, so she remained as she was, admiring him.

"The best madness," she managed, finding her ability to speak once more.

He cupped her cheek, giving her a slow smile. "The best, indeed."

Stuart drew her against his side, lifting the bedclothes over them, and she snuggled against his warmth, her earlier weariness returning. He kissed her crown tenderly. "Get a bit of rest, sweetheart. You must be exhausted after all this travel."

She was, and he felt so wonderful.

"Perhaps for a few minutes," she allowed with a yawn.

He stroked her bare back in soothing motions beneath the covers, and within moments, Rosamund fell headlong into slumber.

CHAPTER 14

"*How* ow much longer do I need to remain still?" Stuart asked Rosamund.

At her request, he was seated on a chair in the sitting room, where she had chosen to set up her watercolors. The sitting room itself was decorated sparsely, much of the furniture outmoded. The chair wasn't particularly well padded or comfortable. But the chamber did enjoy the brightness of the morning's sunshine, thanks to the wall of windows facing eastward. She had chosen it for that reason, she'd told him when she had lured him here after breakfast.

"Just a bit longer," she said, frowning down at her work, her brush hovering over the canvas.

They had settled into a glorious routine here at Gilden Hall, a place he had never particularly cared for until he had brought his wife here. Despite its general shabbiness and the repairs it required, the old edifice had begun to feel like home over the course of their idyll. He'd never expected to enjoy Rosamund so much. But enjoy her—and most thoroughly—he did in every way. As evidence, he was presently sporting a cockstand that no amount of subtly adjusting his trousers or forcing himself to think prick-wilting thoughts could cure.

Because the more he had of Rosamund, the more he wanted her. He would have sworn it was an impossibility, the feverish way he desired her, had he not experienced it firsthand.

"My arse is getting sore," he complained. "Perhaps you might finish your portrait later."

In truth, watching her paint him had proven such exquisite torment that he was nearly going out of his head with desire. How did she expect him to remain perfectly still, in the same room with her, whilst she was wearing a Prussian-blue dress that showed off her lush breasts and her gorgeous curves? To make matters worse, the entire affair had a tempting line of black buttons on the bodice that begged to be undone. He'd contemplated opening them by any means he could devise—fingers, teeth, and even a knife.

"Don't be disagreeable," she chided in the same tone she used for his nemesis, her parrot.

"Or what?" he couldn't resist asking. "You'll not give me my pistachio?"

With a naughty smile, she continued with her brush, dabbing delicately at some of the paint on her palette before applying it to the vignette she was capturing. "Don't be silly. I know it's not pistachios you want."

"You're damned right," he said, maintaining his stillness. "What I want is you."

Rosamund kept her attention on her art, adding a bit more paint from her palette. "If you had your way, you'd be having me all day long."

Of course he would.

His cock liked the prospect of that far too much. He was going to have to invest in looser trousers.

"And the problem with that is?" he asked, hoping she wouldn't take note of the effect she had on him.

Because if she did, he would abandon the chair altogether, and despite her insistence to the contrary, her watercolor was going to have to wait. He would bend her over the settee and fuck her silly.

Damn it, he had to stop all such thoughts at once.

"You'd wear me out," she said lightly.

"Ha!" He grinned. "You're insatiable."

Yes, his formerly innocent spinster had been thoroughly debauched. And much to his delight, he had discovered she had a lusty appetite that matched his. Even better, she went wild when he said filthy things to her. Which was as often as he possibly could. Oh, she still stammered and struggled for words. But the way she had unabashedly embraced pleasure —hers and his—was a dream.

Pink colored her cheeks as she sent him a pointed look. "You mustn't say such things. There are servants about, and they'll hear you."

His grin deepened. "Let them. I'm besotted with my wife, and she cannot get enough of the pleasure I give her. Particularly my tongue and my big cock."

He was being ridiculous, but he couldn't help himself. He liked shocking her.

"Stuart." She bit her lower lip, looking at once scandalized and tempted. "Besotted, you say?"

He raised a brow, holding her gaze. "Do you doubt it?"

He had been following her about like a mongrel after a bitch in heat. He'd not apologize for it. There was something about Rosamund that made him nearly mad with desire. Her beauty, her inner naughty streak, her luscious breasts, her intelligence, her silken hair, her self-possession —these were all qualities he admired, and not particularly in that order. They seemed to be a combination that was uniquely hers, and that combination made him drunk on lust.

He wouldn't apologize for it.

Nor would he allow worries about what would happen when they returned to London to intrude on their happiness. He would fret over his blackmailer, his mother, and his arsehole of a brother when their honeymoon was at an end—and not a moment sooner.

"Is this not how it is for you with all your lovers?" she asked, returning her attention to the portrait, her brush moving again.

"No," he said honestly. "It is not. I've never experienced the heights of pleasure with another that I have with you."

Her honey-brown eyes jolted back to his. "You haven't?"

He shook his head slowly. "No, sweetheart. I haven't."

What they shared was rare and unique, at least based upon his own storied history. He had bedded women aplenty, it was true. But Rosamund was…different.

"Are you bamming me?" she asked softly.

He hated that she doubted what they had. Perhaps her reticence was yet from what had happened with Wesley.

"I would never joke about what is between us," he told her, entreating her with his eyes.

She nodded. "Thank you. I have enjoyed our time together immensely, but as I have no comparison, I wasn't sure what to think."

Such a practical woman, his Rosamund. She strove to view everything through logic. Undoubtedly, it was one of the reasons she had been able to successfully carry on her father's business ventures after his death. She had opened up to Stuart considerably during their time together, and he had been astounded to learn that she alone continued to run Payne's empire, overseeing her man of business, shipping, antiquities, and other ventures.

"It is rare," he reassured her.

"Good." As swiftly as she had allowed her calm mask to slip and her emotions to show, she turned back to her portrait, straightening her spine. "I'm almost finished painting you. If you would just turn your head slightly to the left, toward the window, however. I do believe you've shifted your posture."

Rosamund didn't want to further examine what was happening between them. Fair enough. He didn't want to do that either. For now, he simply wanted to enjoy it. To savor it. To savor *her*. Everything about her and about their marriage was so damned unexpected.

He corrected his posture as she had directed. "How is this?"

"A bit more to the left," she advised, studying him with the cool air of an artist rather than the heated stare of a lover. "A bit more. Now, tip your chin up, just a hint, toward me."

He did as she asked, but then a new idea took hold of him, and he deliberately moved his chin to the window. "Like this?"

"No." She frowned at him. "In my direction, not in the window's direction, if you please. The light has changed with the sun moving, and I want to see if I can have your face bathed in the late-morning glow again."

This time, he made an exaggerated motion with his chin and shifted his right shoulder.

"Let me help you," she said finally, frustration evident in her voice as she replaced her paintbrush in its crystal holder and rose from her seat, shaking out her skirts with a sigh.

She brought with her the seductive scents of rose, violet, bergamot, and ambergris, blended together into a decadent floral lure. He inhaled and maintained the pretense of his confusion, which forced her to lean over him, cupping his face and angling it the way she wanted.

214

"There," she said, sounding breathless as she placed a hand on his shoulder and pressed it down as well. "I do believe this is how you were originally seated, with the light playing across your face just as it is now."

Stuart decided he had grown weary of posing. He had Rosamund where he wanted her. Well, *almost* where he wanted her. That could be remedied, however. He hooked his right arm around her waist and hauled her into his lap with one swift motion. She fell atop him with a squeak of surprise.

"Stuart!"

"I like it when you chastise me," he told her. "Go on. Do it again."

Her eyes went wide as, undoubtedly, through the layers of her gown and undergarments, she felt the exact effect she was having upon him.

"Oh my." Her cheeks were flushed. She was so fucking gorgeous, and her skirts were billowing around her, so bountiful that the two of them scarcely fit together in this bloody chair, and he didn't care.

He had lured her away from her portrait, and now, she was in his arms and he wasn't about to let her go. With his left hand, he smoothed some of her skirts out of the way before settling it on her waist in a possessive hold.

"Do you have any idea how much torture it is to watch you from across the room and not be able to touch you?" he asked, nuzzling her throat.

"It's only been two hours," she protested.

"It felt like bloody eternity," he grumbled, noting the way she softened in his arms, the protest seeping out of her. "Tell me, did you feel nothing as you painted me?"

"Nothing at all," she said, tilting her head back for him to ply her neck with kisses.

Stuart strung a path of kisses to her jaw. "I think you're

lying." Ever so gently, he nipped her there. "But the truth is proven easily enough." He kissed the corner of her lips. "All I need to do is slide a hand beneath your skirts and find the slit in your drawers. If your pussy is drenched, then I know you weren't telling me the truth."

"Why, Your Grace," she protested, pretending maidenly outrage. "I'm shocked that you would suggest something so very untoward."

"I'm a very untoward man," he told her unapologetically. "Shall I prove it to you?"

"I'm trying to paint your portrait," she said, laughing as he drew her hems up past her knees. "I'll never have it finished with so much distraction."

"Do you know what I think, my dear?" He lifted her skirts a bit higher, caressing her outer thigh as he did so.

And promptly discovered that his very naughty minx of a wife wasn't even wearing any drawers.

"You wonderful woman," he praised, dragging her hems even higher. "You seem to have forgotten a rather important undergarment."

"Oh dear," she said, biting her lip as she gazed at him with an unapologetically sensual air. "Have I?" She shifted, parting her legs for him. "You'll have to tell me which one."

He caressed the satiny, warm skin of her thigh even higher, the heat blossoming from her cunny beckoning to him like a lighthouse on shore calling in lost sea captains. This was where he belonged. He knew every inch of her intimately already. Had committed to memory every part of her that earned him the greatest sighs, that made her writhe, that made her wet. And oh, what a glorious education it had been.

He dragged a lone finger over her folds, gratified at the moisture kissing his fingertip. She was hot and soaked, and he was as randy as a young man about to shag his first woman. After the torment of remaining still with her gaze traveling over him like a caress, he couldn't wait to be inside her.

"I do believe it's your drawers that seem to be missing, Duchess," he told her, keeping his voice hushed so that it wouldn't carry beyond the closed sitting room door.

He had no wish to embarrass her. Their games were for the two of them alone. And indeed, whenever they were together, it felt quite as if they were the only ones in all the world.

"Silly me," she lamented insincerely. "Perhaps I was distracted this morning when I dressed."

"Or," he said carefully, parting her folds and finding her swollen clitoris, "you intentionally took them off because you knew you'd be painting me this morning, and because you are a very bad, naughty duchess. One who likes to get fucked often."

He circled her nub once, twice, keeping his touch light and teasing, without giving her the pressure he knew she craved. "Is that why you aren't wearing any drawers, madam? Is it because you wanted me to give you my cock and all the spend I've been saving for you since dawn?"

"Oh sweet heavens, Stuart," she gasped out, her hips chasing his fingers. "Must you say such filthy things to me?"

"Yes, because you love it." He made another light swirl over her pearl, tormenting her, bringing her to the edge. "It makes your gorgeous cunny so very wet."

"I'm wicked, aren't I?" she asked, undulating against his hand, on her knees as she sat astride him, her billowing gown covering everything that was happening.

Pity. He would have loved to see her all pink and glistening. To sink his tongue deep inside her and suck her clitoris until she screamed. But this particular position didn't allow for such luxuries.

He rubbed her harder, faster, rewarding her. "You *are*

SCARLETT SCOTT

wicked, Duchess. And there is only one way to atone for your sins."

She was panting now, riding his finger, her expression a mix of ecstasy and determination. "What is that?"

"Ride my cock," he told her, withdrawing his fingers and moving them instead to the fall of his trousers. With a few deft motions, he had them undone, and his cock sprang free beneath the shielding dome of her skirts.

Somehow, being fully clothed—at least as far as his eye could see—heightened the experience. It made this feel so much more forbidden. He gripped his thick shaft, presenting it to her.

Wordlessly, she rose up, then lowered herself, inch by inch. He held himself still, her entrance finding his cock with unrelenting precision. Slowly, surely, she took him inside her, her greedy cunny bathing him in a vise of tight, slippery heat. It was perfect. *She* was perfect. His head fell back, and he watched her, his beautiful wife, always assured and poised, coming undone for him, his cock wedged deep within her.

If anyone were to open the door, they would see nothing more scandalous than a wife sitting on her husband's lap. He had debauched her most thoroughly during their short marriage, and he didn't regret it one bit. Watching Rosamund embrace her sensual nature was a revelation. A true aphrodisiac.

"Oh, that feels wonderful," she breathed at his cock seated inside her, stretching her wide.

"Fuck me," he urged her. "Take your pleasure. Use me to get what you need."

He didn't need to tell her twice. Rosamund rose until he almost fell free and then sank down on him again, the throaty sound of bliss she made enough to make his cock pulse within her. He had spent himself inside her just that morning. Indeed, each day of their honeymoon had been spent alternately eating, talking, and fucking. If he didn't have her with child by the time it came to an end, he would be amazed.

And somehow, that notion made him harder still.

He surrendered himself to the exquisite sensation of her fucking him, riding his cock as the chair creaked around them, threatening to give way, and the sun shone on them both, gilding them in late-afternoon warmth. It was too good. So good. Exquisitely, wonderfully good. Just as each time with Rosamund had been. He had to clench his jaw to keep his climax at bay as she worked him in and out of her pussy's delicious grip. He longed to rip open her bodice and tear at her corset so he could suck her nipples, but there wasn't sufficient time.

He could feel the pleasure building at the base of his spine, white-hot and potent. His balls ached. More, more, more. She rode him faster, harder. And then, with a cry, she came, clamping down on him, her cunny nearly squeezing him from her velvet depths. He clamped his hands on her waist and held her there, her pussy fluttering around him, so hot, so wet, milking him. A few thrusts of his own, and he was gone, his hips pumping to meet her, sinking his cock deep as he came and came and came, his seed a hot flood within her, his vision going black around the edges.

Stuart drew her to him, giving her a long, slow kiss on the mouth, before releasing her. "Now, sweetheart, you can finish your portrait."

She stared at him, skin flushed, eyes glassy, looking dazed and sated. "Perhaps I can finish it tomorrow instead."

He grinned and kissed her again.

This woman. He was so damned grateful she was his.

CHAPTER 15

*R*osamund gave the wooden boat floating at the edge of the Gilden Hall lake a dubious look.

"Are you certain it's seaworthy?" she asked Stuart.

As a Londoner born and bred, she could not swim. And whilst her husband had assured her that punting could be a wonderful diversion, she was not convinced.

"I don't reckon I would take her on the sea." He flashed her a grin that was almost boyish, looking indecently handsome with the sun shining on his country tweed and dapper hat, his eyes twinkling merrily into hers. "However, I think she'll do just fine on the lake."

When he chose to be charming, the effect was nothing short of devastating. Their honeymoon was soon at an end, which was just as well. Because she needed the stern reminder of the life that awaited them in London to keep her from falling any further beneath this magnetic rake's spell.

Stop mooning over how handsome he is, Rosamund, she ordered herself, turning her attention back to the punt, which looked as if it had been sitting on the edge of the lake, forlornly awaiting its fate, for at least as long as Stuart had been alive.

"How old is it?" she asked suspiciously.

"*She*, sweetheart," he corrected. "A ship is always a female."

The derelict vessel in question was nowhere near a ship. But Rosamund decided not to argue the point.

"Forgive me for my lapse. How old is *she*?" she tried again. "She looks rather…weathered."

"Seasoned," her husband told her, taking up a pole that looked equally as ancient as the punt itself. "Don't let her hear you calling her weathered. Females have very delicate feelings. You're likely to hurt hers. Call her seasoned instead."

He was being absurd, and equally absurdly, she found it impossibly endearing. Over the course of their time together in Hertfordshire, she had discovered that Stuart possessed a lighthearted, silly side she'd never guessed at. He could make her laugh and smile with such dedicated ease that it was almost frightening.

Was he trying to make her fall in love with him?

Rosamund banished the foolish question, shocked her mind had even arrived at such a conclusion. She didn't love Stuart. She was fond of him, yes. She'd enjoyed the time they had been spending together and getting to know him better as well. But nothing had altered. She was still a pragmatic businesswoman who had married him so that she might have a family, and he was still the duke who had married her to pay off his many debts.

"Is something amiss?" Stuart asked, jolting her from her thoughts as she realized he had turned his attention back to her.

She forced a smile. "Of course not. Why do you ask?"

"You look distressed." He frowned, moving toward her. "Are you afraid to go punting? If you are, I'll not force you. I thought you would enjoy it."

She wasn't about to tell him that her unease was caused by the wayward ramblings of her inner musings. Nor about the feelings she was unintentionally developing for him. Let him think it was the old punt that was her greatest source of worry.

"I'm not afraid," she reassured him. "I merely want to make certain the boat won't take on water the moment we're in the midst of the lake."

"If it does, I'll swim you to the shore," he said with a gallant air.

"You can swim?"

"I learned in this very lake as a lad."

For a wistful moment, she tried to imagine what Stuart must have looked like as a young boy, swimming in the sparkling, still waters before them. Then she wondered what their son might look like, were they to have one, and all those warm, fluttery feelings she was doing her utmost to ignore returned.

Clearly, she needed a diversion. Punting on the lake in a dilapidated wooden boat was preferable to lingering on the unsettling feelings that had blossomed for her husband and continued to grow.

"Very well," she relented, needing to keep her mind from such unsettling thoughts. "I'll go punting with you, as long as you promise to save me should we sink."

He took her hand in his and settled it into the crook of his elbow. "I promise. Besides, the lake is filled with silt. It's grown quite shallow. You could likely wade to shore."

She allowed him to lead her to the waiting punt and help her to get in—not a particularly easy feat with the way the boat dipped and swayed as she lifted her hems and stepped one booted foot into the hull. He put a hand on her waist, steadying her.

"I have you," he said softly.

And *oh*, the effect those words had on her. Her foolish, foolish heart. His presence, strong and reassuring at her back, his hands on her, guiding her—it made her feel wonderfully *protected*. Protected in a way she had never felt from a man before.

Father had protected her, of course. He had doted on her too. Cherished her. He had encouraged her, been proud of her. But although she understood she had been fortunate to have a father who treated her as equally as he would have any son, a father who adored her unconditionally, he had still been her father. He had not been a suitor, a beau, a husband.

She had to cease this nonsensical thinking of hers.

With a haste she instantly regretted, Rosamund straightened and jerked away from Stuart's hold, making the old boat rock wildly and the calm waters of the lake splash up the sides. She stumbled, catching her boot in her hems, and nearly pitched over the opposite side into the water. It was only her husband's quick thinking that saved her. A jerk on the rear of her skirts halted her forward motion, and, gasping for breath as her corset cinched her waist from her ungainly pose, she turned to find Stuart had caught her skirts in his fist, keeping her from falling overboard.

His expression was taut with concentration and worry. "Trust me, Rosamund. I won't allow any harm to befall you, this I swear."

"Thank you," she managed as she grasped the edge of the punt, trying to salvage what remained of her pride after nearly falling into the lake. "You can release me now. I won't go overboard. You needn't concern yourself with my welfare."

He gave her an odd look she couldn't quite decipher. "You are mine to look after now, and I intend to do precisely that."

His words were so unexpected that, coupled with her thoughts about Father and her heightened emotions, they caused tears to prickle the backs of her eyes. Her vision swam, but she blinked furiously, chasing that weakness, that insistent vulnerability she refused to acknowledge.

She was made of sterner stuff. She was Rosamund Payne, and she was a businesswoman in her own right.

"I can look after myself," she told him pointedly. "Just as I have been doing."

A slight smile curved his lips. "I didn't say you couldn't look after yourself, sweetheart. You are, without doubt, the most capable and intelligent and independent woman I know. But that doesn't mean I'm not here to catch you when you need me. To keep you from falling headlong into the water, or whatever it is you require in a given moment."

Curse him. Why did he have to somehow always say what she needed to hear?

Rosamund forced herself to remain unmoved, offering him a curt nod. "Thank you."

With painstaking care, she sank onto the bench seat, maintaining her poise as best she could and mercifully keeping the boat from swaying too much. But it was impossible to keep her gaze from Stuart as he stepped into the punt as well, his motions fluid and graceful. Grasping the long wooden pole, and still standing, he used it to push them into the lake.

The boat glided with surprising ease, traveling with a few bobs from side to side. Rosamund cast her eyes around the punt's interior, looking for any indications that they were taking on water, and thankfully found none thus far.

"Searching for leaks?"

Stuart's amused voice had her gaze returning to him with a start, heat creeping up her throat. "I don't see any yet. Should you not sit down now that we are moving?"

He grinned, standing at the bow, apparently unperturbed by the subtle swaying of the boat on the water as he punted them deeper into the lake. "I'm touched by your wifely concern, but I won't fall in, I promise."

Wifely concern. Was that what this feeling was, tight and inescapable coiled within her? She didn't know, nor did she want to examine it, for fear of what she might discover about herself. Because she was beginning to suspect that this feeling was far more than that, that it ran deeper. It was dangerous, this feeling. And she refused to allow herself to entertain it.

"See that you don't," was all she said, turning her head and adjusting the brim of her hat to account for the sun reflecting off the water. "I have no wish to be stranded in the midst of this lake on a rotten old boat."

He chuckled. "The boat is hardly rotten. She is only taking on a bit of water."

She glanced back toward him, alarmed. "It is?"

But her husband was grinning, looking as carefree as she had yet seen him. "I was only jesting, sweetheart. She's as watertight as ever."

She stared at him, that feeling inside her growing, and swallowed down a rising lump in her throat. "You seem at home here. The countryside is good for you, I think."

"Perhaps it is *you* who is good for me," he countered, his smile fading, his countenance serious.

He was being charming again. Gallant. She forced her eyes back to the water, a far safer place.

"You needn't woo me," she said quietly. "You've already won me."

"I don't think I've won you just yet," he said thoughtfully. "But I'm determined to try."

If only he knew. But she wouldn't tell him. Rosamund would never allow herself to be vulnerable again. No amount of drugging kisses, courtly promises, captivating grins, or knowing caresses could change that.

"I'm your wife. I do believe that is as much victory as you shall have," she said primly.

"There is always more."

A seductive note had entered his voice, one she recognized.

"You're being fanciful," she told him.

"There's nothing fanciful about what I want to do to you," he promised. "Have you ever had your cunny licked in a punt in the middle of a lake?"

His words sent molten heat to pool between her thighs even as he scandalized her. "Naturally not."

His pole dipped into the water again with a small splash, and they coasted closer to the lake's center. "Then I shall have to rectify the matter at once."

"Stuart," she protested when he settled the pole inside the hull and stepped toward her, making the boat sway wildly under the force of his motion. "You'll capsize us and send us both into the water."

"No, I won't." He dropped to his knees on the scarred old bottom of the boat, which couldn't have been comfortable at all. "You see? We're still afloat."

"Yes," she agreed breathlessly. "We are. But you're not going to...we cannot...it's the afternoon, and we are out of doors where anyone could see."

Calmly, he removed his hat, revealing the silken dark strands that had hidden gold lights in them brought out by the sun. "You know how hard my cock gets when you turn into a maiden spinster, sputtering over your words."

"Stuart," she tried again, with meaning.

He took her hems in his hands and slowly raised them up her ankles, past her boots, and higher. "Yes, darling?"

"I could never…not in a boat…"

"You can, and you will." Her hems went to her knees now.

She was on fire, and it had nothing to do with the sun blazing overhead. "But…"

"Hush," he interrupted softly, nudging her legs apart as he pooled her silken skirts in her lap. "Allow me to demonstrate."

Her husband's head disappeared beneath her voluminous gown, and she felt the flick of his tongue over her, and all other objections swiftly fled.

"Oh my…" He lapped at her clitoris, then sucked. "Goodness," she hissed.

This was indecent. Scandalous. Depraved. They were in sight of the manor house, even if a spacious distance stretched between the lake and Gilden Hall. But there was something thrilling about being in the open air with him, in this boat, on the water, with the sun gilding them in a warm glow and the birds calling in the trees and the rhythmic, pleasant sound of water splashing at the sides of the punt.

His tongue found her entrance, and he licked into her, the hot, velvet glide almost too much for her to bear. Her every sense was acutely heightened. His hands were on her hips, holding her in place for him to devour. She clenched the layers of her gown and undergarments in a tight grip, keeping them pinned to her lap as his tongue sank in and out of her channel in a wet mimicry of lovemaking. She moaned, scooting her bottom forward on the bench seat, pressing herself to his face.

He growled in response, his efforts growing more concentrated and demanding as he returned to her pearl, licking, stroking, suckling, even nipping lightly with his teeth. As he lavished attention on the greedy bud of her sex, he sank two fingers inside her, thrusting them deep, finding the place that brought all the desire within her to a crescendo.

Her eyes fluttered closed, her head tipping back, and she surrendered herself to the glorious sensation he was visiting upon her. To the pleasure. He sucked hard, his fingers gliding slickly through her wetness, and she came with a cry that echoed off the shimmering water, shattering the stillness of the day. When the last pulse of bliss ebbed from her, he kissed her between her legs and then emerged, flipping down her skirts in the same motion.

His handsome face was etched with desire, his lips glistening as he gave her a slow, beautiful smile that made her toes curl in her boots. "I hope I've given you a new appreciation for punting."

She struggled to find her wits and her breath, before finally answering, "Boating on the lake was far more enjoyable than I anticipated. We should do it again."

"There's my wicked duchess." He drew one of her hands to his lips for a soft, reverent kiss. "I knew I could persuade you."

Rosamund knew in that sun-drenched moment, in the midst of the Gilden Hall lake, that her heart was in grave peril. And she needed to do everything in her power to keep herself from falling for her husband.

"My heavens, this must have been a wonderful edifice at one time," Rosamund exclaimed at his side, her enthusiasm making him smile as they approached the late-fifteenth-century Tudor ruins that had been abandoned back in the early seventeenth century for the present Gilden Hall's manor house.

"It was a grand house at one point," he agreed solemnly.

She was dressed in a bright-blue silk walking gown with black velvet trim and a line of buttons down the bodice that had made his fingers itch to undo them from the moment she'd emerged from her bedroom earlier. On her head, she wore a matching bonnet with a jaunty cluster of silk flowers adorning the brim. She looked absolutely entrancing, and he couldn't wait to return home, strip her out of her gown, and make love to her.

But for now, he was escorting her through the Doric columns on the entry arch that still remained. Because Stuart had discovered a newfound pastime.

He enjoyed making his wife happy.

Not just pleasuring her—although that was another pastime with immense rewards that he'd discovered over the course of their marriage thus far. But making small gestures that made her smile. Humoring her by sitting for multiple watercolors. Finding a book of poetry in the library that he thought she might enjoy. Washing her hair when she was at her bath.

With each day that passed, Rosamund's walls of defense crumbled more and more. He was damned grateful for the progress they'd made, for he had come to realize something startling during the course of their honeymoon. He didn't just *like* his wife. He cared for her.

And a great deal.

So much that it would have alarmed him. The *old* him. The Stuart before Rosamund. The Stuart he was beginning to think had been adrift in a sea of nothingness, waiting for her to lure him to shore.

"Only just think of what it must have been like to walk through this when it was in its glory," she was saying, her voice hushed with awe.

Here was the woman who collected Roman antiquities in her father's mold. He felt embarrassingly profligate in her presence. The ruins had stood here all his life, and whilst he had explored them as a lad, he had never imagined what the old abbey would have looked like when it had been new.

"Queen Elizabeth visited here," he told her, knowing she would enjoy that bit of history which had never particularly interested him. "It would have been quite grand at that time."

"Why did you not bring me here sooner?" she demanded. "To think I might have missed this."

Their honeymoon was, unfortunately, waning. And all too soon, they would have to return to London. But he didn't want to think about that now.

"It's not much to look upon any longer." They walked through the entryway and back into the grass, where crumbling brick and limestone foundations delineated the place a room would have been. "I suppose I've grown rather accustomed to it. I only thought of bringing you here when you spoke of how you longed to see the ancient ruins in Greece. The travel distance to this ruin is significantly shorter, even if it isn't nearly as old as the Acropolis."

"I'm so glad you thought of it," she said, moving away from him, to where one of the original windows was still supported by a dilapidated wall.

The panes had long since been smashed and lost to the passing centuries.

Here was something else he enjoyed: admiring her. She had an expressive face, and her innate curiosity meant that she was often moving, investigating, her clever mind whirling. She also had a genius for a dressmaker. The way her gowns clung to her curves was nothing short of criminal. The day was warm enough that she didn't require a wrap, which meant that the lush nip of her waist was on full display.

Rosamund rejoined him, her countenance pensive. "It

seems a shame for a home so rich with history to simply molder like this. I wonder if we might restore it."

There wasn't much left of the abbey. It was rather akin to the skeleton of a fallen stag he had come upon once as a lad here at Gilden Hall—sparse bones all that remained of the once-proud creature.

"It would require a small fortune and an endless amount of work, I have no doubt," he said. "Such a tremendous outlay of money would never have been possible before."

Before he'd married her, he meant. Before her dowry had revived the Gilden family coffers and before she had brought with her the fortune she'd inherited, hers to direct as she pleased. She was silent for a few steps as they continued their meandering path through the ruins, and he feared he had overstepped by mentioning it at all.

"We have a great deal of other work awaiting us first," she said. "Perhaps one day."

They certainly did. And there was also the matter of keeping his brother's gambling debts reined in. To say nothing of the blackmailer. But those were worries for another day as well.

"Perhaps," he echoed.

They finished exploring the ruins and headed back toward the manor house. The walk wasn't far, and they made the trek while she regaled him with tales of some of her favorite antiquities and how they had come into her father's possession. It wasn't until they were settled into the drawing room, a tea tray laid out between them along with some light confections, that he recalled another subject he had wanted to speak with her about.

"How do you teach the feathered menace words?" he asked curiously, before taking a sip from his cup.

Rosamund had prepared it perfectly for him, just as he liked. Of course she had.

"Why?" She arched a brow, looking amused. "Do you intend to teach Megs something dreadful so that she will embarrass me even further before company?"

He pressed a free hand over his heart with a dramatic air. "I'm wounded that you think I would do something so Machiavellian."

She was not entirely wrong, but Stuart didn't bother to tell her that. It would spoil his fun.

"You must admit that it wasn't out of the realm of reason for me to make the assumption," she said archly.

And he couldn't disagree. She knew him so well already. He would fret over that alarming fact later. For now, he needed to learn her secret means of charming a parrot.

"Perhaps," he allowed, "but I can assure you that I have no nefarious intentions. I'm merely curious. It is quite intriguing how intelligent and loquacious she is. I've never known another parrot before."

Something in her countenance shifted, and there was suddenly a tenderness there that she often kept hidden. He wanted to kiss her. But that would distract her from giving him the information he required, so he tamped down the desire.

"You don't dislike her as much as you claim to, do you?" she asked.

"I wouldn't entirely say the two of us have called a truce, but seeing as how she has many more years to live and I fully intend to have the same, perhaps it is best if Megs and I might reach an understanding. If I know how her mind works, I shall be well ahead of myself."

He was evading the truth, dancing about it lightly. But Rosamund appeared to take him at his word. She nodded.

"Not all parrots are as social and eager to learn as Megs is," Rosamund explained. "Some are much more resistant to training. However, Megs enjoys new words. All she

232

requires is impetus, and it was quite easy once I learned her cues."

"Cues?"

"Her behavior tells me whether she is amenable to learning. If she is moving about and making sounds at me, the chances are far greater that she will enjoy a small session of learning. If she is tired or quiet, I know to wait until her mood improves. If she's in the proper mood, I place her on her perch and make sure no one else is about. It is imperative that she have a calm, quiet room, as she can get easily distracted."

By God, the parrot was not so dissimilar from a person. He didn't know what he had supposed the process would be like, but he hadn't imagined it would require such attention to detail.

"Of course," he offered. "Distraction is the very devil of a thing. I can't begin to count the number of times, just in this day alone, that I've been distracted by your breasts straining against your gown. It doesn't matter the time of day or the frock. Your bubbies look astonishingly lovely in everything you wear, and then I can scarcely concentrate on a word you say. I'm merely staring at you, thinking of the moment when I can strip the silk and corset and linen from your skin, and suck your pretty nipples until you come."

Her lips were parted as he finished, and there was no mistaking the way her pupils had darkened and grown. She was not unaffected by his words, though she remained a safe arm's length away.

Not at all.

He grinned. "Oh dear, have I shocked you, wife? I must confess, I wasn't certain such a thing would be possible. But let us get back to the subject, shall we? You were telling me how our feathered friend must not have any commotions."

Rosamund wetted her lips. "I…you…" she stammered in

that adorable way of hers, looking deliciously flustered. "My breasts are that great a source of distraction to you?"

His grin deepened. "The rest of you as well, my dear. I could go on if you would like."

"No." She shook her head vehemently this time. "That won't be necessary. We were talking about Megs."

If ever there was a topic of conversation that made his rampant prick wilt, here was one. Just as well. He did need to learn how to teach the damned nettlesome parrot to call him something far less insulting than *gormless shite*.

"Ah yes." He kept his tone magnanimous, as if he weren't drowning in lust for her at this very moment. "Do go on, my dear. What happens after the feathered beggar is on her perch?"

Rosamund's frown was instant. "You must cease referring to her by such names, you know."

"Must I? Well then, she is to also refrain from calling me a gormless shite," he said smoothly. "What comes after the perch?"

"When she is settled, I hold a treat before her, making sure it's level with her eyes," Rosamund continued.

Level with her silvery demon eyes? Did that mean he needed to look into them? Stuart barely suppressed a shudder at the notion. But for his wife, he would do anything. Even beguile a parrot.

"Not an entire pistachio for training," Rosamund continued, unaware of his uncharitable thoughts, "but a bit of a crushed one works wonders. I say the word I want to teach her, and then when she makes any sort of sound, I praise her and give her the pistachio. After a few rounds of this, I withhold the pistachio until she makes a sound that is closer to the word I'm trying to teach her. She adores praise, so I tell her what a smart bird she is, what a pretty bird, and then she usually preens. We do this in five-minute increments, with lengthy pauses in between, until she has mastered the word. If she needs a rest or grows weary, she begins to groom her feathers, and I know it's time to give her a respite."

"That sounds as if it requires a great deal of patience and time," he said, trying to quell his inner disappointment.

Of course it couldn't have been as easy as telling the parrot *repeat after me*. He couldn't lie. He'd rather hoped it would have been as simple.

"Teaching her did require some patience," Rosamund agreed. "Of course, she still has a mind of her own, as you have seen. Some of her favorite words tend to be the impolite ones, much to my chagrin. I can only imagine it is because of her former owner."

"You never did tell me how Miss Rosamund Payne became the caretaker of an African grey parrot who belonged to a sea captain," he reminded her.

"He was one of the finest captains in my father's shipping fleet," she explained with a wistful smile. "Captain William Vaughan was his name. Megs kept him company for several years after he was no longer able to captain his ship. He liked to pay calls upon my father at his offices and take coffee with him. He would always bring Megs, and of course, I spent a great deal of time with my father there as well. Megs took to me, as Captain Vaughan said. Just before he died, he told me that if anything were ever to befall him, he wanted me to have her. So I honored his wish."

Her voice broke a bit at the last, a sheen of tears making her eyes glisten. It was akin to a knife being stabbed into his gut, the sight of her grief.

"I'm sorry, sweetheart. If I had known it was a sad story, I wouldn't have asked."

She sniffled, forcing a smile that didn't reach her gaze. "You need not apologize. I miss the captain. But I miss my father as well. There was a great deal of death in a short period of time in my life. I don't suspect I shall ever truly recover from it. Not entirely."

Her raw admission touched something deep inside him. Stuart rose from his chair and opened his arms to her, not knowing any other means of comfort.

"Come here, Rosamund."

She didn't hesitate, setting down her tea and rising to close the distance between them. She burrowed into his chest, wrapping her arms around his waist. He held her tightly, pressing his face to her fragrant hair.

"I wish I had been there to comfort you then," he murmured thickly.

"You are here now," she said, her words muffled into his waistcoat.

Yes, he was, wasn't he? And he was thankful for it. Not because he had needed her fortune to dig himself out of the tremendous hole of debt in which he'd nearly been buried. But because the time he had spent with her recently was the happiest in his memory. She had brought passion and caring and kindness to his world, like a lamp lit to shine into his darkness. How astonishing that she should be his. How wondrous.

He kissed her part. "Yes, I am here now, yours to do with as you wish."

"As I wish?" Her head tipped back, and there was a lone tear that had slipped down her cheek, leaving a trail.

He couldn't resist lowering his head and drying up the salt of her sorrow with his lips. "As you wish," he repeated softly when he had finished.

She gave him a subtle squeeze. "I'm not certain you should give me so much power over you, husband."

"I ceded it to you long ago, whether you realized it or not," he said honestly. "You've changed me, and in the very best of ways, I think."

"Oh, Stuart. I do believe that is the sweetest thing you have said to me."

Another thought rose in his mind.

Marrying you has made me happier than I ever hoped to be.

The words were impetuous, impossible. How could they be true? This wasn't meant to be anything more than a marriage of convenience. He didn't dare speak them aloud for fear he was delusional. Had he fallen and hit his head? Was he feverish? He didn't feel as if he had gone mad, but perhaps he had.

He swallowed hard against a rush of emotion and tried for a lighter tone to disperse the heaviness of the moment. "I rather thought that bit I said about your bubbies earlier was sweet as well."

She laughed, and it was a beautiful sound. One he wished he could capture and store somewhere so that he might listen to it again and again. It was husky and sweet, mellifluous like her voice. But it was also the knowledge that he was the source of her laughter that moved Stuart.

"It was sinful," she told him, "and you know it. Moreover, I cannot believe it's true. I do think you merely wanted to shock me."

"I would never lie about something like that," he assured her. "Shall I offer you the evidence that I spoke truth?"

Her eyes widened. "Stuart."

He liked when she said his name with spinsterish outrage. It made his cock hard.

"Here, give me your hand, darling." He reached for her right hand with his left and brought it between their bodies, settling her palm over his straining cock. "You see? Proof that I'm hopeless when it comes to trying to ignore your potent allure."

Her fingers curled around his length, and she gave him a

brazen stroke from root to tip. "I'm not certain if this is proof," she said slowly.

"Oh?" It certainly felt that way to him.

He was near to coming in his trousers—and not for the first time when she was about.

She nodded, every inch the seductress. "I think you will have to show me to persuade me."

His cock thickened, and he thrust himself into her touch. "My beautiful, naughty wife. I do like the way you think."

CHAPTER 16

*I*t was the last day of their honeymoon.

The afternoon sun was bright and sparkling, the sky was blue, birds were winging through the air and singing their songs, and Rosamund was riding through the Gilden Hall estate with her husband at her side. She had to admit, Stuart seated a horse quite well. She was not nearly as skilled a horsewoman; she preferred city life and traveling in carriages. But she was not a complete novice when it came to riding. She was mustering her side saddle with what she hoped was at least a modicum of aplomb.

"How often do you come here to Gilden Hall?" she asked him as their horses trotted slowly alongside each other.

Her mount was a dappled mare named Lady, and his was a gelding called Alexander. The stables, much like the rest of the estate, were in dire need of restoration and attention. She had already suggested they hire additional hands to help the stable master and to bring in some new horseflesh. Gilden Hall was ripe for rearing horses, the land open and sprawling, a gurgling spring pouring into the lake that would serve well. With some fences and newly erected structures to house the animals, she had no doubt that they could begin thriving again.

"Not often," Stuart admitted, casting a wry glance in her direction. "Perhaps once every few years."

His response shocked her. She couldn't imagine owning such a vast property and yet visiting it so sparingly. "How do you manage it, then?"

"My steward does," he said. "We correspond regularly, and I trust him to make the decisions necessary to the daily running of the estate."

She tried to imagine allowing her man of business to conduct all her affairs without overseeing him. To imagine never paying a call to the shipping yard, never directing the opening of shipments, never visiting mines and factories, nor hearing the voices of those who worked within.

"That is rather ducal of you, I suppose," she allowed, trying to be politic.

She had been born and raised into a different social circle than his. Her father had been in trade all his life. Her mother was from a genteel family that was not aristocratic, but of modest means. Here was another reminder of how differently they must have been raised.

"You disapprove," Stuart said, more statement than question.

"I am merely surprised," she countered. "From the time I was a small girl, my father took me along with him on all his business calls. I didn't realize it then, but he was preparing me to be the one who would one day take the reins. After his death, I assumed his responsibilities. I couldn't do it without my man of business, Mr. Watts, of course. He has sometimes traveled on my behalf to pay calls to our mines and factories in the north, and I regard his counsel highly."

"You were close with your father, then?" Stuart asked.

Her heart gave a pang. "I was very close to him, yes. There

is not a day that passes without missing him." She blinked furiously as tears sprang to her eyes. "I suspect most of his associates thought him quite eccentric for carting his daughter about as he did. When I was small, he would hold me on his shoulder, rather like a parrot. It was a wonderful height from which to view the world."

"Little wonder you are so fond of the feathered menace," Stuart said teasingly, as if he sensed her need for lightness to distract from the heaviness of grief.

She smiled. "I'm sure I don't know who you're speaking of. My Megs is not a menace."

"On this, Duchess mine, we shall agree to disagree," he quipped.

They rounded a copse of trees in silence, the plodding of their horses' hooves and the cries of birds overhead the only sounds. Rosamund was grateful for this time to learn more about her husband.

"What of you and your father?" she asked, curious. "You said he was a wastrel and that your brother is in his mold. Was there no love lost between the two of you?"

It was a probing question, the sort she would never have dared ask him not long ago. But their honeymoon had brought them closer, and she found that she yearned to know everything there was to know about Stuart.

He was quiet for a few moments before he answered her. "I don't think my father was capable of loving anything other than his vices. He was callous at best and mercilessly cruel at worst. He spent the later years of his life gambling his way through what remained of the ducal coffers, drinking himself to oblivion, and bedding his mistress, until one day, he died in her arms. No one, I daresay not even that unfortunate woman, misses him."

The vitriol in his tone said as much as his harsh words did. Her heart ached for him.

"I'm sorry."

"Don't be. It's all over now, and he can no longer hurt anyone. His legacy of misery died with him."

"Did it truly?" She frowned. "What of your brother?"

A muscle tensed in his jaw. "I'll own that Wesley was his whipping boy. For all my brother's failings, it isn't entirely his fault that he's become what he is. Sometimes, I feel as if I'm to blame. I wonder if I had been able to protect him, would he have become the man that he is now?"

"I'm certain you did everything for him that you could, Stuart," she said soothingly.

One thing she had learned about her husband was that he was a good man, compassionate and kindhearted. He was benevolent with his servants, he loved his mother fiercely, and he allowed his brother far more patience than Wesley deserved. He always treated Rosamund with courteous care and concern. He was nothing like the last Duke of Camden. Of that, she was sure.

Stuart shook his head, his countenance taking on a haunted expression. "I could have done more. I should have. Had I known…" His words trailed off, and he sighed heavily.

She longed to comfort him, but she didn't know how.

"You mustn't blame yourself. Lord Wesley is his own man, and he has chosen the path upon which he finds himself."

"I'm sorry for the pain he's caused you," Stuart said, holding her gaze. "If I could take it on myself, I would."

And just like that, the realities of what would face them when they returned to London hit her. She would be beneath the same roof as Lord Wesley again.

"I learned an important lesson from him, one I shan't forget," she said, summoning a smile. "And now I'm made of much sterner stuff. He didn't break me. He only made me stronger."

"He didn't deserve you. I don't either, but I find I'm a selfish man where you're concerned. I'm damned glad your mine, Rosamund."

His words warmed her. She hadn't known how this marriage of convenience would fare. It had been a risk. But thus far, it was one she was pleased she had taken.

"Thank you," she said softly. "That is kind of you to say."

"I mean it," he insisted, his expression earnest.

Part of her still found it impossible to believe that he would want her for herself. That he respected and appreciated her, instead of merely needing her fortune. These were dangerous notions to her pride and her heart. She had trusted once before, and she had discovered just how easily fooled she had been.

But something deep within her wanted to believe this was different. If Stuart had only wanted her for her fortune, he wouldn't have brought her to Gilden Hall on a honeymoon. He wouldn't make love to her as he did. Nothing between them felt like duty. Rather, it had begun to feel alarmingly *genuine*.

And that was a concern as well.

"What will you do about Lord Wesley's gambling debts?" she asked, needing to change the subject.

He sighed again. "I'm at my wits' end with him. Wesley knows that I will do whatever I must to protect our mother, and he has been using that weakness against me for years."

Here was her chance to speak with him about the blackmail as well, she realized. But she would have to do so with care.

"You love your mother very much, don't you?" she asked.

"I do," he instantly affirmed. "She is the only good to have come from the damned house of Gilden. She did everything in her power to keep my father's wrath and the worst of his sins from us. I would lay down my life for her."

Rosamund studied Stuart, sensing the turbulent emotion rolling off him. "What do you protect her from?"

They had approached a small cluster of ash trees, and he slowed his mount. "Let's tether the horses and walk for a few moments."

She followed suit, slowing Lady and then bringing her to a halt. Rosamund watched as Stuart secured Alexander to an ash trunk before he turned to her, offering her a hand to help dismount. Though they both wore gloves, the placement of her hand in his still sent a jolt of awareness through her. She slid from her side saddle and landed on the uneven ground, swaying a bit as she lost her footing. He held her and kept her from falling, his hands on her waist.

"Steady," he murmured.

She couldn't help but to notice how handsome he looked today, wearing country tweed and riding boots, a dashing hat atop his head. It was still something of a shock, after all the intimacies they had shared, that he was her husband. Almost like a dream she had wandered into, too good to be true.

"I'm fine," she reassured him, a trifle breathlessly. "See to Lady."

He nodded and released her, securing her mount to a nearby tree as well before returning, his arm extended. She took it, and they began walking back along the path they had traveled, Rosamund waiting patiently for Stuart to speak.

"My mother is an invalid, as you know," he began. "She suffered a stroke that nearly killed her. In the years since, she has gradually convalesced as best as she is able. However, her physician made it plain that she is not to endure anything that would cause her upset."

"Anything like enmity between her sons, you mean," she said, understanding.

"She was so near to death, Rosamund," he said, his voice cracking with emotion. "I thought she was lost to us forever.

That she recovered at all is a miracle, and one for which I'm willing to pay the devil."

"That is why you pay your brother's debts, then."

"I know how it sounds. I should be able to keep better control over him, but tightening the purse strings only makes him more frivolous. And my mother has always doted on him. Wesley has long been her favored son, in part, I believe, because she feels guilty over the hell my father put him through. She has made me promise to take care of Wesley, and I gave her my oath as a gentleman and as her son that I would."

Her heart hurt for him anew. What a terrible burden for him to bear, saddled with a wastrel drunkard of a brother who ceaselessly gambled away funds and the promise he had made to his invalid mother.

"Have you ever tried speaking with her about your brother's gambling?" she asked gently.

"I have, and it did not go well. She accused me of being distraught over what happened with Lady Flora Seaton."

Stuart's betrothed. Hearing the other woman's name aloud sent a spark of jealousy shooting through her before she could tame it. *This is a marriage of convenience*, she reminded herself sternly. Besides, Lady Flora was in the past. There was no need for Rosamund to be envious.

She gave his arm a gentle squeeze of compassion. "Were you distraught?"

"At the time it happened, of course I was. But it was years ago now, and my anger toward Wesley runs far deeper than that lone betrayal."

Perhaps not entirely the answer she had sought, but she appreciated his honesty. Even if the notion of Stuart being heartbroken over another woman left her feeling vaguely ill.

"Did you explain that to your mother?" she asked.

A muscle in his jaw tensed. "When I tried, she grew

agitated, and I was reminded that I wasn't to upset her in any way. I couldn't bear it if I were to cause her any harm."

"And so you continue paying your brother's gambling debts, allowing him to live at your town house, and sacrificed yourself in marriage to save you all from ruin," she concluded.

He gave her a tender look. "I would hardly call marrying you a sacrifice, sweetheart. It has turned out to be a fine decision. The best I've ever made, in fact."

She wondered if he was saying so for her benefit or if he truly meant those words. Best not to examine it too much, her vulnerable heart decided.

"The secret you've been so intent upon keeping, the reason you've been blackmailed," she said instead, at last addressing the blackmail that had been troubling her, "is it your mother's?"

He stiffened beneath her touch, drawing their leisurely walk to a halt as he turned to stare down at her, his expression rigid. "Rosamund, don't."

"Why not?" She searched his gaze. "If you tell me, perhaps I can help you."

"There is nothing you can do, and the payment has been made. The problem is at an end now. You mustn't fret over it. I've handled it."

"What makes you think this blackmailer of yours—whoever he may be—will settle at this payment?"

"Because I've made it clear that this will be the final payment I offer, and it was a more than ample sum. I'll not beggar the estates again."

"But if you are willing to pay a small fortune to keep this secret, does it not stand to reason that you will pay more?" she pressed gently. "Do you not think this villain will continue to want payment? What shall you do then?"

"I don't know, but I will manage it, should that come to

pass. As I said, you need not worry, my dear. This is my alba-tross to bear, not yours."

He was being polite, smiling at her as if he hadn't a care. But the smile didn't reach his eyes. And she didn't like the distance she suddenly felt, as if he'd retreated into his fortress and raised the portcullis before she could join him.

"I am your wife, Stuart," she said quietly, trying to hide her hurt. "How can I help but to worry?"

He lowered his head to press a chaste kiss to her forehead as if she were his sister, the brim of his hat colliding with hers and jostling it in the process. "I will manage it. This, I swear. The problem shan't affect you."

"You don't trust me," she said, the realization hitting her in the same moment as she spoke the words. "That's the true reason you won't tell me what this secret you keep is, isn't it? You needn't dance around the truth. Just say it."

"Rosamund, please. Let this go."

Likely, she ought to do so. She had no expectations from him, save the children he would hopefully one day give her. This business agreement was mutually beneficial, and no emotions were to be involved. And yet, over the course of their honeymoon, something had shifted. Now, she felt raw and sore inside, like a scraped knee. She felt as if she were allowing herself to feel more than lust for him, regardless of how foolish she knew it was.

"We need a plan in place for if he asks for more," she insisted, trying to approach the matter practically rather than with her jagged emotions. "Surely you agree. As long as the blackmailer is in possession of this secret, whatever it is, you will be in danger. He may ask for more and more until there is nothing left to give again."

But he was stubborn. "As I said, should that come to pass, I will take care of it, just as I have been before we married."

"*Taking care of it*, as you say, was paying this villain everything you had, and still, it wasn't enough," Rosamund pointed out.

"I may have been pockets to let, but I'm not an imbecile, Rosamund. I know all this." He clenched his jaw, an edge in his voice that she hadn't heard before.

Perhaps it was his pride that was stung. She tried to tell herself that, but his cool reticence felt like a rebuke. And after the closeness that had developed between them, it was akin to cold water tossed in her face.

She disengaged from him, needing some space, physically if not emotionally. "I hope you haven't forgotten that I retain control of the bulk of my fortune. I'll not be spending a farthing so that a blackmailer can keep a secret I'm not permitted to know."

His lips twisted into a derisive smile. "You needn't fear, my dear. I could never forget that you bought me."

She recoiled at his words, so harsh and unfeeling. The accusation was ugly, as were the implications. Plain spinster Rosamund. What had she been thinking, that this beautiful man had wanted her for any reason other than her fortune? *Heavens*, what a ninny she was. He had made it plain from the start what he was after. And now he had showered some attention upon her, and she wanted more.

Tears pricked at her eyes, but she refused to allow them to fall.

She held her head high and adjusted her hat, meeting his gaze. "I'm beginning to think I made a poor bargain."

With that, she spun away from him, blindly stalking back toward where their horses were tethered, mouthing at the grass, blissfully unaware of the tension roiling between the people who had left them there.

"Rosamund," he called, the crunch of his boots following after her.

She refused to stop or turn around. He had hurt her, and

she didn't like it. She wasn't meant to feel. She was meant to have children and live her own life. She wasn't meant to have emotions where he was concerned.

"Rosamund, wait," he called.

"I'm going to ride back," she told him. "I find I've grown weary."

Long fingers encircled her elbow from behind, halting her progress. "Please. Don't be cross with me."

She was more than cross with him. But she was vexed most of all with herself for somehow being enough of a fool to allow herself to be charmed by a second Gilden brother. What had she been thinking? This was but a temporary haven away from the rest of the world. Stuart was only making love to her so that he could fulfill his end of the bargain. She must not forget that.

Gathering herself, Rosamund turned back to him, pinning a smile on her lips. "I'm not cross. You've made your opinion clear, just as I have made mine. But I would like to return now. You are free to continue with your ride, of course. I wouldn't want to be a burden."

A muscle worked in his jaw. "You're not a burden."

"I am weary, Stuart," she said quietly. "I wish to return."

His light-blue eyes bored into hers for a long moment, until he finally relented, nodding. "Of course. I'll ride with you."

She nodded, saying nothing, firmly keeping her smile in place. This would serve as her reminder to never allow herself to believe their marriage could be anything more than one of convenience.

CHAPTER 17

*H*e had hurt Rosamund.

And Stuart hated himself for it.

Their carriage ride back to London presently held a funereal air for which he was wholly at fault. After he and Rosamund had ridden back to Gilden Hall yesterday, she had pleaded a headache and taken dinner in her room. When he had knocked at the door adjoining their chambers to inquire after her welfare, she had told him that she was well, but in need of rest. By breakfast, she had still been unsmiling and quiet, avoiding his gaze and keeping her conversation painfully polite.

Even when he had helped her into the carriage, she had kept her gaze carefully averted just as she was now, looking out the window at the slowly passing scenery instead of at him. From her place in her covered cage on the floor between them, Megs made a kissing sound.

"Gormless shite," she proclaimed.

And for once, he was completely in accord with the feathered menace. He *was* a gormless shite, and he deserved to be taken to task for his own stupidity.

"Do behave, Megs," Rosamund chastised in a hushed voice, still keeping her face turned to the Hertfordshire countryside beyond the window.

"She's not wrong," he said. "I *have* been a gormless shite."

And at last, his wife's head turned from the sea of sky and fields out the window to him. "Did I just hear you correctly?"

"Yes, you did." He raked a hand through his hair. "I'm sorry for distressing you yesterday. I was frustrated, and the burden of what awaits me in London was hanging heavily on me, and then my foolish pride had me saying something stupid."

"You said that I bought you," she reminded him. "As if you were a horse. Is that how you truly feel?"

He winced, wishing he could go back in time and recall those truly stupid words. "Of course not. I was being an arse."

"Arsehole, walk the plank," Megs said, then made another kissing sound.

"Language, Megs," Rosamund chided. "You must remember to be a good bird."

"What a pretty bird," Megs responded.

The carriage traveled through a rut that made the conveyance jostle from side to side. The parrot whistled. Stuart was trapped in Bedlam. A Bedlam of his own making, it was true.

"Please forgive me, Rosamund," he tried again. "You did not deserve my anger or frustration. I was being an insufferable, vainglorious prig."

She gave him a small, sad smile. One that didn't reach her eyes. "I think you were being honest, Stuart. We have enjoyed our honeymoon, but the reasons for our marriage have not changed. I overstepped as well. This is a business arrangement between the two of us, and I was allowing my emotions to get the better of me yesterday. It shan't happen again."

He didn't like the sound of that. Not one whit. Nor did he

like the lack of passion and fire in her voice. Or the way she had referred to their marriage as a business arrangement. That stung. Because while it had once been true, what they had shared this last fortnight had taken them well beyond the bounds of a marriage of convenience.

Until he had dashed their tentative happiness to pieces yesterday.

She averted her gaze again, looking back out the window before he could respond.

"Look at me, Rosamund," he commanded softly.

"I am enjoying the scenery," she said.

Damn her. She was being stubborn. He skirted the cage containing Megs, which was on the floor between them, striking his head on the carriage roof in the process, and then knocked his shoulder into the door, adding insult to injury. But finally, he wedged himself onto the Moroccan leather at Rosamund's side.

"Look at me," he repeated.

She did, her expression startled and uncertain. They were pressed together on the squabs, and he was crushing her voluminous traveling skirts, but he didn't give a damn.

"You're crowding me," she accused, frowning. "Go back to your seat, Stuart. I don't want to have a row with you today."

"I have no intention of having a row with you," he countered. "I am trying to make amends for what I said."

"I fear it is too late for that. You made your opinions clear. I am not to know your secrets because you don't trust me, nor am I to interfere in any of your private concerns because I *bought* you." She shook her head. "What we have is a marriage of convenience, nothing more, and yesterday served as an important reminder of that."

She had resurrected the walls she ordinarily kept around herself. And it was his fault, but he didn't know how to dismantle them again.

He stared into the amber-flecked depths of her brown eyes, imploring her to listen. "It doesn't feel like a marriage of convenience when we are together, Rosamund. It feels like a great deal more than that to me."

Her icy mask slipped, indecision reflected on her lovely face for a moment, giving him hope. "My fortune has always been a curse. I thought it might be different with you because, unlike other suitors, you were honest about what you wanted from me. I didn't buy you. I made a bargain with you."

She was clinging to those stupid, thoughtless words of his still. Stuart couldn't blame her for it.

He reached for her, unable to resist, cupping her cheek. "It is a bargain I hope you don't regret."

"Stuart."

She was still frowning at him. He hated being the cause of her distress.

He traced the fullness of her lower lip with his thumb. "I'm sorry, sweetheart. Please say you'll forgive me."

She sighed softly. "Of course I forgive you."

The unspoken was there, hanging in the air between them. She would forgive him, but she would not so easily forget. He had chipped at her defenses, but he hadn't yet managed to obliterate them. He could only hope that he hadn't foolishly ruined everything they had built during their honeymoon.

"Thank you," he said simply.

The carriage rocked on, bringing them ever nearer to London and the reckoning that awaited them.

THE STREET SURROUNDING the town house was a throng of carriages. Quite unusual for this time of day. The moment their conveyance rumbled to an abrupt halt in the sea of broughams and landaus, Rosamund sensed that something was amiss. At her side, Stuart stiffened before peering out the Venetian blinds and cursing.

"Wesley," he growled. "What the devil has he done now?"

She couldn't deny it—his brother seemed a reasonable conclusion. Nor could she deny that returning to London after their honeymoon in Hertfordshire felt like a grim harbinger. The confluence of carriage traffic and their arrival was apropos.

"Gormless shite," Megs chirped from her cage.

"Megs," she scolded quietly, "you really mustn't."

"I'll not protest the name for my brother either," Stuart said grimly. "Damn it, why aren't we moving?"

He gave the roof an irritable rap. And still, the carriage remained where it was, blocked from further travel by the snarl of conveyances ahead. A few more moments of irritated silence and stillness ensued before Stuart surrendered with a heavy sigh.

"Remain where you are," he told her, a muscle in his jaw working as proof of his quiet fury. "I'll see if I can ascertain what is happening and why all these blasted carriages are blocking the street."

She nodded, because they were too far from the town house to carry Megs in her cage, and she would not abandon her beloved companion. Poor Megs would be frightened to be suddenly alone in the cramped confines.

"What do you think it could be?" she asked.

He stuffed his hat on his head. "If it's what I fear it is, then my brother needs a sound drubbing."

Those words did nothing to dispel her worry. But she didn't have time to tell him as much, because in the next breath, he was wrenching open the carriage door himself and leaping to the street below.

"Stuart!" she called after him.

He turned back, looking over his shoulder, his countenance hewn of marble.

"Don't do anything you will regret," she implored.

"You needn't worry over my brother," he said coolly.

And then without another word, he stalked away, far too quickly for Rosamund to tell him that it wasn't Lord Wesley she was concerned about at all. Rather, it was him.

A servant swung the carriage door closed, leaving her alone with her beloved African grey.

"Well, Megs," she murmured, unable to keep the sadness from her voice, "I don't know what will become of this."

"Walk the plank," her parrot said. "Handsome duke."

The last two words took her by surprise. She bent down, flipping back the covering on Megs's cage to find the bird gazing up at her.

"What did you say, Megs?" she asked.

Megs made a kissing sound and cocked her head to the side. "Handsome duke. Megs want pistache."

"That devious man," she breathed, wondering when Stuart had been spending time with the African grey without her knowledge. "He's been teaching you to say that, hasn't he?"

Megs extended her wings. "What a pretty bird."

"You are the prettiest bird," Rosamund agreed solemnly, that strange, pernicious fullness in her chest returning.

The one that had been steadily present, growing ever larger and more imperative during the idyllic days of her honeymoon. The one that Rosamund was beginning to fear was the beginnings of love, or something like it.

≈

HIS TOWN HOUSE looked as if it had been invaded by a phalanx of marauding enemy soldiers. Stuart stood in the entry, staring aghast at the river of people parading all over his house. These were not the lords and ladies of a Mayfair ballroom. No, indeed. These were the rabble with whom Wesley had no doubt been consorting at the filthy gambling warrens he inhabited. Stuart had suspected as much on his walk as he had spied many hired hacks in the congestion. But here was his proof, unveiled before his eyes.

The drunken revelries before him were nothing short of depraved. Men and women wandered about, shouting over the top of one another, in various states of dishabille. Stuart had attended many house parties hosted by the Wicked Dukes Society, and all of those paled in comparison to what he witnessed now. A bare-breasted woman laughed as she clutched a bottle of wine in one hand, a red-faced older gent not far behind her. In the main hall, a man had a woman pressed to the faded damask wall, her skirts up and his hand beneath them. Two women were locked in a heated kiss in the doorway of his blasted drawing room.

The floor was sticky with spilled wine. The raucous voices and laughter were hideously loud. And there were at least three different tables where cards were being dealt and dice were being cast. In his absence, his brother had turned the town house into a combination of a house of ill repute and a gambling den.

"Fleetwood!" he called out, hoping his poor, sainted butler was somewhere within earshot. "Fleetwood, are you in here?"

But his butler was nowhere to be found. Instead, an unfamiliar fellow with a long mustache stumbled past Stuart before tossing up his accounts in a nearby potted palm.

By God.

"Where is Lord Wesley?" he hollered over the din of revelries.

"Wot's that, luv?" asked a red-haired woman who stumbled into his chest, her bubbies bursting out of her bodice. "Did you say yer lookin' fer Alice? I'm right 'ere, m'luv."

He took her arms in a gentle yet firm hold and thrust her away from him, feeling nothing but ill. "The host of this fête," he shouted above the din. "Where is he?"

"Who is it?" she asked, her eyes wide. "I 'aven't seen him, luv. Supposed to be a grand duke's house, this is. Wot do ye think?"

He was going to throttle his brother for this abomination.

He had just arrived back home with his wife, their relationship tentative, thanks to his own foolish mistakes, and his carriage was being waylaid by traffic because Wesley was having a goddamned bacchanal. Without Stuart's approval and expressly against his wishes.

"I'm the damned duke!" he shouted, trying to be heard and to vent his fury all at the same time. "This is my house! *Out*, all of you!"

Alice blinked at him blearily, mouth parting in an *O* of complete confusion. No one else even paid him any heed.

And a sudden thought overcame every other consideration in his mind.

Mother.

Good God, where was his mother as all this mayhem was carrying on? His heart leapt into his throat. If one of these drunken fools had dared to hurt her in any way, he would tear them apart with his bare hands.

Mindless with worry now, he waded through the revelers, passing two laughing men who were smoking cheroots and a woman who had slumped against a doorway and was presently snoring. Everyone was a blur of sound and color as he stalked to the staircase. A strident whoop preceded a strange woman sliding down the banister wearing nothing but a corset and drawers. She hiccupped and landed on her feet by sheer luck, the impact jostling her abundant breasts from her undergarment. They sprang forth, ruddy-tipped and blue-veined.

Stuart stormed past her, up the stairs, taking them two at a time. He didn't even give a damn about Wesley. All he wanted was to find his mother and reassure himself that she was well. By the time he reached her chamber, he was ready to commit murder.

"Mother?" He pounded on the closed door. "Mother, it's Stuart. Are you in there?"

"Your Grace?" A hesitant voice on the other side reached him.

One he recognized.

"Yes, it's Camden. Norton, is my mother within?" he asked, barely restraining himself from putting his shoulder to the door and bursting over the threshold by force rather than awaiting a response.

"Yes, Your Grace," came the faithful lady's maid voice.

The door opened to reveal the domestic, clad in her customary drab gray attire. She sighed with relief as she saw him, an uncharacteristic action for the ordinarily stalwart woman.

"Oh, Your Grace. Thank heavens you have returned."

He crossed the threshold, closing the door at his back lest any of the revelers attempt to elbow their way into his mother's private apartments. "Not a moment too soon, it would appear," he observed grimly.

"Stuart?"

His mother was seated at her writing desk as usual, looking flustered, her left hand, which was also weaker than her right following the stroke, resting on the polished mahogany surface. The cap on her head was slightly askew, and he wondered if she had plucked at it in her distress.

"Mother." He rushed to her, belatedly offering a bow when he had reached her side, his gaze searching her familiar form for any hints of ailment or duress. "Are you well?"

"I suppose I am as well as I'm able to be," she said, sounding indignant. "What is happening, Stuart? There has been all manner of noise, and Norton has had to hide within. Fleetwood and the others have decamped belowstairs."

"I know as much as you do," he explained grimly. "I've only just returned from my honeymoon with my wife."

"Your honeymoon," his mother repeated, smiling brightly. "How was the fortnight, Stuart? I do so hope I shall have a babe to fawn over soon."

Heat crept up the back of his neck. "Mother."

It was all he could say. In truth, he hoped that Rosamund was with child. They'd certainly made an excellent concerted effort of getting her *enceinte*. But that didn't mean he wanted to speak about such matters before the woman who had birthed him. And particularly not here and now, with her lady's maid present.

"I want a grandchild," his mother said, unaffected by his chastisement. "I do so wish I'd had a chance to speak with your wife before you left."

"We are returned now," he said firmly, "and there shall be ample time for that. All we need to do is return the house to a modicum of sanity. Have you any idea what is happening? I've no doubt this is all Wesley's doing, of course."

"He said he wished to host a ball," Mother said, her voice sounding small as she fixed her gaze on her writing desk, as if she were studying the sheets of paper and inkwell atop its surface. "This is not a ball, is it?"

"It's madness," he said honestly. "You are uninjured and in good health?"

"Of course. Wesley would never do anything that would cause me harm," Mother told him, utterly certain of her words.

Stuart, meanwhile, was no longer convinced his brother was incapable of doing their mother harm. This wild soiree was proof of that. Wesley and the servants were nowhere to be found. The town house had been overrun by all manner of drunkards and wastrels and even light-skirts. Anything could have happened to Mother. He shuddered to think what would have occurred had his return to London been delayed or had he and Rosamund decided to linger in Hertfordshire and their charmed honeymoon for just a bit longer.

He shook his head. "Mother, I know you wish to believe the very best of my brother, but you have not seen what is happening in this very house. I was afraid to come to you for fear you had been defiled or worse."

"Camden," his mother rebuked. "You mustn't speak of such dreadful things. You would shock your lady wife, I am sure. Where is your new duchess?"

"Awaiting me in our carriage," he gritted, "on account of the abundance of conveyances approaching, lingering at, and leaving our home."

"Oh dear," his mother murmured, taking her weak hand into her lap and resting the other atop it. "It is a dreadful return for the two of you."

"Yes," he agreed, bending to press a kiss atop his mother's head. "But what is important is that you are well. The rest, we shall deal with presently. I will chase the unwanted guests below and return."

He spun on his heel, intent upon the task awaiting him and eager to be rid of the *hoi polloi* destroying his home below.

"Stuart?" his mother called after him.

With a heavy sigh, he paused, turning back to her. "Yes, Mother?"

"I didn't want to trouble you with this, but I've searched everywhere for months, and there is only one conclusion for me to reach. They are gone."

He blinked, not understanding. "What is gone, Mother?"

"My journals," she elaborated. "I have been keeping them all my life."

His gut twisted. He cast a glance in Norton's direction. The servant was busying herself in a task, but she still possessed ears. And yet he didn't dare to dismiss her, sending her belowstairs for fear of what she would find on her way there.

Stuart looked back to his mother. "When did they go missing?"

"I can't be certain, but months ago, I fear," Mother answered, her lower lip trembling. "Stuart, no one must read my writings. They were meant for my eyes alone."

A sickening sensation blossomed in his gut as suspicion began to take root.

"Has Wesley paid you a visit in the last few months?" he asked.

"Yes, of course he has, dear." Mother frowned. "Why do you ask?"

Because everything was beginning to make sense. Stuart had wondered where the blackmailer had come upon the information in the letters he'd received. He'd supposed it was a former acquaintance of his mother's who had somehow recognized her after so many years.

"No reason," he lied, not wanting to burden his mother with more worries until he had proof that Wesley was behind the blackmail letters. "I must clear out the house now, but I will return. Don't open your door to anyone but me."

"Of course, dearest," his mother agreed.

Stuart left her room and stalked down the hall to the chamber his brother kept. Not even bothering to knock, he threw open the door with so much irate force that it slammed into the wall, making a deep divot in the plaster with the door handle. But he didn't give a damn. He was a man on a mission, intent to find some manner of evidence to prove Wesley had been behind the blackmail letters.

The room was, as usual, strewn with garments that had been left where they'd been thrown. Stuart started with the writing desk, finding nothing but blank paper, a pen, and a capped inkwell. He moved to the bedside table next, then the wardrobe, systematically making his way through every piece of furniture in the room.

Nothing.

"Damn it," he muttered, returning to the desk.

There had to be something somewhere. Stuart shuffled through the papers a second time. Still nothing but empty pages. He was about to stop his search when he suddenly recalled that the writing desk, which had once belonged to his father, had a hollow secret compartment. Running his fingers over the bottom lip of the desk, he searched for the hidden mechanism that allowed the desk drawer to open. He found the cool metal of the catch and pressed.

The drawer popped open a scant few inches, and Stuart pulled it the rest of the way. There it was, the evidence of his brother's complicity. The compartment was brimming with papers, letters, and small bound-leather books. Correspondence from Messrs. Dolan and Rowe, drafts of notes written to Stuart, the wording precisely the same as the missives he'd received, then burned to ash. There was no other way for these letters to be in his brother's possession other than he had written them himself. It was apparent that Wesley had made an effort to disguise his handwriting. Flipping open the books revealed his mother's tidy penmanship and private words.

Stuart's gut churned.

His brother had stolen their mother's private journals and had not just read them, but then used the information within to blackmail Stuart, knowing he would do anything in his power to protect their mother and her delicate health. Little wonder Wesley had been thick in funds. Undoubtedly, the thousands of pounds he had claimed to have won at the tables had been unwittingly provided by Stuart himself.

Grimly, Stuart collected everything from within the hidden compartment. Arms laden with journals and incriminating letters, he stalked to his own chamber, secreting everything in his wardrobe. Then he descended the stairs to the mayhem below.

It was time to face his bastard of a brother.

CHAPTER 18

"Out!" Stuart shouted above the din of the unruly and uninvited revelers filling his house. "Get out of my house, all of you. Now!"

Some had already begun filing out of the town house, leaving a mess in their wake of discarded gloves, hats, and even shoes. A corset had been left dangling over the banister of the staircase, its owner either too soused to care or woefully ignorant of its whereabouts.

There was a pile of vomit in one of the potted palms thanks to the mustachioed chap, and another palm stank wretchedly of piss. The faded carpet was an abandoned battlefield of broken glass and spilled spirits and only God knew what else. The men and women who had been carousing for what must have been hours staggered past him in bleary-eyed shock that their den of sin was being so abruptly curtailed.

Order, unfortunately, would take a great deal of time to be restored.

The town house was virtually in ruins. And in the midst of it all, his brother stood, eyes bloodshot and glazed, wearing the same trousers and stained shirt and waistcoat he'd likely been sporting for days.

Stuart had never wanted to plant someone a facer more.

"What the devil do you think you're doing?" Wesley wanted to know.

He held his brother's gaze, so much righteous fury ignited in his chest that his hands trembled with its force. "I'm doing what I should have done years ago. I'm taking control over this bloody mess you've made. You need to leave."

Wesley barked out an incredulous laugh. "Leave? This is my home."

He shook his head, his decision made. "Not any longer, it isn't. You are not welcome here."

His brother sobered, apparently sensing the intent in Stuart's voice. "But we've been through this before. Mother would never want you to deny me a place to live. It is bad enough that you've stolen my birthright. You cannot keep me from a roof over my head. I belong here every bit as much as you do."

"You would be wise to keep our mother's name out of your mouth," he snapped. "After all the sins you've committed, it's the least you can do. Moreover, I didn't steal your birthright. I am the firstborn, and I am the Duke of Camden. You are nothing but a drunken wastrel who has preyed upon everyone in your life like a leech sucking the blood from its host."

More revelers moved past them to the door, stumbling over the various abandoned objects littering the floor. Stuart didn't pay them any heed. His servants had reemerged from hiding belowstairs, and Fleetwood and a pair of burly footmen were now applying themselves to the task of chasing a pair of lingering interlopers from the house.

The door closed on the last of the intruders, and the domestics moved into other rooms quietly, beginning the endless task of cleaning up after the mayhem that had so recently reigned. Stuart had no doubt that they were giving him and his brother some privacy as well. He didn't care who heard what needed to be said now, however. He had held his tongue long enough. Wesley had to pay for what he had done.

"Fuck you," Wesley spat. "Why should you have everything while I have nothing?"

"You've had more than your fair share," he said coldly. "But apparently I didn't give you enough funds to support your gambling and whoring habits. You needed to blackmail me for more, did you not?"

Wesley paled, realization dawning on his countenance. "I didn't blackmail you. What the hell are you talking about?"

His frayed patience snapped, and Stuart caught his brother's rumpled cravat in his fist, giving him a shake. "Don't lie to me. I know everything. I saw what you've been keeping in the hidden compartment of your writing desk. I know you are the one who has been blackmailing me and threatening to go to *The Times* with delicate family secrets that would destroy our mother's frail health and send her to her grave. I know what you've done, and I'm not going to tolerate another bloody second of it. Do you hear me? *Not another second*. Get out of my fucking house!"

He was shouting by the time he reached the last words of his tirade, but it couldn't be helped. Stuart didn't recall ever being so overcome with anger. He was seething. He'd had more than enough of his brother's manipulations and deceptions. They ended today.

But Wesley remained defiant, pushing Stuart off him. "I need money, damn you. I'm not going anywhere without collecting what I'm owed."

"I just paid you a fortune a fortnight ago," he snarled, ready to tear down the walls with his bare hands. "Use that until you run out of funds. I don't give a goddamn what you do after that. Just don't come here. You'll not get another farthing from me."

"I spent that already. I need more." Wesley's demeanor had changed, some of the customary smugness seeping away.

"How the hell did you spend ten thousand pounds in a fortnight?" he demanded.

"I had a bad night at the tables," his brother said. "And then I needed supplies for tonight's soiree, which you've thoroughly ruined."

"If you don't get out of here now, I'm going to beat you to within an inch of your life," he warned, meaning those words to his core. "I will never forgive you for what you were willing to do to our mother just so that you could continue gambling."

"You truly intend to cut me off without anything?" Wesley demanded.

"Yes," he answered without hesitation. "I do."

Wesley's jaw clenched. "But I'm your brother."

"You're no family of mine. Now, leave."

"What makes you think I won't go to *The Times* with the story now?" Wesley asked, his bravado ringing false.

Stuart's lip curled. "You have no evidence. The journals are in my possession. And I have every intention to make it known that you've gone mad. Who do you think polite society will believe, a drunken wastrel who can't even be bothered to wear clean clothes or a peer of the realm?"

And Stuart would do it, too. Wesley had hurt Rosamund, and he had threatened their mother. He had manipulated, deceived, and stolen. It was time for him to pay for his sins.

Wesley went ashen. "But Stuart, you can't do that. I have nothing. Nowhere to sleep, nothing to eat, not a farthing to my name."

He refused to allow himself to be moved. "I don't bloody well care, brother. Get. Out."

"Go to hell," Wesley roared.

And then he spun away, storming from the entry hall, and from Stuart's life. He hoped that this time, it was for good.

ROSAMUND STOOD in the entryway of Stuart's town house, surveying the damage before her. She wasn't sure which was more appalling, the scent of sour spirits and urine assaulting her senses or the curious assortment of abandoned belongings strewn about. She took a tentative step forward, and the sole of her boot crunched on a piece of glass. To be sure, this was most certainly not the return to London she had anticipated.

"Where would you have your parrot settled, Your Grace?" asked the footman at her side who was bearing the cage containing the African grey, the cover pulled back so that Megs might see her surroundings.

With so much transpiring, Rosamund had been forced to entrust the young servant with her beloved companion.

"Walk the plank," Megs announced.

"Please see that she is taken upstairs to her normal spot," she told the footman with a tight smile. "I'll be awaiting His Grace in the drawing room for some tea."

If tea was even to be had in this disaster, that was.

"Of course, Your Grace," huffed the footman.

He was a strapping fellow, but Megs's cage was large and heavy. Thankfully, the crush of conveyances had moved away from the town house. She had watched from the carriage, nonplussed, as men and women had swarmed out the doors. Stuart had come to fetch her at last, giving a cursory explanation of what had occurred.

"My brother was hosting a fête," he had said curtly, displeasure dripping from his voice, his jaw hard as granite. "You needn't worry he will cause us any further trouble, however. He is no longer welcome in our home."

Without saying more, he had helped her to alight from the carriage and had remained outside to give directions to the servants overseeing the unpacking.

She moved toward the drawing room, picking her way through shards of glass, forgotten stockings, and what appeared to be a lady's shoe. The footman followed in her wake.

"Dear heavens, what has happened here?"

The shocked gasp from above had her turning to find an older woman dressed in a gown that was quite fine, if outmoded by a decade. Her silver hair was confined in a neat chignon at her nape, and she clutched a cane in her right hand as she slowly descended the staircase, each step looking painful.

It was the dowager duchess, Rosamund realized.

Before she could answer, her husband came striding into the main hall. "Mother, what are you doing out of your bedchamber?"

"Attempting to see what manner of mayhem has been happening," she answered, working her way down another step.

"You shouldn't see this," he argued gently. "It's far too distressing."

But his mother continued her descent, looking determined. "It is distressing to remain in my room, not knowing what has been unfolding down here. I heard a great deal of cacophony, Camden."

"You ought to be resting," Stuart fretted. "The servants are cleaning and restoring the house. You needn't worry about anything."

"Too late for that," his mother said sadly.

"Perhaps you would both care to join me in the drawing room for some tea," Rosamund suggested, trying to smooth the waters between the two.

Her mother-in-law smiled. "That would be lovely, my dear. You must be my Camden's duchess. I hope you can forgive me for missing the wedding and for not having the opportunity to speak with you before you left on your honeymoon."

"Of course," she replied dutifully. "The wedding was a whirlwind, and then we were off to Hertfordshire the very next morning. How are you feeling today, Your Grace?"

The dowager reached the bottom of the stairs at last and, out of breath, sighed, her pale eyes so much like her son's that it was startling. "I am feeling my age today."

"I wonder if you are also feeling like a woman who ought to have remained where she is most comfortable," Stuart grumbled pointedly, though he dutifully offered his mother the use of his arm for the hand not holding her cane.

The dowager took it, and together, the two walked to the drawing room, which had not fared much better than the rest of the house, though it did appear that some of the servants had swept the carpets of debris. A tea service was already awaiting them, a welcome sight.

The three of them sat, and Rosamund took it upon herself to pour.

"This was Wesley's doing, was it not?" the dowager asked Stuart.

"Mother," he protested, looking torn.

She thumped her cane on the floor for emphasis. "Tell me, my son. I need to know."

"Yes," he allowed, his tone grudging. "Wesley is responsible. He was soused, he'd just gambled away what was left of his funds, and he decided to host a party for an assortment of unscrupulous characters from his gaming den. When I arrived with Rosamund, it was to find the house teeming with strangers who were drinking, carousing, and engaging in all manner of scandalous behavior."

Rosamund had finished preparing the tea, and they each had a cup steaming before them. It didn't escape her notice that none of them took a sip. The air was too fraught with tension and uncertainty.

"He is forever finding himself in one scrape or another," the dowager said. "But inviting the rabble to your home is beyond the pale, even by his standards."

"I'm afraid that's not the worst of his sins," Stuart said, passing a hand through his hair, his expression pained.

"What else has he done?" his mother asked, looking concerned.

"He stole your journals," Stuart said. "He was using them to blackmail me."

Rosamund gasped. "Your brother is the one who has been blackmailing you?"

The dowager looked shocked. "Wesley stole my journals? How can you be sure?"

"Because I found them secreted in a hidden compartment in his writing desk," Stuart answered. "Along with correspondence from the solicitors he was using to collect the funds I provided and copies of the missives he sent me. He appeared to be practicing them so that he could sufficiently disguise his handwriting and make it difficult for me to recognize it."

The dowager looked ashen and small, the teacup trembling in her hands. "What was he threatening to do?"

"To go to *The Times* with secrets you had written in your journals," Stuart explained. "He knew I would do anything to protect you from scandal. I never imagined it was him until you told me today that the journals were missing. I didn't think he knew about…the past."

So, the secret Stuart sought to protect *was* his mother's. Rosamund had been correct. Her heart ached for both Stuart and his mother at the knowledge that a member of their family would be malicious enough to use his mother's scandalous secret for his own gain. Worse, that he would be willing to reveal it. He had stolen his mother's private journals and used them against her.

"He didn't know," the dowager said quietly. "No one knew except you and your father. And you only knew because you overheard that dreadful row we'd had…"

Her words trailed away as she was presumably caught in the throes of a memory.

Rosamund couldn't begin to imagine what her mother-in-law's secret was, scandalous enough to drive Stuart to pay a small fortune he didn't have to keep his blackmailer silent.

"The secret will remain safe," Stuart told his mother. "The journals are no longer in Wesley's possession. After all that he's done, to you, to my wife, and to me, I cannot in good conscience continue to provide him with funds or to allow him to live beneath this roof."

"You have cut him off." The dowager looked dazed by the pronouncement.

Stuart cast a meaningful glance in Rosamund's direction, his gaze burning into hers. "I have. I am sorry, Mother. I have no wish to cause you upset, but he has gone too far."

The dowager at last took a sip of her tea, remaining quiet for a few moments, the only sound in the chamber the faraway din of the domestics restoring the town house to order. Until finally, she spoke again.

"I agree with your decision, son," she said. "I fear I am to blame for always believing the best of your brother. You did try to warn me of what he had become, but I didn't want to hear it. I didn't want to believe that he could be so like his father. I was wrong."

Rosamund took a sip of her own tea, devastated for Stuart and his mother both. For the first time, she realized just how torn her husband must have been. And the betrayal of realizing Wesley had been the one blackmailing him all along... It must have been terrible for him. Little wonder she'd been abandoned in the carriage with Megs for the better part of an hour.

"I allowed him to carry on with his destruction for far too long," Stuart told his mother then. "I am to blame as well."

She shook her head. "I had no notion you were being blackmailed on account of me. Why did you not say anything?"

His voice was earnest, like his expression. "To protect you."

"You needn't protect me any longer," the dowager said firmly before turning her gaze upon Rosamund. "You are family now. You may as well know the secret Camden was so desperate to keep on my behalf."

"You need not feel obligated, Your Grace," she protested.

"You may call me Mother as Camden does," the dowager countered. "I shall call you Rosamund. And now, my dear Rosamund, I will tell you also the terrible truth about me. When Camden's father and I met, it was my first night at a very infamous brothel. He took me home with him for a handsome price, and then he whisked me away to Hertfordshire, where we married, much to the horror of his poor mother. She never forgave me for marrying her son." She paused and flashed a small, wry smile. "We had that in common, at least. Because I never forgave myself for marrying him either."

The dowager had been a courtesan.

It was a secret Rosamund hadn't imagined.

"Thank you for telling me," she told her mother-in-law. "You have my word that your secret is safe with me."

"I believe you, my dear. I see the way Camden looks at you. The two of you are happy together, are you not?"

Rosamund's gaze flew to her husband, who was watching her with a look that had softened considerably. There was an unmistakable tenderness in his eyes. She understood now what he had meant when he'd said the secret was not his to reveal. And she admired him deeply for his loyalty and love for his mother. He was a good man. Not the brother she had once thought she would marry, but she realized in that moment that what she'd once felt for Wesley had been naught compared to what she felt for Stuart.

She had never been in love with Lord Wesley Gilden.

But she *had* fallen in love with his brother.

True love. Real love. Deep and abiding love. And now she knew the difference. It terrified her, being so vulnerable, but she couldn't change the way she felt. It was indelible.

Rosamund turned back to the dowager, smiling even as tears swam in her vision. "We are quite contented together, yes."

She could only hope that one day he might grow to return her feelings and that their marriage of convenience could blossom into a love match.

CHAPTER 19

The day was a dreary one, a fine mist falling and the sun blotted out by fog and clouds hanging overhead. Rosamund pulled her wrap about her more closely and hastened her steps. She had paid a call to Mr. Watts this afternoon, a necessary visit to her man of business after having been gone from London for a fortnight. The news had been good, and yet she couldn't seem to shake a knot of dread in her stomach. A deep-rooted feeling of foreboding that seemingly had no source.

It was likely silly.

She was overreacting.

Their ignominious return to London the day before had left her at sixes and sevens. And it was understandable with so much upheaval, from the dreadful mess awaiting them in the town house, to Stuart's unexpected revelations about his brother, and realizing she'd fallen in love with her husband. Naturally, she was guarding that discovery close to her heart. If she confessed her feelings to Stuart and he didn't return them, she would be devastated.

No, it was best to bide her time and—

A hand gripped her elbow in a harsh grasp at the same time something hard was shoved into the small of her back. The scent of spirits and hair grease and unlaundered clothing assailed her.

"Don't make a sound, or I'll put a bullet in your back," Wesley warned in her ear.

"What are you doing?" she asked, fear making her mouth go instantly dry.

He led her in a different direction and pushed her toward a waiting carriage that wasn't hers. "Walk."

Her instinct was to run. To tear away from him and flee. But the damning pressure of the pistol's barrel in her back told her that running would be a terrible mistake. If Wesley shot her, she would die in the street.

And she couldn't die. Not now. Not when she and Stuart were just beginning their life together. Not when she was so close to having the family she had always yearned for.

"This is madness," she hissed, frantically looking around for someone who might aid her somehow.

But no one was looking in her direction, the busy street filled with merchants and hacks and horses, everyone going about their day, so caught up in their own routines that no one took note of her plight.

"Shut up," Wesley bit out, jamming the pistol into her back with so much force she knew it would leave a bruise.

He moved close to her, keeping a tight hold, the pistol hidden from view. To any observer, they likely looked as if they were a couple, Lord Wesley escorting her to their conveyance. Not like a desperate man with a gun, attempting to spirit away his unwilling sister-in-law for heaven knew what purpose.

Icy fear licked down her spine.

She was afraid she knew what purpose.

"You can't kidnap me like this," she countered. "Wesley,

please. Let me go, and I won't mention this to Stuart. I'll pretend as if it never happened."

"I said, shut your bloody mouth," he growled, increasing his pace and giving the pistol another painful shove into her back.

They reached the carriage, and he yanked the door open, urging her inside with menacing force. She nearly fell as she scrambled within and settled on the worn squabs. Wesley clambered up and into the conveyance as well, his pistol trained on her as he slammed the door closed and then rapped on the roof. The vehicle swayed into motion.

There was no way to escape. Nothing she could do with the barrel of a gun pointing at her. She could scream, but who would hear her? And she would run the risk of further inciting his wrath. In this moment, he seemed capable of anything.

Even her murder.

"My dear Rosamund," he drawled, his tone nasty. "How lovely it is to see you again."

"What do you want, Wesley?" she demanded tightly, trying not to allow him to see her inner terror.

"What do I want? Ah, such an excellent question. I'm so glad you asked." He leaned forward, his lip curling. "What I want is what I am owed, and you're going to help me get it."

Her mind whirled. "If it is funds you need, consider them yours. Please, just take me home, and I'll see that Stuart gives you what you want. He was angry with you yesterday, but I'm sure he'll see reason."

"Do you think me an idiot, my dear?" he asked. "You're not going home. You're staying with me."

"Please, Wesley," she pressed. "I'm begging you. Take me home, and we can forget all about this. Stuart will help you. There is no need to hurt anyone—"

"Enough!" he snapped, interrupting her. "Stop talking.

Nothing you say will alter my course. My brother has left me with no other choice."

"There is always another choice," she countered.

"He cut me off without a farthing. Threw me into the street like a common thief." Wesley shook his head. "No, no. The time for choices is done. I'm doing what I have to do. What I should have done a long time ago."

"What is that?" she dared to ask, fear making her stomach clench.

He smiled, and it was an ugly smile, a sinister smile. The smile of a man with nothing left to lose.

"Taking what's rightfully mine."

"How was the house party at Wingfield Hall?" Stuart asked the Duke of Kingham as they sat, nursing brandy and soda water in his study.

Thanks to his wedding and honeymoon, he had missed the most recent house party being held by their club. Not that he minded. While their wild house parties had once held endless allure to him, their appeal had waned. He was a new man now. A married man.

A married man who was hopelessly, helplessly besotted with his wife. And although the old Stuart would never have been able to conceive of such connubial bliss, the new Stuart wouldn't change a bloody thing. Because he'd realized something astounding last night as he'd held Rosamund in his arms.

He had fallen in love with her.

He just hadn't told her yet.

"It was deadly dull," King said, taking a meditative puff of his cheroot. "Whitby spent the entirety of the house party sniffing the skirts of a scandalous divorcée. Riverdale was as exciting as a wheel of moldy cheese, Richford was in one of his terrible moods, and neither you nor Brandon attended because you're *married*."

King shuddered dramatically at the last word.

"You make it sound as if we've contracted the plague and died," he observed wryly.

"Because I've scarcely seen or heard from you in weeks," King returned, giving him a disdainful look. "Although, if I were wearing a fusty waistcoat like that, I would hide myself away at home too."

Stuart glanced down at his waistcoat. "What's wrong with it?"

King shook his head. "My poor lad, have you learned nothing from me?"

He grinned. "Not to drink any of your potions before half past eight in the evening?"

"A wise lesson," his friend agreed. "But please, for the love of all that is pure and holy in this world, stop wearing paisley waistcoats during the day. You're in desperate need of paying a visit to my tailor, and now that you're flush in funds, I strongly encourage you to do so."

Stuart laughed. "Send me his direction, and I'll make the time."

"Damned right you will, or I'll refuse to be seen in public with you," King grumbled good-naturedly. "Now then, do tell me why your study stinks of stale piss."

"Does it?" Stuart sniffed the air. "All I smell is your cheroot."

"I have a sensitive nose, as you know," King drawled. "There is a distinct odor in here. I recommend having the carpets replaced."

"Blast. I can thank my arsehole brother for that."

"Your brother has a propensity for pissing in the corners of rooms?" King asked mildly, as if they were discussing something as mundane as the weather, before taking a slow inhalation of his cheroot.

"No, he has a propensity for making me want to throttle him," Stuart growled, before explaining the chaos he had returned to the day before and how he had finally banished Wesley from the town house and his life.

He had just finished his tale when a rap at the study door interrupted them.

"Come," Stuart called, frowning as he wondered what could be the cause of the intrusion.

The door opened to reveal a pensive-looking Fleetwood. "Forgive me for interrupting, Your Grace. However, there is a matter of some urgency which I thought you might like to immediately be apprised of."

He didn't like the sound of that.

"Go on," Stuart urged. "What is it?"

"Her Grace's carriage has returned without her," the butler said. "The coachman says that Lord Wesley told him to proceed home, that he would escort Her Grace. He also gave him this missive."

Dear God.

Wesley had taken Rosamund.

Dread and fear colliding within him, Stuart rose to his feet, striding across the room like an automaton to take the missive from his butler's hand.

"Thank you, Fleetwood, that will be all," he muttered, tearing open the missive and reading its contents.

The butler bowed and took his leave as Stuart's world shattered around him.

"What is it?" King's voice cut through the din in his brain. "What's happened?"

The words swam before him. "My brother has kidnapped my wife and is holding her for ransom. This is instructions for where I am to meet him and how much money I'm to bring."

He felt numb.

Helpless.

Stupid.

How had he failed to realize that Wesley would retaliate? Why had he allowed Rosamund to leave for her father's offices? Why had he not accompanied her?

"You're not going alone," King told him, giving him a reassuring clap on the back. "I'm coming with you."

ROSAMUND WAS SEATED ON A DIRTY, uncomfortable chair in a dim little room, her hands tied behind her back. Wesley had brought her to the unkempt flat where he kept a room for, as he had so succinctly phrased it, sleeping and fucking. The place was littered with empty gin bottles and it smelled of soot and old water, and she'd seen a mouse skittering about in a corner.

"Why have you brought me here?" she asked, trying to distract him so that she might work at the bindings on her wrists without his noticing.

"To have tea," he said snidely. "Why do you think?"

"So that you can lure Stuart to you," she guessed. "That is what you hope, is it not? That he will come for me? What do you hope to gain, then? Money? If that is what you are after, I would gladly give it to you. All you need to do is release me."

"That's part of what I want, yes." He lifted a bottle to his lips and took a long drink from it before wiping his mouth with the back of his hand. "But that's just the beginning."

He had been drinking steadily since their arrival, and he was beginning to slur his words ever so slightly. She didn't know if she should be hopeful that he would become too inebriated to do her harm or fearful that he would shoot her by accident. The pistol was on the table before him, the barrel facing her in a grim reminder of the danger she was in.

She wetted her dry lips. "What do you mean, this is just the beginning?"

"I want to be the duke. I should have been the duke. Sheer luck and a little over a bloody year, and it would have all been different."

Cold dread iced through her.

Dear heavens, he intended to kill Stuart.

"But you cannot be the duke," she reminded him, wriggling her wrists subtly at her back in an effort to loosen the ropes holding her. "You are the second son."

He smiled evilly. "Soon enough, I'll be the *only* son. And I have you to thank for it."

"You can't murder him," she burst out. "You'll go to prison."

He took another sip of spirits. "No, I won't. I'll be the grieving brother, heartbroken over his brother's and sister-in-law's deaths."

He intended to kill her as well, then. But of course he did.

"You cannot believe you can murder a duke and duchess and that no one will be the wiser," she said, still struggling with her bonds.

Wesley gave a bitter laugh. "Of course I can, you stupid cow. You were having an affair with a commoner, you see. Good old Stuart catches you here in your love nest. In a fit of rage, he shoots you and then himself. It will be a terrible tragedy. A horrid scandal."

Every part of her was numb. Cold.

Terrified.

Wesley had thought of everything, and she had allowed herself to be neatly caught in his trap. And now, she and

Stuart would both be murdered if she didn't do something to stop this madman. But her wrists were tied so securely, and it seemed that the more she struggled, the tighter the rope became, cutting into her wrists until they were burning and raw.

A knock sounded at the door.

"Ah, there is brother dearest now," Wesley said.

"Stuart, don't!" she cried out, wanting to save him. "He's going to kill us both!"

"You fucking whore!" Wesley snarled, launching himself across the table and slapping her soundly. "Shut your mouth."

Pain exploded in the side of her face, a hot trail of blood trickling from her lip, down her chin. Everything that happened next was a blur of color, sound, and motion. The door burst open, and Wesley scrambled for the pistol, bringing it to her temple.

"Welcome, brother," he greeted. "Come inside and close the door."

Stuart's eyes locked on her. "Rosamund. What has he done to you?"

"I said come inside," Wesley repeated sharply. "If you don't, I'll put a bullet in your wife's head. Is that what you want?"

"No, of course not," Stuart said. "Don't hurt her. You have no quarrel with Rosamund."

"In," Wesley ordered him.

"Don't," she begged Stuart, pleading with her gaze.

"Stubble it," Wesley said, grabbing her chignon and pulling so hard that tears sprang to her eyes.

"Stuart, I love you!" she cried out, the words torn from her. Words she had been too proud to say, too scared. Words she should have given to him freely, from the warmth of his embrace as they lay side by side in his bed.

But if she was going to die, she would do so with him knowing how she felt for him.

"I said, shut up!" Wesley snarled, shaking her.

"I love you too, Rosamund," Stuart said, his gaze locked on hers as he crossed the threshold slowly. "Put the pistol away, Wesley. We can talk about this. I'll give you whatever you want. Just please, don't hurt her."

"Close the door," Wesley commanded, the cold, hard barrel of the pistol biting into her temple.

"Cam, old chap," called another masculine voice from the hall.

Wesley snatched the pistol away from her temple as the Duke of Kingham suddenly came into view at the threshold. He was dressed elegantly, as out of place as a zebra in this hovel.

Kingham sauntered over the threshold, closing the door smartly at his back. "What is taking so long, Cam? I have a dinner engagement awaiting me this evening, and I do so detest being tardy." He glanced toward Wesley and Rosamund then, wearing a look of surprise. "Hullo, Lord Wesley, Duchess. As charming as it is to see you both, I cannot imagine why you'd wish to meet Cam in such a distasteful little slum."

He was carrying on as if they were engaged in a social call. Was the man a fool?

"What are you doing here, Kingham?" Wesley demanded, his voice sounding shaken.

Rosamund wondered where the pistol was. Had he hidden it in his coat? Was it pointing at her back? Surely Kingham could see that her lip was bleeding.

"Waiting for Cam," Kingham said calmly, reaching into his waistcoat. "Sweet God, is that a rat?"

Rosamund turned to follow the direction of the duke's

gaze out of sheer habit, so she only saw the flurry of movement in her peripheral vision before the crack of a pistol rent the air. Behind her, something fell to the floor as a cloud of smoke billowed from a gun in the Duke of Kingham's hand.

"Rosamund!" Stuart cried.

Gasping, she looked over her shoulder to find Wesley slumped on the floor, a pool of blood around his head growing larger by the moment. A scream tore from her throat, and in the next second, Stuart was upon her, cutting her hands free and taking her into his arms.

"Rosamund," he said her name, over and over again, holding her so tightly she could scarcely breathe, but she didn't care because she was alive and so was he. "My love. You're hurt. What did he do to you?"

She inhaled the beloved scent of him, sandalwood and musk and the man she loved, his heart a steady, reassuring thump in his chest. "I'll be fine. What about you? What happened?"

"You're safe now," he said grimly. "We all are. It's over."

"Did the Duke of Kingham…" She allowed her words to trail away, unable to finish her question.

"Yes," Stuart said simply. "Wesley is dead. He can't hurt you or anyone else ever again."

Her eyes fluttered closed, and a sob shuddered through her, shock making her knees go weak. Stuart gathered her up in his arms, keeping her from falling, and she didn't protest, beyond speech.

"I'm going to take you home now, sweetheart."

"Yes," she said, half plea.

Dimly, she was aware of him making arrangements with Kingham, who spoke coolly and calmly, as if he had not just killed a man and saved their lives. The dichotomy of the fashionable rake and the merciless hero was something she would make sense of later, when her overwrought mind could properly function again. For now, it was enough that he had saved her and Stuart both with his unwavering precision and clever distractions.

She clung to Stuart tightly, burying her face in his chest, and somehow they were in the carriage and it was rocking over the rutted streets, taking them away from the death and horrors in that dank room. He held her on his lap, his face buried in her hair, and for a few moments, neither of them spoke.

They just held each other.

"What did he do to you, my love?" Stuart asked at last. "Will you tell me?"

"He…he came upon me when I was leaving Mr. Watts at my father's offices," she managed, her breath catching. "He pressed a gun to my back and f-forced me into a carriage and took me to that room. He was intending to kill the both of us. H-he wanted to be the duke. He planned to make it look as if I was having an affair and y-you had caught me and killed me and then yourself."

"My God, sweetheart," he murmured, tipping her head back so that he could see her face, tenderly caressing her bruised cheek. "I am so sorry. I had no notion he was capable of something like this. If I had, I never would have let you out of my sight this morning. To think that I could have lost you…"

His eyes glistened, and wetness shone on his cheeks. Stuart was weeping, she realized, and so was she.

"You didn't lose me," she said. "I'm here."

"Did you mean what you said to me?" he asked softly, his gaze searching hers.

Rosamund swallowed down a lump of emotion in her throat. "That I love you?"

286

He nodded. "That."

"Of course I meant it," she answered, cupping his cheek gently and smoothing her thumb over the wet trail of a tear he'd shed over her. "I love you, Stuart. I never expected to fall for you. This was meant to be a business arrangement and nothing else. But the more I grew to know you, the more I realized I couldn't resist you. You are loyal and charming and witty, and you grudgingly adore my parrot."

"I don't know about adore," he teased. "That's a rather strong word for the winged demon."

She smiled, grateful for this man, for this love. For this life, for the air in her lungs and the hearts beating in both of them, for the catlike instincts of the Duke of Kingham, for the carriage that was taking them home where they belonged.

For the future that awaited them.

"You adore her," she insisted.

"I do," he allowed, giving her a tender smile. "But I love you most of all, Rosamund. You've changed everything for me. When I thought I was going to lose you today, I could scarcely breathe. I don't want to live in a world without you in it. I love your sharp mind and your determination, your kindness and your stubborn streak and the way you stammer when you're embarrassed and... Hell, I just love you, sweetheart, full stop. I love you more than I ever imagined possible."

"Oh, Stuart." More tears blurred her vision of his handsome face. Tears of happiness and sorrow, of shock and fear and relief, all coming together as one.

"Hush, love. Don't weep. I'm here. I have you now." He kissed her slowly, softly, and her split lip ached, but she didn't care because they had faced death and emerged alive, and because she loved him so much it hurt. They kissed and kissed until at last he lifted his head and they gasped for precious air, staring at each other in awe.

"I have you forever," he added.

And Rosamund believed him. Because here, in the loving circle of her husband's arms, was exactly where she had always belonged.

EPILOGUE

"*H*andsome duke," Megs chirped. From her perch, the African grey flapped her wings and made a kissing sound.

"What a pretty bird you are," Stuart praised her, extracting a nut from the pouch Rosamund kept filled with Megs's favorite treat. "Would you like a pistachio?"

The parrot made another kissing sound with her beak. "Megs want pistache. Handsome duke."

Rosamund laughed at both of their antics, then flattened her palm over her bodice. "Soon, you'll have to teach her a new word again."

"Oh?" Stuart held out the pistachio, and Megs took it in her beak. "And what word is that?"

"Baby," Rosamund told him, happiness rising within her, like the sun ready to glow and give new life to everything in its path.

His head jerked toward her, a question in his expression. "Baby?"

She nodded, then gently patted her stomach. "Baby."

"You're…" he began, only for the rest of his words to trail

away as he spluttered. "We're…it's…" He ran his fingers through his hair. "Truly, sweetheart?"

"Truly." Rosamund laughed, amused by his awestruck countenance and his stunned reaction. "You sound like I do whenever you say something wicked to me because you want to make me blush."

Stuart grinned at her. "We're having a baby."

"We are."

They stared at each other, a myriad of emotions passing unspoken between them. This news, which she had been keeping to herself until she could be certain, was thrilling, terrifying, and what they had both been hoping for. What she saw in her husband's eyes was love, unrivaled and unchecked. So much love. And she knew that was what he saw in her gaze as well.

"Gormless shite," Megs announced into the silence.

She and Stuart both broke into startled laughter.

"We're going to have to teach her better manners as well," he said, crossing the room to Rosamund and pulling her against him. "She can't be teaching our innocent children such words."

"Why not?" Rosamund quipped. "She has already taught both our mothers."

To their mutual delight, Rosamund's mother had been spending a great deal of time with the dowager. The companionship was good for the both of them. They gossiped, drank tea, and bonded over their mutual desire for grandchildren.

"My mother was quite scandalized by our Megs," Stuart agreed, dipping his head to give her a slow, delicious kiss that had her melting into him and wrapping her arms around his neck.

"*Our* Megs?" she repeated when their mouths broke apart. "No *feathered menace* or *winged demon*?"

"I'm going to be a father. I need to learn how to behave."

She smiled back at him, love overflowing in her heart. "Yes, you are. But don't behave too much. I like you when you're just a bit naughty."

He kissed her again. "Don't worry, sweetheart. I'll be as naughty as you want me to be. You only have to ask nicely and make sure you aren't wearing any drawers."

She couldn't contain her half-scandalized giggle.

"You will?" This time, it was her turn to press her lips to his, and she did, giving him a kiss that was long and slow and achingly thorough.

A kiss that made hunger pulse between her legs as their mouths parted once more.

"I will," he promised, his lips grazing hers as he spoke.

"Walk the plank," Megs declared.

He rested his forehead against Rosamund's. "But only when we're alone. No birds or babies about."

"I think I require a demonstration," she told him.

"With pleasure." In one graceful motion, he swept her into his arms, gathering her to his chest.

She clung to him, peals of laughter echoing through the town house as the Duke of Camden carried his duchess away to his bedroom in the midst of the day before happily demonstrating that he would, indeed, be as naughty as she wanted.

THANK you so very much for reading *Duke with a Debt*! I hope you loved Rosamund and Stuart's unexpected happily ever after and that you're ready for more wicked dukes laid low by the intrepid women who steal their hearts. Speaking of which, do read on for a sneak peek of *Duke with a Secret* (Wicked Dukes Society Book 3), featuring Lady Miranda

Lenox and the Duke of Whitby. Warning: contains a sinful wager, a secret mistress, a whole lot of steam, a rake who falls hard, and a woman following her dream. Also, naughty romps that possibly involve ice cream and other desserts.

Please stay in touch! The only way to be sure you'll know what's next from me is to sign up for my newsletter here: http://eepurl.com/dyJSar. Please join my reader group for early excerpts, cover reveals, and more here: https://www. facebook.com/groups/scarlettscottreaders. And if you're in the mood to chat all things steamy historical romance and read a different book together each month, join my book club, Dukes Do It Hotter right here: https://www.facebook. com/groups/hotdukes because we're having a whole lot of fun!

Now, do read on for that sneak peek of *Duke with a Secret* I promised!

Duke with a Secret
Wicked Dukes Society Book 3

Rhys Northwick, Duke of Whitby, has unabashedly devoted himself to a life of debauchery and hedonism. With his friends falling prey to the despicable institution of marriage, the responsibility of hosting the sinful Wicked Dukes Society house parties has fallen largely on his shoulders. Rhys doesn't mind. He'll happily seduce bored widows and wives out of their drawers any day. Until an encounter with a tempting divorcée leaves him longing for the only woman in London who is immune to his rakish charms...

After a scandalous divorce from a coldhearted earl, Lady Miranda Lenox is finally free to pursue her dreams of operating a school of cookery. If she wants to continue attracting a polite clientele, however, Miranda needs her reputation to remain above reproach. What she doesn't need is a rakish duke determined to lure her into further disgrace.

But Rhys will stop at nothing to get what he wants—the delicious Miranda in his bed. He's so assured of his success that he offers her a wager. If she can resist his seduction for the duration of the next house party he's hosting, he will abandon his pursuit of her. But if she succumbs, she'll be his mistress in secret for a month.

It's the perfect bargain. Except that once Rhys wins, he realizes one month with Miranda will never be enough. Nothing less than forever will do. But Miranda refuses to marry again, even as each clandestine encounter with Rhys leaves her one perilous step closer to ruin.

Chapter One

THERE WAS ONLY one thing Rhys Northwick, Duke of Whitby, enjoyed more than a luscious pair of naked, bountiful bubbies and a wet, inviting cunny.

And that was why his carriage was presently parked outside a Marylebone school of cookery. And also why he was peering out the Venetian blinds like a house cracksman watching a street of homes to decide where it would be most opportune to strike first and where he might find the most silver.

Rhys wasn't planning to rob the cookery school, of course. Rather, he was planning to cozen its owner into allowing him to hire a student for the house party he would be hosting in a week's time.

Ordinarily, he wouldn't give a damn about something as bourgeois and feminine as a school of cookery. Hell, he wouldn't even be awake at this ungodly hour, for he was firmly of the opinion that mornings were either for fucking or for sleeping and sometimes both, but absolutely *never* for anything as taxing as being awake and—ye gods—*fully clothed* at half past eight.

His valet had been astonished and confused. But Lavenue had dutifully shaved him and dressed him, and now Rhys was awaiting the blasted owner of the cookery school who had so maddeningly refused his request. Not just once, but thrice.

"Bloody fool," Rhys muttered, reaching into his waistcoat and extracting his pocket watch to consult the time.

He wasn't certain whom he spoke of—himself or the cookery school's stubborn owner. The bastard hadn't even possessed the courtesy to respond to Rhys's perfectly polite and more than generous request himself. Instead, he'd had a secretary dash off one insulting refusal after the next. No matter how hard Rhys tried to persuade the fellow and regardless of how much money he offered, a meeting between the school's owner and the Duke of Whitby would not occur. *On account of His Grace's reputation*, the final missive had so damningly said.

Rhys had ripped that particular epistle in two, and then he had thrown both halves into the fire, delighting in watching them catch flame and curl into gray ash. He had also decided that enough was enough. The arrogant arse would see him today. And he would also give Rhys exactly what he wanted.

Or else.

A carriage drew up to the cookery school, coming to a halt before Rhys's equipage. Hastily, he stuffed his pocket watch back into his waistcoat. Drumming his fingers on his thigh, he waited. Watched. Yesterday, he had arrived in the afternoon—at a decent time—only to be turned away because the owner had left for the day. He had demanded to know from the stammering lackey who had attended him just when the owner deigned to arrive each morning. Nine o'clock, he had been told.

He had been here for one quarter hour already. Biding his time. And now, his patience was about to pay him dividends. He would not give up until he had what he wanted.

The carriage door swung open. Rhys held his breath and watched as the owner of the cookery school emerged. A pair of dainty, embroidered boots first, a flash of stockings, and then the hems of a pale-gray day gown, a wrap draped over small shoulders, a bonnet atop her head.

What was this? An early student? He knew well enough that classes did not begin until ten o'clock. What was the woman doing here now?

Realization descended.

The owner of the school of cookery couldn't be a woman. Could it?

Her profile was proud, head held high as she descended from her carriage. She cast a frowning look in the direction of his conveyance before she hastily walked up the front steps with the self-assured posture of a woman who knew her place in the world. And despite himself, he was intrigued.

Perhaps she *could* be a woman. A vexing, maddening woman who was about to be stunningly routed in this little war of theirs.

He slid off the Moroccan leather squabs and flung open his carriage door, leaping to the pavements and ignoring the steps. She was almost inside now, and he wasn't about to let her escape him.

"Madam," he called.

She stopped, glancing over her shoulder, too far away for him to see the details of her countenance. Her hair was a sleek ebony confined at her nape beneath her millinery. From here, she looked vaguely familiar to him, but then he had met—and bedded—more than his fair share of women. It wasn't impossible that their paths had crossed somewhere along the way.

She cocked her head at him, rather in the fashion of a curious bird. "Sir?"

He approached her, his long-limbed strides closing the distance between them easily. She was lovely, he realized, taking her in: high, elegant cheekbones, dark brows arched over eyes that were a vibrant emerald, full lips that were made to be kissed, a retroussé nose, and a stubborn chin. But he hadn't come here to admire her.

"Allow me to introduce myself," he offered. "I am the Duke of Whitby."

Her eyes widened, those sensuous lips parting before she gave her head a vehement shake. "No."

With that one, lone word, she spun about and hastened into the building.

What the devil? He watched her skirts bustling away for a moment before gathering his wits and following in her wake. Gray silk disappeared inside the door in the second before it slammed closed.

Well, almost closed because Rhys had braced his forearm against it and wedged his boot over the threshold just in time.

"You are not welcome here," she told him frostily, pushing on the door as if she truly believed she possessed the strength to overwhelm him and snap it closed.

He hated to tell her, but she didn't. He would play along for now, however.

"Madam," he tried politely, "I insist you let me in. I need to speak with the owner of this establishment."

"You are looking at her," she snapped, "and I've already told you that my school of cookery will have nothing to do with a man of your reputation. Now please leave."

Tenacious wench.

He pushed against the door, overpowering her with ease, and stepped inside, closing it at his back. "There we are. This is a much better way to conduct business, do you not agree?"

Her lips thinned to a firm, grim line that made him think about kissing them to restore their fullness. "You cannot be here."

Rhys grinned, immensely entertained by her icy disdain. "And yet, here I am."

Footsteps sounded then, scurrying into the entry. A bespectacled woman with white hair surged into view. "My lady, forgive me. I sent Mr. Lucas for more ice, or he would have been at the door."

My lady? The luscious termagant before him grew more intriguing by the moment. This bit of information could certainly be used to his advantage.

"Don't fret, Mrs. Kirkeland," his reluctant hostess told the older woman. "You may return to your duties. I shall see to my guest."

"Of course, my lady." The woman bobbed, her dark skirts fluttering, before she disappeared again.

He turned back to the beautiful woman who was glaring at him as if he had just flung horse dung all over her entryway.

"Please leave, Your Grace," she said sternly.

"After you give me an audience, I'll do as you like," he said reasonably.

Rationally.

Because he had come here to offer the silly woman a fortune. And she was attempting to toss him out on his ear.

"I have already informed you that I have no wish for an association between yourself and my cookery school," she said primly.

"And I have a thousand pounds that says you will change your mind after you hear what I have to say," he countered.

She stared at him, her mouth still compressed, unsmiling and unspeaking. Until finally, she relented, nodding with the regal air of a queen. "Very well. Follow me, Your Grace."

Without waiting for his response, she turned and swept from the entryway in a glide of dove-gray skirts. He prowled after her, a predator intent upon his prey. It was a testament to her culinary prowess that he was here, but he wouldn't allow her the upper hand. Not for a second.

Even if her prowess was the stuff of legends. He knew because he'd tasted it.

He had made the startling discovery purely by coincidence. A fortnight ago, he had been to a small, private dinner gathering where his hostess had proudly served a confection called *cornets à la crème* for dessert. The apple and ginger cream ice had been a decadent delight when paired with a crunchy cornet decorated with chopped pistachios and royal icing. He'd never had anything quite like it, and neither had the rest of his fellow guests.

Rhys had politely inquired after the origin of the course, quite unique in addition to being delicious. The dish was a novelty that he had instantly known would be perfect for the indecent house party he would be hosting soon. His hostess had been annoyingly tight-lipped about the cornets until she had finally admitted their origin: a cookery school in Marylebone.

Finding the school had been easy. Finding its elusive owner had not. Time was running low, however, and so was Rhys's patience. He was bloody well going to have the *cornets à la crème* and she was going to have to accept it.

Because once the Duke of Whitby settled his mind on something he wanted, he didn't stop until it was his.

Want more? Get *Duke with a Secret* now!

DON'T MISS SCARLETT'S OTHER ROMANCES!

Complete Book List
HISTORICAL ROMANCE

Heart's Temptation
A Mad Passion (Book One)
Rebel Love (Book Two)
Reckless Need (Book Three)
Sweet Scandal (Book Four)
Restless Rake (Book Five)
Darling Duke (Book Six)
The Night Before Scandal (Book Seven)

Wicked Husbands
Her Errant Earl (Book One)
Her Lovestruck Lord (Book Two)
Her Reformed Rake (Book Three)
Her Deceptive Duke (Book Four)
Her Missing Marquess (Book Five)
Her Virtuous Viscount (Book Six)

Wicked Dukes Society
Duke with a Reputation (Book One)
Duke with a Debt (Book Two)
Duke with a Secret (Book Three)

Christmas Dukes
The Duke Who Despised Christmas (Book One)

League of Dukes
Nobody's Duke (Book One)
Heartless Duke (Book Two)
Dangerous Duke (Book Three)
Shameless Duke (Book Four)
Scandalous Duke (Book Five)
Fearless Duke (Book Six)

Notorious Ladies of London
Lady Ruthless (Book One)
Lady Wallflower (Book Two)
Lady Reckless (Book Three)
Lady Wicked (Book Four)
Lady Lawless (Book Five)
Lady Brazen (Book 6)

Unexpected Lords
The Detective Duke (Book One)
The Playboy Peer (Book Two)
The Millionaire Marquess (Book Three)
The Goodbye Governess (Book Four)

Dukes Most Wanted
Forever Her Duke (Book One)
Forever Her Marquess (Book Two)
Forever Her Rake (Book Three)

Forever Her Earl (Book Four)
Forever Her Viscount (Book Five)
Forever Her Scot (Book Six)

The Wicked Winters
Wicked in Winter (Book One)
Wedded in Winter (Book Two)
Wanton in Winter (Book Three)
Wishes in Winter (Book 3.5)
Willful in Winter (Book Four)
Wagered in Winter (Book Five)
Wild in Winter (Book Six)
Wooed in Winter (Book Seven)
Winter's Wallflower (Book Eight)
Winter's Woman (Book Nine)
Winter's Whispers (Book Ten)
Winter's Waltz (Book Eleven)
Winter's Widow (Book Twelve)
Winter's Warrior (Book Thirteen)
A Merry Wicked Winter (Book Fourteen)

The Sinful Suttons
Sutton's Spinster (Book One)
Sutton's Sins (Book Two)
Sutton's Surrender (Book Three)
Sutton's Seduction (Book Four)
Sutton's Scoundrel (Book Five)
Sutton's Scandal (Book Six)
Sutton's Secrets (Book Seven)

Rogue's Guild
Her Ruthless Duke (Book One)
Her Dangerous Beast (Book Two)
Her Wicked Rogue (Book 3)

Royals and Renegades
How to Love a Dangerous Rogue (Book One)
How to Tame a Dissolute Prince (Book Two)

Sins and Scoundrels
Duke of Depravity
Prince of Persuasion
Marquess of Mayhem
Sarah
Earl of Every Sin
Duke of Debauchery
Viscount of Villainy

Sins and Scoundrels Box Set Collections
Volume 1
Volume 2

The Wicked Winters Box Set Collections
Collection 1
Collection 2
Collection 3
Collection 4

Wicked Husbands Box Set Collections
Volume 1
Volume 2

Notorious Ladies of London Box Set Collections
Volume 1
Volume 2

The Sinful Suttons Box Set Collections
Volume 1

Stand-alone Novella
Lord of Pirates

CONTEMPORARY ROMANCE
Love's Second Chance
Reprieve (Book One)
Perfect Persuasion (Book Two)
Win My Love (Book Three)

Coastal Heat
Loved Up (Book One)

ABOUT THE AUTHOR

USA Today and Amazon bestselling author Scarlett Scott™ writes steamy Victorian and Regency romance with strong, intelligent heroines and sexy alpha heroes. She lives in Pennsylvania and Maryland with her Canadian husband, their adorable identical twins, a demanding diva of a dog, and a zany cat who showed up one summer and never left.

A self-professed literary junkie and nerd, she loves reading anything, but especially romance novels and poetry. Catch up with her on her website https://scarlettscottauthor.com. Hearing from readers never fails to make her day.

Scarlett's complete book list and information about upcoming releases can be found at https://scarlettscottauthor.com.

Connect with Scarlett! You can find her here:
    Join Scarlett Scott's reader group on Facebook for early excerpts, giveaways, and a whole lot of fun!
    Sign up for her newsletter here
    https://www.tiktok.com/@authorscarlettscott

facebook.com/AuthorScarlettScott

x.com/scarscoromance

instagram.com/scarlettscottauthor

bookbub.com/authors/scarlett-scott

amazon.com/Scarlett-Scott/e/B004NW8N2I

pinterest.com/scarlettscott

Printed in Dunstable, United Kingdom

67135372R00177